DEADLY OBSESSION

A DETECTIVE JANE PHILLIPS NOVEL

 ₹YAN

1

WEDNESDAY, FEBRUARY 3RD

His hot breath steamed up the glass on the front door as he fumbled to get the key into the lock. His hand was shaking and his heart raced, adrenaline coursing through his veins. He swallowed hard and took a deep breath. Finally, he managed to get the key into place, then turned the Yale lock to the right and gently pushed open the door. The warmth of the hallway caused his cheeks to flush and skin to tighten as he stepped inside. For a moment blood rushed to his face, causing him to feel light-headed and a little nauseous.

Closing the door quietly behind him, so as not to wake his wife and young son sleeping upstairs, he turned to look at his reflection in the mirror positioned next to the door. He allowed himself a smile of admiration, then removed his leather boots, winter coat, ski hat and thick scarf. Standing in the silent hallway for a long moment, he listened for any signs of life from upstairs. When he was satisfied everyone was asleep, he padded through to the open-plan kitchen and switched on the light. That woke Lola. Crouching, he greeted the doe-eyed black Cockapoo, scooping his hands under her chin. 'Hello, Lola,' he whispered in a child-like tone. 'Who's Daddy's girl, hey? Who's Daddy's favourite girl?'

Lola obediently raised a paw and placed it on his knee as he moved his right hand onto her head and rubbed it vigorously. 'Daddy's been busy tonight, Lola,' he whispered again, allowing his smile to return. 'Very busy.'

The dog continued to look up at him, completely oblivious to her master's activities.

Just a few hours ago, he had passed the point of no return and stepped into a whole new world, experiencing a level of power and exhilaration he could never have imagined possible. What was even more shocking, though, was just how easy he had found it, *to take a life*.

He closed his eyes and replayed the final moments in his mind once again; the excitement he had felt as the pulse faded to nothing and finally stopped. He could almost hear the ghostly silence that had fallen in the room at that exact moment, and a shiver shot down the length of his spine.

Opening his eyes now, he kissed Lola on her head, then stood and made his way to the sink, where he filled the kettle, switched it on to boil and placed a teabag in his favourite mug, which was emblazoned with the slogan, 'World's Best Daddy'. As he waited for the water to boil, he noticed the adrenaline dissipating, to be replaced by agitation and anxiety. He desperately wanted to maintain the newfound sense of power and euphoria that had gripped his body in the immediate hours that had followed the murder, but with every minute that passed, it faded away. Much to his chagrin.

Steam began to rise from the kettle spout and, when the

tiny LED light flicked off, he filled his mug and left it to brew for a minute. Standing there in the kitchen, waiting, his stomach began to churn. For a split second, the enormity of what he had done seemed to weigh heavy on his shoulders. To distract himself, he spooned three sugars into his tea, then poured in the milk and gave it a stir.

'Time for bed, Lola,' he said softly as he turned back towards the dog and pointed in the direction of the large basket positioned in the corner of the room. Lola obediently followed his direction. A moment later, she appeared content as could be, curled up in a ball on top of her tartan blanket. 'Night night, sweetheart,' he said as he switched off the light, then made his way along the hallway and up the stairs to bed.

On reaching the landing, he could see the door to the bedroom was slightly ajar. Pushing it gently open, he peered inside. Lying on the side of the bed closest to the door, his wife, Jodie, opened her eyes and smiled, then put her finger to her lips as she cast her gaze down to the tiny Moses basket next to her. Their three-month-old son, Noah, lay sleeping, arms bent at ninety degrees, his hands next to his ears.

Opening the door wider, he tiptoed into the room, passed Noah and went round to the other side of the bed. He placed his mug on the bedside table.

'Long night?' asked Jodie, turning to face him.

'Yeah. It was, actually,' he replied, slipping off his T-shirt and jeans.

'You're working too hard, Gabe. We hardly ever see you.'

He smiled softly before pulling back the duvet and slipping in next to her. 'I know, love, but I'm the new boy and when the work's there, I have to take it.' He drew her close. 'This partnership is important to me, and besides, we need the money.'

'I get that, but we also need you *here*,' added Jodie.

'Please don't start that again, babe. I'm doing what I can.'

'I'm not starting anything. I'm just finding it hard on my own, that's all.'

At that moment, Noah let out a high-pitched moan.

They both held their breath, but a second later, the now-familiar wail of a hungry baby filled the bedroom.

Jodie's face contorted and sagged. 'He can't be hungry already! I only fed him an hour ago.'

He kissed her on the forehead and let out a sigh. 'I'll do it,' he said. He climbed out of bed and made his way over to the Moses basket.

Noah's screaming had reached fever pitch by the time he picked him up and cradled him in his bare arms. 'I'll take him downstairs for a feed. You get some sleep,' he said.

'I always said you were an angel, *Gabriel*,' said Jodie with a wry smile.

He nodded softly before turning and making his way out onto the landing. Out of sight, he chuckled to himself as he headed down the stairs, thinking back to the events of that evening. 'I'm an angel all right, love. An angel of *death*.'

2

THURSDAY, FEBRUARY 4TH

A few years back, when her mental health had taken a turn for the worse, running late had been an occupational hazard for DCI Jane Phillips. Being shot in the line of duty had taken its toll for a very long time. Still, after many hours of therapy and implementing better lifestyle choices, she had worked her way back to good health and habits. All of which made the fact she was twenty minutes late leaving home this morning all the more frustrating. Especially so, considering she was due to meet her newly appointed chief superintendent at 9 a.m. sharp.

She checked the clock on the dash; 8.53 a.m.

Ashton House – headquarters of the Greater Manchester Police – was situated five miles north of her current location and at least twenty minutes away in light traffic. Sadly, not something Manchester was famous for at this time of the day.

As the squad car surged up the on-ramp to the Mancunian Way towards Failsworth, her heart sank at the stationary traffic on the road ahead of her. With no way of turning the car around and the nearest exit over two hundred metres away, she was well and truly stuck.

'Damn it!' she yelled as she brought the car to a stop and slammed her hand down onto the steering wheel. 'Jesus, Jane. He's only been in the job a couple of weeks. This is hardly gonna endear you to him, is it?'

Navigating her mobile phone through the in-car system, she located Detective Constable Entwistle's number and pressed the green dial button on the screen. After a couple of rings, he answered.

'*Morning, Guv.*'

With her patience at zero and her frustration mounting by the second, Phillips wasted no time with pleasantries. 'Are you in the office?'

'*Yeah. I've just this minute sat down. Why?*'

'I'm due to meet Carter at 9 and I'm stuck in traffic on the Mancunian Way, just where it intersects the university. Can you check the traffic feed for me? I need to know what I'm up against before I call him and let him know I'm gonna be late.'

'*Sure, let me pull them up for you,*' said Entwistle before going silent.

Phillips could hear the click of his mouse on the other end of the line as he searched for the traffic updates.

'*Looks like there's been a lorry fire just ahead of you, about half a mile ahead, by the railway bridge. It says emergency services are at the scene, but it could take a while to get it under control.*'

'Bollocks! That's all I need,' barked Phillips.

'*Can't you put the siren on and push your way through, Guv?*'

Phillips took a moment to ponder his suggestion. Strictly speaking, driving under blues and twos – using the siren and lights – was restricted to police emergencies only. As much as she hated being late to meet her boss, this wasn't an emergency.

Just then, Phillips's phone began to beep, indicating she had another call coming in. Picking up the handset from the central console next to her, she could see it was coming from her second in command at the Major Crimes Unit, Detective Sergeant Jones. 'I've gotta go, Entwistle, Jones is calling.'

With that, Phillips cut him off and activated the call with Jones. 'Jonesy, what's up?'

'Where are you, Guv?' he asked, his South London accent reminding Phillips of a young Michael Caine.

'The car park that is now the Mancunian Way. Apparently there's been a lorry fire ahead of me. I'm gonna be so late for my 9 a.m. meeting with Carter, it's not even funny.'

'So you're stationary, then?'

Phillips felt her brow furrow. 'Yeah, I bloody am. Why do you ask?'

Jones let out a loud breath. *'I need you to see something, Guv. I'm gonna switch to a FaceTime call.'*

A second later, the scrawny, gaunt features of Detective Sergeant Jones appeared on her phone screen.

'What on earth's going on, Jonesy? Where *are* you?'

'I'm at the Cedar Pines Residential Care Home in Longsight.'

'What the hell are you doing there?'

Jones's mouth fell open for a moment as he appeared to be struggling to find his words. *'It's probably easier if I show you,'* said Jones. He flipped the screen on his phone so the camera showed the room in front of him.

It took a moment for the lens to adjust to the low light

before Phillips saw what he was looking at. 'Jesus. What's that?'

Jones narrated from behind the camera. *'One of the residents, a Michael Yates, deceased. The nurses found him like this about two hours ago and called in uniform, who then called me.'*

Phillips stared at the contorted frame of the old man lying on the bed. He lay facing upwards, his expression fixed in agony, back arched and arms pulled against his chest in a pugilistic pose, almost as if frozen in the middle of some kind of fit. 'What's happened to him?' she asked, her voice low.

'That's just it. I've no idea and nor does anyone else. I've never seen anything like it.'

'Where did you say you were?' asked Phillips.

Jones flipped the screen back. *'The Cedar Pines Care Home in Longsight.'*

'Right, in that case, I'm five minutes away,' said Phillips. 'I'll head over to you now.'

'What about the traffic, Guv?'

Phillips grinned. 'Emergencies like this are what blues and twos are for.' She hung up and switched on the siren and lights.

As the cars in front of her began to move left and right to create enough space to let her through, she called Chief Superintendent Carter through the in-car system.

He answered promptly, his soft Newcastle tones a stark contrast to Jones's London drawl. *'Jane, I was just about to call you. I'm in the canteen. Do you want a coffee for the meeting?'*

'About that, sir. I'm gonna have to come and see you later on this morning. Something urgent's come up.'

'*Oh?*' He sounded slightly disappointed. '*Is that your siren I can hear?*'

'Yeah, it is.'

'*What's happened?*'

'I'm not sure, in all honesty,' said Phillips, edging her car forwards through the traffic, 'but it looks like a suspicious death at an old people's home in Longsight. I'm heading there now to meet Jonesy.'

'*Suspicious, how?*' Carter asked.

'I'll bring you put to speed when I see you, sir. It's a bit hard to explain at the moment.'

'*Very well. Keep me posted, won't you?*'

'Yes, sir.' Phillips rang off. A warm feeling of relief washed over her at having avoided being late to meet her new boss, mixed with the rush of anticipation she always felt on her way to a brand-new crime scene.

A moment later, the last of the cars finally parted in front of her, and she could see clear road ahead. Slamming her foot to the floor, she sped off in the direction of the care home.

3

Jones was waiting by the main entrance doors as Phillips pulled into the Cedar Pines car park, next to the police patrol car. The building itself was typical of British residential homes built in the eighties and nineties, comprising a single storey with large windows facing out to the main road. As she stepped out of the vehicle, she could see a host of elderly faces on the other side of the glass. Some stared out towards Phillips's position with glazed expressions, while others appeared to be snoozing in the high-backed chairs. She pulled her collar up against the bitter February wind and strode towards the double front doors to meet with Jones, his skinny frame wrapped in a black trench coat.

'Are you ready for this?' he asked.

'As I'll ever be.'

Jones turned and led the way. 'It's one of the weirdest things I've ever seen, Guv.'

As they stepped inside, Phillips was struck by the familiar smell of industrial disinfectant mixed with overcooked food and strong urine. It was something she had grown accustomed to during visits to see her beloved grandfather, who had died in a similar home a couple of years ago. A wave of sadness washed over her as she remembered him in his final days, lying motionless in the high-sided bed, a shadow of his former self in so many ways.

Jones recalled her attention to the reason she was there. 'I haven't called in SOCO yet. I wanted you to see him first.'

Phillips nodded as they came to a stop outside room sixteen, where two uniformed officers stood. 'Are you the guys that called it in?'

'Yes, Ma'am,' replied one of the officers.

'And who called you?' asked Phillips.

'The care home manager, Ma'am. Dianna Kirby. As soon as we saw the body, we called MCU.'

'Well, get yourself a drink or something for the moment. We'll call you if we need you. Ok?'

Both officers nodded in unison, then walked away down the narrow corridor back towards reception.

'He's in here, Guv,' said Jones, and moved inside.

Phillips followed him, and stopped in her tracks as she laid eyes on the body. It was even more grotesque in the flesh, contorted and frozen; the head and feet were connected to the bed, but the rest of the body arched upwards and the arms bent inwards like a boxer's. The expression on the waxy face appeared to be one of abject agony. Pulling on a pair of latex gloves and a surgical mask, she moved closer before bending forward to get a better look. 'What the hell could've caused this?'

'I honestly have no clue. Never seen anything like it in over twenty years on the job,' Jones said.

Phillips straightened and turned to face him. 'Get Evans and the rest of SOCO down here immediately, and let's cordon off the room. I don't want anyone in here from now on, including us.'

Jones nodded and reached into his jacket pocket for his phone.

'In the meantime, I need to talk to the manager.'

A few minutes later, Phillips rapped her knuckles on the door emblazoned with the words *General Manager*.

'One moment,' said the voice from the other side.

A mix of low voices came from within the room before the door was pulled open. 'Can I help you?' said the woman abruptly. She was smartly dressed in a trouser suit, with curly brown hair and glasses.

Phillips presented her police ID. 'Detective Chief Inspector Phillips from the Major Crimes Unit. I'm looking for Dianna Kirby.'

The woman's face softened and she offered a warm smile. 'That's me. Please come in.' She gestured into the small office space.

Phillips stepped inside. She was greeted by two more tear-stained faces, staring back at her from a couple of office chairs.

'These are the carers that found Mr Yates,' said Kirby, by way of introduction. 'Nadia and Cassidy.' She dragged over a plastic chair from the wall and offered it to Phillips. She took the seat as Kirby returned to hers on the other side of the desk.

'I need to ask you all some questions. Is that ok?' said Phillips.

'Of course,' said Kirby, which triggered the two carers to nod their heads in unison.

Phillips took out her notepad and pen. 'Who was the first person to find Mr Yates?'

'That was me,' said Nadia. Her accent was thick Eastern European. She was a petite blonde, pretty in an unconventional way.

'What time was that?'

'It was the first medication run, so around seven this morning.'

'And how did he look at the time?' asked Phillips.

Nadia's elfin face twisted. 'Like the devil had stolen his soul,' she said dramatically, as tears streaked down her cheeks.

Phillips made a note. 'Was his body contorted, as it is now?'

Nadia nodded, and thrust a well-used tissue up to her nose.

'And when did *you* see him for the first time?' said Phillips, looking directly at Cassidy, who seemed to dwarf Nadia next to her. 'Big-boned,' Phillips's unforgiving mother would have called her.

'A few seconds later,' said Cassidy, her accent nasal and unmistakably Manchester. 'I heard Nadia scream and ran in to his room. It was awful.'

Phillips nodded. 'What happened next?'

'I came down here to speak to Mrs Kirby,' said Cassidy.

'And I called 999,' added the manager.

Phillips turned her attention towards Kirby now. 'Paramedics or police?'

'Paramedics initially, but when they got here, they took one look at the body and said I should call the police.'

'I see. Can you tell me who was the last person to visit Mr Yates last night?' asked Phillips.

Kirby's eyes flickered in Cassidy's direction.

'It was me,' said Cassidy. 'We're short-staffed, so I did a double shift. Lates last night, then earlies this morning.'

'So what time did you last see him alive?'

'Just before I finished, which would be around 10 o'clock.'

'And how did he seem to you?'

Cassidy shrugged. 'Normal, I suppose. Quiet and half asleep, like he always is... Sorry, I mean *was*.'

Phillips returned her gaze to Kirby now. 'Who looks after the residents overnight?'

'At the moment, we have one carer on that shift.'

Phillips's brow furrowed. 'Just one? For how many residents?'

Kirby's neck flushed and she swallowed hard. 'Fifteen residents currently. I'd like more but it's so hard to get the staff.'

'And who was working last night?' said Phillips.

Kirby opened her laptop and began typing. 'It would have been an agency worker. I like to keep my best girls for day times.' She found what she was looking for. 'So last night it was Eddie Randall from the Safe and Well Care Co. He was on until 6.30 this morning.'

'Do you have an address for him?' asked Phillips.

Kirby shook her head. 'No, but I can give you the number for the agency.' She scribbled it down on a Post-it Note and handed it to Phillips.

'Did Mr Yates have many visitors?'

Cassidy cut in now. 'No, not at all. It was quite sad, really. No family, no friends, just us and his doctor.'

Phillips's attention was piqued. 'Which doctor would that be?'

'Dr Goodwin from the Manchester Central Surgery just

down the road,' said Cassidy. 'She comes to see him at least once a week.'

Phillips made a note of the name. 'So, no other visitors?'

Cassidy shook her head. 'No, none. It's such a shame, considering Mr Yates helped so many kids when he was a teacher.'

Phillips looked up from her notepad. 'He was a teacher?'

'Yes. He told me he'd done thirty years when he was forced to retire with ill health,' said Cassidy.

'Do you know what school he taught at?'

'I can't remember the name, but it sounded funny and it was out near where he used to live in Didsbury.'

'St Aloysius?' asked Phillips.

'That's the one,' grinned Cassidy. 'He tried to teach me to spell it once, but it was too hard! Do you know it?'

'You could say that. How old was Mr Yates?'

Kirby typed into her laptop once more and answered a moment later. 'He was sixty.'

'Isn't that a little *young* for a care home?' said Phillips.

'Ordinarily, yes,' replied Kirby, 'but as Cassidy already mentioned, Mr Yates had no family. When his health deteriorated and he could no longer live by himself, social services brought him to us.'

Phillips nodded. 'Could I get a list of everyone who was working this week?'

'Of course. I'll print the rota off for you now,' said Kirby.

'Thank you.' Phillips returned her notepad to the inside pocket of her coat.

The small printer in the corner of the room sprang to

life. A moment later, Kirby collected the printout. She handed it to Phillips, who stood.

'Well, you've all been very helpful. Either myself, or one of the members of my team, may need to talk to you again, but for now I think I have what I need.'

'Whatever we can do to help, don't hesitate to ask,' Kirby said, and offered her outstretched hand.

Phillips shook it firmly and took her leave. As she opened the door, she turned back to the room. 'Oh. I should probably warn you. The scene of crimes officers will be here very soon, and they'll need your full cooperation. Plus each of your fingerprints.'

Kirby's mouth fell open, and both Nadia's and Cassidy's eyes widened.

Phillips offered a reassuring smile. 'Purely for elimination purposes,' she said, then left.

4

As Phillips moved back along the corridor, she spotted Jones stood outside Yates's room, watching on as Senior CSI Andy Evans and his SOCO team began setting up their equipment in the corridor. Evans was already wearing his white protective suit, blue shoe coverings and purple latex gloves when Phillips joined them.

'Jane. Fancy seeing you, here,' joked Evans as she approached.

'Andy, you didn't waste any time getting here,' she replied, before getting straight to business. 'So, what killed him?'

Evans scoffed. 'Give us a chance, will you? I've just walked in. I'm in forensics, not bloody clairvoyance.'

Phillips thrust her hands in her coat pocket. 'Sorry. I'm just keen to find out. Have you ever come across a body like this, before?'

'Not *exactly* the same with regards to the arched position, but I have seen them with the hands and arms drawn into their chests like that.'

'And what happened in those cases?'

'Poisoned,' said Evans, pulling his protective hood over his head.

Jones raised his eyebrows. 'Do you think that's what might have happened here, then?'

'That's a job for the pathologist, but it could well be a possibility. Equally, maybe he had a stroke, or a fit or something else…'

'How long will you be here for?' asked Phillips.

'Hard to say until we get in and review the room properly.'

Phillips nodded. 'Ok. Well, call me if you find anything, won't you?'

'Of course,' said Evans, then headed into Yates's room.

'We need to pay a visit to Yates's doctor,' Phillips said to Jones, then turned on her heels and marched back to the car park at speed.

As they ventured out into the cold morning air, Jones caught up. 'Are you ok, Guv?'

'Yeah, I'm fine.'

'Really? You don't seem fine.'

Phillips offered a faint smile. 'You don't miss much, do you, Jonesy?'

'That's what makes me such a great copper.' He grinned. 'Plus, I've worked with you for so long now, I can usually tell when something's bothering you.'

'Get in the car, and I'll tell you.' Phillips released the central locking before jumping into the driver's seat, then turned on the engine to get the heater running again.

'So, what's up?' asked Jones.

'I know him.'

'Who?'

'Yates. I know Yates.'

Jones recoiled. 'As in the old fella in there?'.

'Yeah.'

'*How?*'

'He was my sixth form teacher at St Aloysius College when I first came back from Hong Kong.'

'Are you sure?'

'Well, as much as I can be at this stage. I mean, I can't say I recognised his face when I first saw him, but then it *was* all contorted out of shape. Plus, I haven't laid eyes on him for almost thirty years. But one of the carers said he was a teacher at St Aloysius in Didsbury, where he lived. The manager also confirmed he was sixty, which would make him the right age.'

'Bloody hell,' said Jones. 'How well did you know him?'

'We were close. Well, as close as anyone can be to a teacher. He was a great guy who really took me under his wing when I needed it. I was a typical teenager, you know, all messed up and confused about what I wanted to do with my life, and he helped me through. In fact, if it wasn't for him, I would never have joined the police.'

'How so?' asked Jones.

'Well. At the time I was choosing my A-levels, my mother was adamant I should be doing sciences so I could go onto medical school, like my brother.'

'And you wanted to be a copper like your dad had been, in Hong Kong?' said Jones.

'*Exactly.* Mr Yates told me it was my life – not my mother's – and I should do what *I* wanted with it. Not allow myself to be bullied by her and her own shortcomings. So that's what I did, and that's why I'm a murder detective today."

'Much to your mother's total and utter dismay, of course?'

Phillips chortled. 'Have I told you this story before?'

Jones chuckled. 'Once or twice.'

Phillips shook her head and exhaled loudly. 'Jesus. What a way to end up, Jonesy. No family, no kids, no visitors. Dying alone in a care home, surrounded by lost souls.'

Jones's tone was gentle now. 'That won't happen to you. You know that, don't you, Guv?'

Her 2IC really did know her inside out. 'Won't it? Yates dedicated his whole life to his work at the expense of a family. Sounds pretty familiar to me.'

'I know it hasn't happened for you yet, but you'll find the right person, boss. I'm sure of that.'

Phillips was keen to change the subject. 'Right, well that's quite enough Oprah chat for one day. Let's go and see Yates's doctor,' she said as she engaged reverse and the car began to move backwards.

MANCHESTER CENTRAL SURGERY was just a short drive from the care home. A few minutes later, Phillips and Jones walked through the automatic doors into the building.

After introducing themselves to the young receptionist behind the desk, they followed her instructions and took a seat in the packed waiting room. A few minutes later, an officious-looking woman wearing a cream blouse and black trousers approached the reception desk, where she spoke for a moment before turning and striding towards them. A large NHS lanyard hung around her neck. 'DCI Phillips?' she asked, her face stern.

'Yes, and this is DS Jones.' They both stood and flashed their IDs simultaneously.

'I'm Dr Goodwin. How can I be of help?'

Phillips cast her eyes around the busy space. 'Is there somewhere more private we could speak?'

Goodwin raised an eyebrow for a moment before nodding. 'Follow me.'

A few minutes later, they each took seats at a large conference table in a cold, musty-smelling meeting room. Jones pulled out his pad to make notes.

'Sorry. It's bloody freezing in here, but we never use it,' said Goodwin. 'Now, how can I be of help?'

Phillips took the initiative. 'Am I right in thinking that this practice is responsible for the residents of Cedar Pines Care Home?'

'That's correct. Why do you want to know?'

Phillips ignored the question. 'And was Michael Yates under your care specifically?'

'Yes, I look after Michael. What do you mean by "was under my care"? He still is.'

Phillips looked her straight in the eye to monitor her reaction. 'I'm afraid he's dead.'

Goodwin appeared incredulous. 'He's *what?*'

'He's dead.'

'Since when?'

'His body was found in the care home this morning,' said Phillips.

'Why wasn't I told? He's my patient. I should've been notified immediately.'

'At this stage, we're treating his death as suspicious.'

'Suspicious? Why on earth is it suspicious?'

Phillips deliberately avoided the question and pressed on with her own. 'When did you last see Mr Yates, Doctor?'

'Tuesday night. I called in to check on how he was responding to his new medication.'

'How was he during your visit?'

'His usual self: sleepy and a little confused, but very much alive. I can assure you of that.'

'And where were you last night, Dr Goodwin?' asked Phillips.

Goodwin fixed Phillips with an icy glare. 'On stage, presenting at the Manchester Medical Association quarterly meeting. My partner in the practice, Dr Singh, and I were there together, talking about health care within the inner city. You can check with him yourself if you don't believe me. That said, you'll need to come back tomorrow, as he doesn't work Thursdays.'

Phillips flashed a smile. 'I'm sure that won't be necessary, Doctor.'

'So how did Michael die?' asked Goodwin.

'I'm afraid it's too early to say.'

'Well, when will you know?'

'Again, it's too early to say at the moment.' Phillips detected a faint snarl on Goodwin's lips.

'Well, unless there's anything else, I'd like to get back to my patients, if you don't mind?' said Goodwin.

Phillips glanced at Jones and nodded. 'Of course. Judging by your waiting room, you must be very busy.'

'We are.' Goodwin stood and gestured to the door. 'I'll show you back to reception.'

A few minutes later, outside and out of earshot, Phillips and Jones stopped to debrief.

'Well. I'm not sure I'd want the Ice Queen to be *my*

only visitor if I was in a care home on my own,' said Jones playfully.

'You're not kidding. She had one helluva bedside manner, didn't she?'

'And a cast-iron alibi too, Guv.'

'Maybe. But it doesn't hurt to get Entwistle and Bov to check it out, though, does it?' Phillips pulled her phone from her pocket. 'Hold this, will you?' she handed the Cedar Pines staff rota to Jones, then took a picture on her phone. Next, she dialled Entwistle.

As ever, he answered promptly. *'Guv?'*

'Are you with Bovalino?'

'Yes, he's sat opposite me.'

'Great,' said Phillips. 'Get your digital spades out. It's time to do some digging.'

5

Gabe stepped into his father's foisty old kitchen and placed his workbag on the battered wooden table in the middle of the room. 'Dad, it's me,' he shouted.

No response came as he cast his eyes over the cluttered worktops, each filled with discarded takeaway containers, dirty dishes and ancient, yellowing newspapers. 'Dirty old bugger,' he mumbled under his breath, then picked up his bag and made his way into the bedroom.

As he stepped inside, he was greeted by his father's sullen face. Albert – or Bert to those who knew him – lay in his bed, facing the door. The small television on the chest of drawers to Gabe's left was turned on.

'Where've you been?' asked Bert, wheezing. His voice was gravelly and rasping after a lifetime of smoking forty-a-day.

'Working. Like I told you,' said Gabe. He moved to the side of the bed and hitched his buttocks onto the high mattress, then placed his bag on his knees.

'I need you here. You can't keep leaving me on my own. I'll die in this bloody room if you do.'

'Stop being so dramatic. I was here yesterday, and the day before that, and the day before that.'

'I'm a sodding prisoner in my own home!'

'How many times do we have to go over this? The reason you're stuck in here is because you're not strong enough to get out of bed at the moment. The chemo makes you weak.'

'*You* make me weak, more like. Keeping me dependent on that muck you're shoving into my veins.'

Gabe exhaled loudly. 'Well, if you'd like me to get the doctor, you only have to say.'

'No. No doctors. They'd have me in a box as soon as look at me.'

'Well, in that case you're stuck with me, aren't you?'

'I've been stuck with you your whole bloody life, boy!' rattled Bert.

'Oh, don't start all that shit again.'

'I'll start what I bloody well like. This is my house, and I can say what I want.'

'This is your house? Really? You've never mentioned it,' Gabe said, sarcastically.

Bert sneered for a long moment before speaking, 'Did you get my ciggies?'

Gabe shook his head, then reached into his bag and pulled out four packets of Marlboro Reds. 'Isn't it time you quit?' he said as he placed the cigarettes on his father's bedside table.

'What would be the point of that? *You've* stopped me drinking, so this is the only vice I have left.'

Gabe said nothing.

'I'm as good as dead, anyway. I'll be joining your mother soon enough...' Bert began coughing, heavily.

When his father brought up his dead mother, Gabe knew only too well what was coming: a torrent of abuse levelled at him and the Almighty.

'I'll never understand why God took *her* from me and left me with *you*.'

Gabe bit his lip and stepped up off the bed to remove himself from the direct firing line. It was a well-practiced routine aimed at stopping himself from throttling the old man.

His father continued, unabated. 'Imagine it? Detective Sonny's boy. More interested in books than girls; pathetic and weak!'

Gabe reached the bottom of his father's bed and turned to face his tormentor. The years of resentment felt like they would burn a hole in his stomach. 'I am *not* weak,' he said through his clenched jaw.

Bert scoffed. 'It's all you are. All you've *ever* been.'

Gripping the bed end so tightly his knuckles turned white, Gabe stared at his father.

'Look at you. You look like you're gonna cry!' Bert goaded. 'You're as weak as piss, boy!'

Gabe finally snapped. 'Weak, am I?' Pulling his phone from his pocket, he opened the photos folder, found what he was looking for, and marched back to his father's side. He presented him with the image on the screen. 'If I was so weak, how could I have done *this?*'

Bert flinched, then his eyes narrowed as he tried to focus on the picture in front of him. He stared at the screen for a long moment, then moved his gaze to meet his son's. 'What have you done?'

Gabe could feel his chest swelling as he recalled the events of the previous evening. A shot of adrenaline surged through his body. 'I killed him,' he said with pride.

Bert's mouth fell open momentarily. 'You did what?' he wheezed.

'I killed him.'

'Why, for God's sake?'

Gabe stared his father in the eye, his gaze unflinching. 'Because I *could*.'

'You're insane,' Bert hissed.

'Yeah? Well, who's fault is that?'

'You can't blame me for your problems, now.'

'Well, who else is to blame? No one else ever came near this fucking house of horrors!'

'I was a single parent, and I did everything I could to mould you into a man I could be proud of.'

'By belittling me? Beating me?'

Bert scoffed. 'Your mother made you soft. You needed toughening up.'

'So I could be like *you*? An old-school copper who cared more about dead strangers than his own son?'

'I did my duty!' shouted Bert, as loudly as he could through his ravaged larynx. 'I was CID. I didn't get to choose when people were murdered.'

'Oh, spare me the excuses. You were pissed most of the time; you bloody reeked of booze when you did finally come home.'

Bert turned his face away towards the television.

Gabe wasn't finished. In fact – finally – he was just getting started. 'You may have taken away my power for the last thirty years, but you'd better believe me when I say, *I'm taking it back.*'

Bert locked eyes with Gabe once more. 'Pah! By killing a defenceless old man?'

'All that matters is, I took a life. His age means nothing to me.'

'Well, it will to the police. You'll get life for this.'

Gabe smiled, thinking of what was still to come. 'They'll have to catch me first.'

'They'll catch you, boy. You'll never get away with this.'

'Oh, I will,' Gabe chuckled. 'Just you watch me, because I'm like *nothing* they've ever seen.'

Bert shook his head in disgust. 'I hate to break it to you, boy, but killing pensioners is nothing new in this town. Harold Shipman got there before you. Murdered over two hundred of them, and he was a pathetic excuse for a man. *Just like you!*'

Gabe swallowed his anger down. 'I'm nothing like Shipman,' he said calmly. '*His* arrogance meant he got sloppy. *I'm* too clever for that.'

Bert let out a loud cackle. 'And so said every other lifer in Hawk Green Prison. They'll catch you, boy. And when they do, I'll be cheering them on.'

Gabe strode back to his father's side and leaned in close. When he spoke, his voice a sinister whisper. 'That's assuming you'll be here to see it.'

Bert's eyes widened, and he swallowed hard. His breathing laboured. 'What do you mean by that?'

'Don't worry,' said Gabe, straightening. 'I'm not going to kill you, dear Daddy. That would be letting you off the hook. No. I'm going to make you suffer. You're going to watch *me* – your pathetic, *weak* son – ruin the only thing you truly ever cared about.'

'And what's that?'

Gabe flashed a smile. 'Your good name and your legacy as a copper. By the time I'm finished, no one will remember you as a decorated police officer. Instead, you'll only ever be known as one thing...the man who spawned Manchester's greatest-ever serial killer!'

6
FRIDAY, FEBRUARY 5TH

Phillips took the stairs from the ground floor down to the basement, towards the mortuary where the newly married chief pathologist, Dr Tanvi Chakrabortty, was located. A few minutes later, she was buzzed through the secure door and wandered into the silent reception area. By now, she knew to wait until she was attended to.

It wasn't long before Chakrabortty's tall, slender frame appeared wearing freshly pressed green surgical scrubs, her straight, jet-black hair tied up in a ponytail. Her brown skin was darker than normal, thanks to her recent trip to the Maldives.

'Good morning *Mrs Leonard*,' Phillips said theatrically. 'How was the honeymoon?'

Chakrabortty smiled. 'It was wonderful, Jane. Three weeks in heaven on earth. And I'm keeping my own name, so less of the Mrs Leonard nonsense.'

Phillips raised her hands in mock defeat. 'Sorry. Dr Chakrabortty it is.'

'Tan will do, thank you very much.'

Phillips chortled. 'So, how did you get on with the Yates post mortem?'

Chakrabortty signalled for Phillips to follow her, and they headed for her office. A minute later, she took a seat at her desk and Phillips took the chair opposite.

Chakrabortty passed over an iPad. 'Evans's assumption was correct. Yates was poisoned.'

Phillips scanned down, through the report. 'What with?'

'Strychnine. A large dose was administered directly into his cannula.'

'Jesus,' said Phillips. 'So, he was murdered?'

'Looks that way. Unless he somehow administered it himself, which is highly unlikely.'

'Strychnine's not used in medicine, is it?'

Chakrabortty shook her head. 'God, no. It's absolutely lethal and has zero medicinal properties.'

Phillips found herself staring at the image on the screen, of Michael Yates's body prostrate on the examination table. Rigor mortis had still not passed, and mercifully the lower half of his body was covered with a green sheet, but it was still difficult for her to see the man she had once admired so much in such a twisted, emaciated state. 'He was my teacher at school,' she heard herself saying out loud, before lifting her gaze to meet Chakrabortty's.

The doctor's brow furrowed. 'You knew him?'

Phillips nodded. 'He was a big influence on my life when Mum and Dad moved us back from Hong Kong. My A-level tutor.'

Chakrabortty's face softened. 'God. I'm sorry, Jane. If I'd have known, I'd have warned you about the images.'

Phillips forced a thin smile. 'It's ok. I saw it in the flesh at the care home. Plus, it was a long time ago. It's just hard to believe it's the same guy. The Mr Yates I knew was so full of life, funny and charming.' Phillips returned her gaze to the iPad screen. 'Which is why it's so sad to know he died alone, and like this. Would it have been painful, Tan?'

Chakrabortty bit her bottom lip, then nodded gently. 'I'm sorry to say so, yes.'

'Was it at least quick?'

'Not quick enough, I'm afraid. With strychnine poisoning, death comes from asphyxiation caused by paralysis of the neural pathways that control breathing – or by exhaustion from the convulsions it inflicts. Most people usually die within two to three hours of exposure.'

Phillips laid the iPad down on the desk in front of her. 'Poor, bugger.'

'That said, I can say with some certainty that even without the strychnine in his system, he would likely have been dead within twelve months, due to chronic heart failure.'

'His GP did say he had issues with his heart.'

Chakrabortty nodded. 'Plus his lungs were packing up, due to what appears to be a lifetime of smoking. He had the onset of emphysema.'

'Time of death?'

'I'd say between 1 and 2 a.m.'

Phillips said nothing for a moment as she processed the information. 'If he was so poorly, could it have been a mercy killing?'

'With strychnine? No way. As I said before, it's hardly a comfortable way to go, is it? Now if it was morphine, I could see that, but strychnine? Not a chance,' said Chakrabortty.

'But what if whoever killed him couldn't get hold of morphine? If they felt strongly enough, maybe someone could justify two to three hours of pain to relieve Yates of twelve months stuck dying in that place?'

Chakrabortty blew her lips. 'That's for you to decide, Jane, but in my view, anyone looking to euthanize another human being they cared anything for would never use something as toxic as strychnine. It really is a horrible way to die.'

Phillips felt her face and shoulders sag as her mind pictured Michael Yates's last hours alive. Chakrabortty obviously noticed. 'Sorry, Jane. That was insensitive of me.'

'Don't be silly.' Phillips waved her away. 'Whether I knew him or not, I need all the facts and unpleasant details. This can be no different to any other murder I investigate.'

The pair sat in silence for a long moment. Chakrabortty finally broke the deadlock as she pulled her laptop across the desk and began typing. 'I'm emailing my report over to you now.'

'Thanks, Tan.' Phillips exhaled loudly. 'Right. Is there anything else I need to know?'

'Those are the main headlines.'

Phillips stood. 'I'll be getting back, then.'

Chakrabortty followed her out. 'So, how's life after Fox, then?' she asked as they walked side by side down the corridor.

'Well, strictly speaking, now she's chief constable, I am still kind of working for her, but day to day, I must say, it's much easier under Carter. He's a totally different animal altogether.'

'I've heard good things about the new chief super,' said Chakrabortty. 'He's from the North East, isn't he?'

'Yeah. He's a Geordie and a massive Newcastle United fan,' said Phillips as they reached the door.

Chakrabortty smiled. 'Well, we won't hold that against him.'

Phillips returned her smile. 'Thanks Tan, and sorry for getting a bit choked in there.'

'You're only human, Jane. As much as it's my job to examine dead bodies every day, even I get upset with some cases. So cut yourself some slack, hey?'

Phillips patted her on the arm and nodded. 'I will, Tan,' she said, as she opened the exit door, then stepped through.

Ten minutes later, the barrier to the car park lifted and she edged the squad car out into the midmorning traffic and back towards Ashton House.

THIRTY MINUTES LATER, Phillips walked into the MCU office. Jones was sat alone at one of four desks positioned in the middle of the room. 'Where is everyone?' she asked.

Jones looked up from his computer as she dropped into the chair opposite him. 'Bov and Entwistle have gone to the canteen to get a bacon roll each. Their "second breakfasts", they called it.'

'Entwistle's having a second breakfast? That's not like him. For Bov, that's standard, but Entwistle?'

'Apparently he's doing a triathlon next month and needs the calories,' said Jones.

Phillips exhaled loudly. 'I really don't know where he gets the energy.'

At that moment, the office door opened behind her and chatter filtered into the room. Phillips swivelled in the chair to see the remaining members of her core team, DCs

Bovalino and Entwistle, making their way in, each with a sandwich in one hand and a hot drink in the other. The two men could not be more different in size and shape; at six-foot-four and nineteen stone of muscle, Bovalino was unusually tall and wide for a man of Italian descent, but still boasted the trademark swarthy skin and dark hair of his lineage. Entwistle, on the other hand, although also over six feet tall, was slim and athletic, his mixed-race features chiselled and always smooth-shaven and moisturised.

Phillips spied their quarry. 'Anything for a hungry DCI in that lot?'

Both men looked at their food and drink, then back at Phillips.

'No. Sorry, Guv,' said Bovalino. 'I can go back and get you something if you like?'

Phillips smiled. 'You would, too, wouldn't you?'

'Of course. Anything for the boss,' replied the big Italian.

'Brown nose! Brown nose!' teased Jones.

'Piss off, Jonesy,' said Bovalino with a grin.

Phillips let them both off the hook. 'I'm fine. I'll get something in a minute. For now, I want to talk to you about Yates.'

Both men took seats at their desks and for the next few minutes, whilst they devoured their sandwiches, Phillips brought them up to speed on the results of the post mortem.

When she was finished, Jones was the first to speak. 'So, Evans was right and we're looking for an old-school poisoner?'

'It's all a bit Victorian, isn't it?' said Bov.

Phillips placed her palms flat on the desk in front of her. 'It's certainly not something I've ever come across in twenty years of policing.'

Entwistle finished his sandwich and threw the wrapper in the waste bin. 'Jones mentioned you knew the victim, Guv.'

Phillips raised an eyebrow and glanced at her second in command. 'Did he, now?'

Jones blushed slightly. 'It just sort of came out, Guv.'

Phillips turned back to Entwistle. 'Yes, I knew Michael Yates – or Mr Yates – when he taught me in sixth form. He was a good guy. In fact, I can't quite believe the brilliant man I knew ended up alone in a care home.'

Bovalino shuddered. 'If I ever get like that, take me to the bottom of the garden and shoot me, will you?'

'There'll be a queue, mate,' chuckled Jones.

The big man responded with a playful V-sign.

Phillips continued. 'So, what can you tell me about the last thirty years of Yates's life?'

Bovalino opened his notepad. 'I've spoken to the headmistress at the school—'

'What was her name?' Phillips cut him off.

Bovalino glanced at his notes. 'Mrs Braithwaite. Was she one of your teachers?'

Phillips shook her head. 'No. Must've joined after my time.'

He continued. 'Anyway, Yates took early retirement at fifty-five based on health grounds. Seems he had a heart condition that became very serious a few years after he stepped down. According to the headmistress, Yates hadn't kept in touch with anyone from the school, but she had heard from one of the parents that he was unable to live at home because of his issues. Soon after, he was placed into care by social services.'

'Anything else?'

'Just that he was resolutely single and was rumoured to

have left everything in his will to the South Manchester Dogs' Home.'

'According to whom?' asked Phillips.

'Another one of the parents. At least, that's what the headmistress said.'

Phillips rolled her eyes. 'That sounds exactly like the gossipy old biddies that live in Didsbury. My mother included.'

'Is that the lot?'

'So far, Guv, but I'll keep digging,' said Bovalino.

'Do. And take a proper look at his will, will you? Let's see if anyone stood to inherit from his estate – or if it was changed recently. You're looking for anything unusual. You know the drill.'

Bovalino nodded.

Phillips turned to Entwistle. 'And what about Dr Goodwin's alibi?'

'Solid as a rock. There's even video on the society's Facebook page of her and Dr Singh presenting at the dinner. Stood on stage in front of a hundred guests.'

'Anything in her background of note?'

'No, Guv. It seems she's a pillar of the community.'

Phillips scoffed and folded her arms against her torso. 'And so was *Harold Shipman*. Let's not forget he was lauded by *his* community right up until they realised he'd murdered over two hundred and fifty of his patients. So, no matter how saintly Goodwin might appear, keep an open mind. Ok?'

'Yes, Guv,' said Entwistle.

'What about the rest of the staff at Cedar Pines. What have we got on them?'

'All DBS-checked, Guv,' said Jones. 'No records, and all legally allowed to work in the UK.'

'Including the night manager, Eddie Randall?'

'Yep, including him.'

'I expected as much. Anything else would be far too simple for this unit, wouldn't it?' said Phillips facetiously, before changing tack. 'So, who can tell me anything about strychnine?'

Jones shrugged. 'I can't say I've ever come across it.'

'Me either,' said Bovalino.

Entwistle was already typing into his laptop when Phillips turned to face him. 'Come on, Entwistle, you must have something for me?'

'For the moment, only what's available online, Guv,' he replied. His eyes narrowed as he stared at the screen in front of him.

'Which is?'

Entwistle turned the laptop so the screen was visible to Phillips as well as him. 'It says here that in its natural form, the most common source is from the seeds of the Strychnos nux-vomica tree.'

'Well, why didn't you say so? I've got one of those in my garden,' said Jones, his tone sarcastic.

'Have you?' said Entwistle brightly.

Jones's face twisted. 'Of course not, you daft bugger!'

'Ignore him,' said Phillips, chuckling.

Entwistle continued. 'It's highly toxic, colourless, and can be inhaled, swallowed or absorbed through the eyes or mouth.'

'Or fed into a cannula,' added Phillips.

'Indeed. Its most common use is in the pest-control industry to kill rodents such as rats and mice.'

Phillips took a moment to process the information, then turned towards Jones. 'Did you notice any pest-control boxes at the care home when we were there?'

'No, Guv. But then I wasn't looking for them.'

'Me neither,' Phillips said. 'Why don't you and Bov head back over there and take a look. See if they have a contractor for pest control. Most businesses with large waste bins do.'

Jones and Bovalino nodded in unison.

'And while you're there, talk to the staff on duty the night Yates was killed. A DBS certificate is one thing, but I want you to look into their eyes and see if there's anyone that stands out. It'll probably come to nothing, but it can't hurt to speak to them.'

'Consider it done,' said Jones.

'What do you want me to do, Guv?' asked Entwistle.

'I'm still not convinced by Dr Goodwin, so I want as much information as we can muster on her life, as far back as it'll go – including her finances. Let's see if we can find out who she *really* is.'

'On it,' said Entwistle as Jones and Bovalino stood up from their desks.

Phillips followed their lead. 'Right. Well, I'd better get upstairs and update Carter. I'm only two days late for my meeting,' she said with a grin, then made her way out of the door.

7

THURSDAY, FEBRUARY 11TH

Gabe sat on the high stool at the breakfast bar in the kitchen, holding Noah in his left arm whilst feeding him formula milk from the bottle in his right hand. Lola was in her basket, sleeping as usual. His son seemed desperate to drain the bottle of formula as quickly as possible, greedily guzzling on the teat with all his might. Breakfast television played on the screen on the wall in front of him, but he wasn't paying much attention, too engrossed in his own thoughts and plans for the coming evening.

A moment later, Jodie walked into the kitchen wearing tight-fitting sportswear, her wet blonde hair hanging free around her shoulders. 'Do I look fat in this?' she asked.

'Not at all. You look great.'

'Well. I don't feel great. I feel like a right fat cow.'

Gabe let out a silent sigh of frustration. No matter what he said to the contrary, or how many times he said it each day, Jodie was adamant she looked terrible, that her post-baby figure was repulsive.

She continued. 'I'm taking Noah to baby yoga at eleven and I just want to look nice. Instead, I look like a bloody elephant.'

'Babe, you look really good. And don't forget, it's only been three months since you had him.'

Jodie's eyes narrowed as she rested her hands on the breakfast bar in front of her. 'So you're saying I *do* look fat?'

'No. That's not what I'm saying at all.'

'That's it. I'm not going,' she said, slamming a clenched fist on the bench.

'Oh, don't be so bloody dramatic,' said Gabe, beginning to lose patience. 'It's only a baby class, for God's sake. And besides, everyone there will be the same as you.'

'What? Fat, you mean?'

Gabe let out a low growl and stood up from the stool, still feeding Noah. 'I don't know why I even bother. There's no talking to you when you're like this.'

'Like what?'

'Like a crazy woman. You had a baby *three* months ago. You're taking him to a class filled with other new mums – whose bodies have also changed after carrying a kid for nine months – yet you're making it out like everyone there will be a supermodel dressed in designer gear. It hardly warrants a bloody meltdown, does it?'

'Oh, that's just typical of you, isn't it?' said Jodie.

'And what's that supposed to mean?'

'You're still pissed off because I'm taking the full twelve-months maternity, aren't you?'

Gabe's mouth fell open for a moment. 'I've *never* had a problem with you doing that.'

'Really? In that case, you should try telling your face once in a while.'

'When have I ever said anything negative about your maternity leave?'

Jodie folded her arms across her chest with all the petulance of an angry teenager. 'Maybe not directly, but it's there. I can feel it.'

'What the hell are you talking about? *Feel* what?'

'Your passive aggression. You're always telling me how many hours you're doing, how hard you're working and how difficult it is for you with no sleep.'

'That's got nothing to do with your maternity leave,' said Gabe. 'It's just how it is at the moment. Noah's got colic and cries all night, and work's manic, so I'm just knackered all the time. Tell me how any of that is about *you?*'

'Because you think I'm a terrible mother. Don't you?'

'Oh, for fuck's sake,' Gabe muttered as Noah finally finished his bottle.

'It's not easy being at home all day with him, you know. Nothing but feeds, nappies and never-ending piles of washing. I'm going insane, stuck in this house on my own.'

Gabe placed a muslin cloth over his shoulder, then rested Noah on his chest and began rubbing his back, attempting to get his wind up.

Jodie continued. 'I'm an experienced finance lawyer, Gabe. I'm used to intellectual conversation every day. All I get round here is bloody baby talk.'

'So what do you want *me* to do about it, hey?'

'Well, you could start by being here once in a while, instead of always working or spending time at your dad's.'

Gabe continued to rub Noah's back, but so far, the satisfying sound of a little burp eluded him. 'Look. Everything costs money and your maternity money runs out soon.'

'So you *are* blaming me?'

Gabe finally lost his cool. 'Well, you're the one who wanted the expensive house—'

'Yes, but only so we had room to raise a family!' Jodie cut him off.

'*You* want the flash holidays to Australia, not me.'

'So Noah can meet his auntie and uncle. They're the only ones he has.'

'And *you're the one* obsessed with sending him to that stupidly expensive private school!' shouted Gabe.

Jodie pointed a finger at him. 'You want him to go to St David's just as much as I do!'

At that moment, whether it was colic or the raised voices, Gabe didn't know, Noah began to wail. Gabe could take no more. 'Here!' he said, and handed the baby to Jodie. 'You deal with him. I'm already late for work.'

Jodie pulled Noah into the nape of her neck as tears streamed down her face.

As he left the room, Jodie followed him. 'That's right. Do what you always do: walk away!' she shouted after him.

Gabe grabbed his bag and coat from the hallway and headed for the front door. As he opened it, he turned back to see her standing in the doorway of the kitchen. 'I'm working late tonight. Don't wait up,' he said, then stepped outside, slamming the door behind him.

8
FRIDAY, FEBRUARY 12TH

'I'm coming up to Dunham Massey Park now,' said Phillips, as she exited the roundabout and headed along Dunham Road.

'Take your first left onto Farm Walk, we're down there at the scout camp,' said Jones on the other end of the call. 'The track's not been gritted and it's pretty icy down here, so be careful, Guv. Thankfully Bov was driving, so we made it in one piece.'

'I will,' said Phillips as she slowed the car and turned left off the main drag.

Jones had not exaggerated when he said the conditions were treacherous. It was a typical February morning in Manchester, cold and wet with temperatures below zero, and even though the time was approaching 8 a.m., the dawn was still struggling to break through. Sticking the car in first gear, she edged her way along the rough, icy road and through the trees, following the distinctive purple and white signs for the scout camp. Up ahead, she spotted the blue flashing lights of a patrol car as well as the cluster of unmarked vehicles parked up next to a quad bike, which was attached to a small trailer. After a few more tense minutes of driving, she saw Jones, stood with his back to her, on the edge of the track. He turned as she made her final approach and walked slowly towards the driver's door. Bringing the car to a stop, she opened the electric driver's window. 'Am I all right to leave the car here?'

Jones nodded. 'Yeah, the body's just over the other side of those huts.' He pointed to a grouping of small wooden buildings.

Phillips closed the window and stepped out onto the frozen ground. She was thankful she'd had the foresight to put on her walking boots this morning. Closing the door, she pulled her collar up against the biting wind that blew across the camp site. Jones had done the same thing, and the high collar of his black Mac, coupled with his bony features, gave him the appearance of Christopher Lee's Dracula – albeit a much less imposing version.

'She's down here, Guv,' he said, as he led the way.

A couple of minutes later, they rounded the scout huts and found their way onto a piece of open ground that featured a tall flagpole concreted into the middle, as well as large logs that had been laid out in a wide circle. Phillips assumed this was where the scouts would sit around the campfire on summer evenings. Up ahead, a number of uniformed police stood in a cluster. Bovalino was positioned just behind them, staring down at the ground near his feet, which were hidden behind another log. His massive body was wrapped tightly in a blue padded coat with a fur collar.

As Phillips approached, one of the uniformed officers stepped forward and introduced himself. 'Morning, Ma'am.

I'm Sergeant Rees, I called it in,' he said, his breath visible in front of him.

'Who found her?' said Phillips.

'One of the groundsmen – a Jerry Cooper – spotted her clothes first, and then the body. He's in the back of our patrol car if you'd like to talk to him?'

Phillips shook her head. 'He'll have to wait for a minute. I need to see the girl first.'

Bovalino made his way over. 'Morning, Guv,' he said, then handed her a large torch. 'The light's getting better by the minute, but you'll need to use this for the time being. It's pretty dark over there.'

'Lead the way, Bov,' said Phillips.

The big Italian obliged, and a moment later she cast her eyes over the naked body of a young woman, lying in a cruciform position on the other side of the log. Her eyes were black and wide in death. Phillips took a moment to process the macabre scene.

'The groundsman reckons she was like this when he found her,' said Jones.

'What was the temperature last night?' Phillips asked.

'The forecast said it would be minus three,' said Bovalino. 'Poor thing will be frozen solid by now.'

'Which will cause serious issues with figuring out the time of death.' Phillips knelt to get a closer look. 'What's with the cruciform position?'

'Dunno, Guv, but it sent shivers up my spine when I first saw it,' Bovalino said. 'It's almost as if she was left here as a sacrifice, or something.'

Phillips nodded. 'Accidental homicide is one thing, but when a body is left like this, it usually means…'

'A planned attack.' Jones finished her sentence.

Phillips stood. 'Carried out with purpose and likely by someone wishing to make a statement.'

Jones and Bovalino nodded in unison. They'd been Major Crimes detectives for long enough to recognise this was not a straightforward murder.

'Have you called in SOCO?' asked Phillips.

'Yes, Guv,' Jones said. 'Evans called me just before you arrived. He reckoned he'd be here by 8.30.'

'Do we know who she is?' Phillips asked.

'We found a couple of bank cards and a travel pass in the clothes. If they're hers, then her name's Gillian Galloway. No photo ID, though,' said Jones.

'Ok, well, that's a start at least. Get Entwistle onto the banks and see if we can get an address.'

'Already done, Guv. I called him straight after I called you.'

'Good work, Jonesy,' Phillips stared down at the frozen, naked body. Activating the camera function on her phone, she took a couple of pictures. 'Whoever she is, I'm guessing she can't be any older than early twenties.'

'I'd say so.' Jones's phone began to ring. Pulling it from his pocket, he activated the speaker function. 'Entwistle. The Guv's arrived. What have you got?'

'*Gillian Galloway's registered address is in Woodhouses. flat 14A on Newfield Road.*'

'Anything else?' asked Phillips. 'Any pictures of her?'

'*That's it for now, but I'll be able to get more after 9, once I'm at my desk and the rest of the world starts work.*'

'As soon as you have anything, call it through, won't you?'

'*Of course, Guv. I'm leaving the house now, so I'll be in the office in half an hour.*'

'Ok. You'd better get off then,' said Phillips.

A second later, Jones ended the call.

Phillips said nothing for a long moment as she gathered her thoughts. Shaking her head, she locked eyes with Jones and Bovalino. 'This is some weird-looking shit, guys, and I don't like it one bit. Not one bit.'

'So what now, Guv?' asked Jones.

Phillips turned in the direction of the uniformed police. 'Let's talk to the groundsman, see what he has to say for himself.' She set off tentatively across the frozen ground towards the patrol car.

A few minutes later, she opened its rear offside door. 'Would you mind stepping out of the car, Mr Cooper,' she said, gesturing for him to get out.

Jones and Bovalino appeared at her side.

Cooper did as instructed. Phillips was struck by how young he looked. She wasn't sure why, but she had expected an older man. Wearing a heavy-duty Dunham Massey-branded fleece, beanie hat and gloves, Cooper was of slight frame, standing at about five feet ten inches by Phillips's reckoning. A light stubble covered his top lip and chin.

'Can you tell us what happened when you came across the body this morning, Mr Cooper?' asked Phillips.

Cooper appeared sheepish as his eyes darted from Phillips to Jones, and then to Bovalino. His voice was quiet when he spoke, the accent thick Mancunian. 'I was emptying the bins on the camp site and found an open bag of clothes in one of them. It looked like new gear, so I had a glance inside and realised it was women's clothing. I thought nothing of it at the time. People are always dumping their old rubbish in the park, so I chucked the bag on the back of the trailer and carried on clearing the site. Then, when I reached the last bin on the camp, something caught my eye over by the logs. It was still dark, so I went to get a better look. I then realised it was a body.'

'And what did you do then?' asked Jones.

'Called you lot.'

'What time was that?' Phillips cut back in.

Cooper shrugged his shoulders. 'Dunno. About half-six, seven this morning, I guess.'

Phillips continued. 'Who else has access to the site out of hours?'

'There's a few of us working shifts. I'm on earlies this week, but one of the lads is sick, so I've been double-shifting doing lates as well.'

'And were you on lates last night?' Asked Phillips.

Cooper nodded.

'What time did you finish, then?'

'Just after six. The park closes early this time of year, so we knock off earlier, too.'

Phillips pushed her hands deep into her coat pockets to fend off the cold. 'Can the public access the camp site if the main park is closed?'

'Not the camp site, no...' Cooper pointed behind them, towards the main road. '...but they can drive up as far as the barrier, which is locked each night.'

Phillips turned and noted the long metal barrier some thirty yards away. It was fixed open to a post currently. She turned back to Cooper. 'Did you see anything unusual last night?'

'No. Nothing,' he replied without emotion.

'No headlights on the road? No voices, shouts or screams, perhaps?'

Cooper shook his head. 'Not that I remember.'

'And did you touch the body at all?'

'God, no,' said Cooper vehemently.

'So you found the clothes, then the body, and you called us? Is that what you're saying?' asked Phillips.

'Yeah. That's right.'

She studied Cooper's face intently, but saw nothing that made her believe he was lying. 'Ok. Well, that should be everything we need for the time being.'

'Does that mean I can go now?' asked Cooper.

'Yeah,' said Phillips. 'We'll be in touch if we have any more questions.'

Cooper didn't reply. He turned and walked at pace towards his quad bike.

When he was out of earshot, Jones stepped closer to Phillips as she watched him closing the rear gate on the trailer. 'You want me look into his background, Guv?'

Phillips produced a wry smile. 'You read my mind, Jonesy, but Bov can do that. I want you to come with me to Galloway's place.'

'Whatever you say,' said Jones.

Phillips turned to Bovalino. 'Are you ok to wait for Evans and the rest of SOCO?'

'Of course, Guv.'

'Once you've briefed them, get yourself back to HQ. I want you and Entwistle to get as much information on Galloway and Cooper as you can.'

The big Italian nodded.

Phillips rubbed her hands together against the cold. 'Come on, Jonesy. Let's go and see if Gillian Galloway is our victim.' She headed off in the direction of her car.

9

Phillips parked the car in the small communal car park in front of the two-storey block of flats and killed the engine. Then she pulled out her phone and scanned the last SMS message sent by Entwistle to remind herself of the address as she opened the driver's door to get out.

Jones followed suit, and a few minutes later they found the flat, to the rear of the seventies-looking brick building. As they knew nothing of Gillian Galloway or her life, they took the precaution of ringing the doorbell in the hope she might live with someone. If she did, it would speed up the identification process massively. With no answer following the first ring, Phillips tried again as Jones took a step back and inspected the building and surrounding area. As was to be expected in such a small apartment block, a neighbour twitched curtains and peered out at the unknown visitors. A few moments later, the front door to flat 14A opened on the chain and a dishevelled young woman looked out.

'Can I help you?' she asked.

Phillips stepped closer and presented her credentials. 'Detective Chief Inspector Phillips from the Greater Manchester Police. Do you live here?'

A puzzled look appeared on the girl's face behind the chain. 'Yeah, why?'

Phillips ignored the question. 'Does Gillian Galloway live here, too?'

The girl nodded.

Phillips glanced left as the neighbour twitched the curtain again. 'Could we come inside for a moment?'

The door closed momentarily as the girl released the chain before opening the door wide. Then she pulled her thick grey dressing gown tightly around her torso, folded her arms and headed back into the flat. Phillips followed her through, with Jones in tow, as the girl guided them into the small lounge at the end of the narrow hallway. She took a seat on one of the armchairs.

'Do you mind if we sit?' asked Phillips.

'Go ahead.' The girl's eyes were full of suspicion.

Phillips and Jones took seats on the small sofa opposite. 'Can I ask your name?' said Phillips.

'Kelly,'

'Kelly, what?'

'Kelly Windsor. Look, what's this about?' said the girl with an air of petulance.

Phillips didn't answer, and noted the girl's wild hair and red eyes. 'Sorry, Kelly. Did we wake you?'

Windsor nodded. 'Yeah. I'm on nights this week, so I'd just got off to sleep when you rang the bell.'

'And what do you do?' said Jones.

'I'm a nurse at Wythenshawe Hospital. Look, what are you doing here, and why do you want to know about Gilly?'

Phillips's voice softened as she spoke. 'Kelly. When did you last see Gillian?'

Windsor's brow furrowed. 'Last night. Look, seriously. What's going on?'

Phillips shifted towards the edge of her seat. 'I'm very sorry to have to tell you this, but we found a body in Dunham Massey Park this morning that we believe could be Gillian.'

Windsor's eyes widened and her mouth fell open as she raised her hand to cover it.

Phillips continued. 'We don't know that for certain, but we found a bank card in Gillian's name in the vicinity of the body.'

'Oh my God,' whispered Windsor.

'I know this is a lot to take in,' said Phillips, 'but do you have any pictures of Gillian we could take a look at, to help us know for sure?'

Windsor swallowed hard, then nodded her head slowly. 'I'll get my phone,' she mumbled as she stood up from the chair and left the room.

A moment later, she returned and retook her seat. The phone shook in her hand as she attempted to unlock it with her fingerprint. After a few false starts, it opened and she flicked through a number of images until she found what she was looking for. As she handed over the phone, Windsor's eyes oozed fear.

Phillips looked down at the screen and was taken aback by the pretty, smiling face looking back at her. There was no mistaking it. The body in the park was Gillian. But the contrast between the cold, dead face they'd witnessed just an hour ago and the warm, beautiful young woman in the photograph made her feel physically sick.

She handed the phone to Jones and turned her attention

to Windsor once more. 'Kelly. Based on that image, I'm very sorry to tell you that the body we found *is* Gillian's.'

A wave of shock and grief appeared to smash down over Windsor as she blinked furiously and began to stutter. 'Th-th-th-that's not true. I-i-i-it can't be.'

'I'm sorry, Kelly. We found her body this morning,' said Phillips.

Windsor dropped her face into her hands and began to sob. Quick as a flash, Phillips was out of her seat and moving across the room to comfort her. Jones was up as well, grabbing a box of tissues from the small coffee table next to the TV, which he passed over.

Phillips wrapped a protective arm around Windsor's shoulder. 'I'm so sorry, love. I know it's a shock.'

Windsor continued to cry.

'Jonesy. Why don't you make us a nice cup of sweet tea?' Phillips suggested.

Jones nodded, and made his way out of the lounge room and into the adjacent kitchen.

A few minutes later, he reappeared with three cups of tea on a tray, which he placed on the small, metal-framed glass table in the middle of the room. He handed one of the cups to Windsor, who tentatively took a sip of the steaming drink.

'I know this has all come as a huge shock, and I'm sure it's the last thing you want, but would you be ok to answer some more questions for us?'

Windsor nodded as she took another sip of her tea.

Jones pulled out his notepad and took a seat back on the sofa, with Phillips following suit.

'When exactly did you last see Gillian?' Phillips asked.

Windsor took a moment before she answered. 'Last night. As I was leaving for work.'

'And what time was that?'

'My shift started at seven-fifteen, so I would have left just after six. She was in the bath, getting ready to go out.'

'Where was she going?'

'On a date.'

'Do you know who with?'

'Kind of. It was some guy called Conrad that she met on Tinder.'

'I see,' said Phillips. 'Did she go out on dates a lot?'

'God, no! Gilly is...' Windsor seemed to run out of words for a moment, before regaining her composure. '... sorry, I mean Gilly *was*, super shy.'

'So how did she end up with a Tinder account? That's not exactly for the shy type, is it?' Jones interjected.

'I set up her profile on my phone without her knowing. I did all the swiping left until I found someone I thought she might like. She literally had no clue what I'd done until a guy asked her for a date. At which point I told her.' Windsor's shoulders sagged. 'It's my fault she's dead, isn't it? If she hadn't gone out last night, she'd still be alive now, wouldn't she?'

'You can't blame yourself, Kelly,' said Jones, his tone paternal. 'At this stage we still don't know for sure how or when she died.'

'Do you have a picture of the guy you set her up with?' asked Phillips.

Windsor nodded, and began flicking through her phone. 'This is him.' She turned the screen so Phillips and Jones could see the man.

Phillips took the phone and examined the image closely. The young man smiling out from the picture was extremely good looking, with chiselled features and thick, curly blond hair. His profile said his name was Conrad Eve and the photo had been taken on a beach somewhere hot. It was hard to tell whether the image was real or a fake. She handed the handset to Jones, who pulled out his own phone and took a picture of the young man's profile. He then handed the phone back to Windsor.

'Do you know where she was going on the date, last night?' Phillips asked.

'The Pig and Whistle in Altrincham, as far as I know.'

Phillips took a moment as she tried to place the pub in her mind's eye.

'Is that the one near the bus station?' asked Jones.

Windsor nodded. 'I think so. I've never been, but she mentioned it was easy to get to because it was near to her bus stop.'

'But that's an old man's boozer, isn't it?' said Jones.

Windsor didn't answer, and instead wiped her nose with a tissue before blowing it loudly.

'If she was so shy, then how did you manage to get her to go on the date?' asked Phillips.

'Well, *you've* seen his picture. He's gorgeous. Even Gilly couldn't say no.'

'I see what you mean, yeah,' said Phillips, smiling softly. 'Can you tell us what Gillian did for a living?'

'A nurse, like me. She worked on the kids' ward at Wythenshawe; loved it.' Tears began to well once more in Windsor's eyes as her lower lip trembled. 'How am I going to explain this to her mum and dad?'

'Please don't worry about telling Gillian's parents, Kelly,' said Phillips softly. 'That's down to us. Our officers will break the news later this morning. Do you have an address for them?'

Windsor got up from the chair and left the room for a minute, then returned with a small address book. She opened it and presented it to Phillips, who took a picture on her phone.

'Would you mind showing me that photo of Gillian, again?' asked Phillips.

Windsor obliged, and Phillips once more took a snapshot on her phone. She glanced at Jones, who nodded. As ever, he knew what she was thinking: Windsor had had enough questions, for now.

Jones folded his notepad and placed it inside his coat pocket.

'We'll leave you to it, Kelly.' Phillips stood and handed over her business card. 'If you think of anything else that might help, give me a call, day or night. Ok?'

Windsor glanced down at the card in her hand, then back at Phillips. 'I will.'

'You should get some rest,' said Phillips, her soft smile returning, then took her leave. Jones tucked in behind her and followed her out.

A few minutes later, they were back in the car.

Phillips turned towards Jones. 'What were you getting at back there, when you said the Pig and Whistle was an old man's pub?'

'Well, it seemed an odd venue, that's all. Look, I'm no Casanova, but if I was a good-looking lad like Conrad Eve, trying to impress on a first date, I'm not sure an old man's boozer next to the bus station would be my first choice of venue, that's all.'

'You've got a point there,' said Phillips.

'I really don't know Altrincham town centre very well at all, but I'm sure there's a lot more trendy places they could have gone.'

'So why choose that one?'

'Beats me, Guv.'

Phillips fell silent for a moment, before straightening and switching on the ignition. 'Let's get back to Ashton House and catch up with the guys. And then I want you and Bov to pay a visit to the Pig and Whistle. See if anyone saw Gillian and our mystery man last night.'

'Sounds like a plan.'

Phillips continued. 'I'm not a betting woman, but if I was, I'd put money on the fact the gorgeous-looking man in Conrad's profile picture was not the actual person who turned up at the pub.'

'What makes you say that?' asked Jones.

Phillips slipped the car in reverse and edged backwards. 'Because if you're that good looking, you don't need dating apps.'

10

After a full debrief of all the information gathered so far on Gillian Galloway and Jerry Cooper – none of which was remotely remarkable or of any help in finding her killer – Phillips had despatched Jones and Bovalino to the Pig and Whistle in Altrincham. A couple of hours later, they were back.

'It appears Galloway did meet a man in the pub, but it certainly wasn't Conrad Eve, the beach bum from Tinder,' said Jones.

Bovalino interjected. 'The barman's description was a little bit different, Guv.'

'How so?'

'He said her date looked like a Thunderbird.'

Phillips frowned. 'What did he mean by that?'

'Apparently he looked like he was wearing a wig, and had thick-rimmed glasses,' replied Jones.

'So, what else did the landlord say?'

Jones continued. 'He reckons they had a couple of drinks and left after about an hour, but that when they did, she was a bit wobbly on her feet and her date had to help her out the door.'

'So, she was drunk?'

'That's what the landlord seemed to think, Guv,' Bovalino said. 'But he did say it seemed a bit odd considering she'd only had a couple of vodkas.'

'Galloway's flatmate said she hardly ever went out, so maybe she wasn't much of a drinker?' added Jones.

'Maybe not,' said Phillips. 'Did the landlord notice anything else about Galloway's date?'

Jones shook his head. 'Nothing of any real value. Said he was wearing a lot of aftershave and relatively well spoken. That's about all he remembers.'

'What about *her*?' asked Phillips.

'Nothing that stood out to him other than the fact she appeared to be drunk. Apart from that, he described her as pleasant, but quite quiet.'

'You mentioned they left together?'

Bovalino nodded. 'That's what the landlord said, yeah.'

'Does the pub have CCTV?'

'No, Guv, it's a right dump. Nothing worth nicking, according to the landlord,' said Jones.

'What about outside? Any council cameras? Neighbouring buildings?'

'Nothing, Guv,' Jones replied. 'We checked all around, but the pub's in a total blind spot.'

Phillips eyes narrowed. 'Which means our guy is either incredibly lucky, or he knew that was the case.'

'That's what we were thinking,' said Bov.

Phillips said nothing for a moment as she considered the next steps. 'Ok. Check the cameras in and around that area of town. See if our man shows up on any of them.'

Jones and Bovalino nodded in unison, then made their way back to their desks.

Phillips turned her chair to face to the window and stared at the treetops swaying in the wind outside. Her mind was awash with questions, one of them being that if Galloway *had* been expecting a good-looking beach bum like Conrad Eve, why had she settled for a man who purportedly looked like a Thunderbird? It had been a very long time since she had been on a blind date – or any date for that matter – but even she knew that just didn't make sense.

11

MONDAY, FEBRUARY 15TH

Phillips walked into the Pathology Department of the MRI just before noon, where she was met by Chakrabortty. The chief pathologist was drying her hands on a large blue paper towel and her green surgical scrubs were covered in small wet patches that Phillips chose to assume had come from the water she'd just used to clean up.

'Morning, Jane,' said Chakrabortty, as she pressed the foot pedal on the orange bin in front of her and tossed in the towel.

Phillips was keen to know how Galloway's post mortem had gone, so got straight to the point. 'What have you got for me?'

'Let's go to my office,' said Chakrabortty. The stench of bleach and cleaning fluid was pervasive. Thankfully, Phillips thought to herself.

Once they were both seated, Chakrabortty picked up a clipboard from the desk and scanned the top page for a long moment before she spoke. 'It's quite a complex case, this one.'

Phillips nodded. 'I had a feeling it might be.'

'The cause of death was asphyxiation, by strangulation. The size and shape of the bruises on her neck are consistent with a man's belt, or something of a similar width and weight, but aside from her throat, there wasn't another mark on her. In fact, the body had been cleaned. Which means no fingerprints and no DNA.'

'Damn it!' said Phillips.

'I know. I'm sorry, Jane.'

'Had she been sexually assaulted?'

Chakrabortty's nose wrinkled. 'That's the odd thing. There was no sign of intercourse at all, but her blood showed traces of rohypnol.'

Phillips recalled Jones's debrief on the Pig and Whistle the previous evening. 'That would fit with our witness statements. They said she appeared wobbly on her feet and had to be helped out of the pub the night she died.'

'Judging by the size of the dose, I'd say it would have eventually rendered her unconscious, but not quickly and not for any great length of time.'

'Long enough to strangle her without her putting up a fight?' said Phillips.

'Almost certainly.'

'Time of death?' asked Phillips.

'The cold temperatures make it difficult, but somewhere between 10 p.m. and midnight.'

'You mentioned the body had been cleaned. What with?'

Chakrabortty sifted through the sheets on the clipboard until she found what she was looking for. 'We found large traces of benzalkonium chloride all over her body, which is an organic salt used in cleaning agents. If you want its official status, it's classified as a quaternary ammonium cationic detergent. It's basically the main ingredient found in most household cleaners.'

'Which means it's almost impossible to identify a specific brand,' said Phillips, sagely.

Chakrabortty nodded. 'I'm afraid so. However, we did find some dirt embedded in a crack on her right heel that contained small traces of nitrogen, potassium and phosphate.'

Phillips eyes narrowed. 'And?'

'I take it you don't watch Gardener's World, Jane?'

Phillips scoffed. 'I barely have time for sleep these days, Tan, never mind TV.'

'Well, if you did, you'd know that the most common place you'll find a combination of nitrogen, potassium and phosphate is in a bag of common-or-garden fertiliser. And the good news for you is that not all fertilisers are the same. In fact, many of them are quite bespoke.'

Phillips pursed her lips as she processed the information. 'In that case, it should be possible to trace it to a specific manufacturer. Can I get a copy of the chemical makeup of the sample?'

Chakrabortty smiled and passed over a printout. 'Already done for you.'

'Always one step ahead, aren't you, Tan?' Phillips eyes scanned down the long list of the chemicals on the sheet in her hands. 'Looks like a job for Entwistle.'

'Rather him than me,' said Chakrabortty with a chuckle.

'Was there anything else of note?'

'She was almost certainly killed, and the body then moved to the final location. As you'd expect, we found mud on the back of the body where she was laid, but the cleaning agent was located on the skin, underneath the mud—'

'Meaning she was cleaned, then dumped,' Phillips cut in.

'Precisely.'

Phillips ran the information over in her mind for a moment, then summarised the evidence she had so far. 'So, by all accounts, Gillian Galloway meets her date for a drink in the Pig and Whistle in Altrincham at around 8 p.m. An hour later, witnesses see her leaving in the arms of her date, looking worse for wear. The reason being, we now know, was because her drink was likely spiked with rohypnol. Then, sometime within the next three hours, her killer strangles her, strips her naked, cleans her body, and then places it carefully in a cruciform position in Dunham Massey Park.'

'We see some weird shit in this job, don't we, Jane?' said Chakrabortty.

'Yeah, we really do.'

'You know I normally leave the policing to you, but do you remember the Suffolk Strangler?'

'It rings a bell,' said Phillips.

Chakrabortty continued. 'The guy's name was Steve Wright. He killed five sex workers in Ipswich in 2006.'

'Oh yeah, I remember now.'

'Well, he used to clean his victims and leave them in the cruciform position. The similarity struck me.'

'Wright's still inside though, isn't he?' asked Phillips.

'Oh, yeah. He got a whole life tariff, but the cruciform position reminded me of that case. So I googled it before you arrived. The similarities are evident for all to see.'

'So, are you suggesting we have a copycat killer?'

Chakrabortty raised her hands in mock defence. 'Like I

say, Jane. I leave the detective work to you. All I'm saying is, there are definite similarities.'

Phillips exhaled loudly. 'Jesus. That's all I need – a bloody copycat killer.'

Chakrabortty offered a sympathetic smile.

'So, is there anything else I need to know?'

'That's your lot. She's all yours,' said Chakrabortty.

'Can you email me a copy of the report?'

'Already done.'

'Of course it is. What would I do without you?' said Phillips, standing. 'Right. Well, I'd better be getting back. I need to debrief Carter on all of this.'

'Good luck,' said Chakrabortty as she turned to face the laptop in front of her.

As Phillips reached the door to the office, she turned back to face Chakrabortty. 'Tan?'

Chakrabortty looked up from the screen. 'Yes?'

'If Galloway *was* knocked out by the rohypnol when he strangled her, would she have known it was happening?'

'I very much doubt it, Jane, but you can never know for sure in these cases.'

Phillips flashed a thin smile, then stepped out into the corridor. A few minutes later, she strode across the windswept car park towards her car, keen to get back to Ashton House to update the team.

12

Phillips used to dread being summoned to the fifth floor to see her old boss, Chief Superintendent Fox; a woman widely regarded around the headquarters of the Greater Manchester Police as a functioning sociopath. Famous for her unflinching ambition, as chief superintendent she had ruled the Major Crimes team with an iron fist for almost a decade before finally securing her dream of promotion to chief constable. Now she ruled the *entire* Manchester force with the same iron fist.

Fox had been replaced in MCU by Chief Superintendent Harry Carter, who couldn't be more different. Suddenly, Phillips found that she quite looked forward to her visits to the fifth floor to talk to her new boss. His style and approach were polar opposites to the previous regime. Gone were the constant dressing downs, the ever-present condescending tone and the total lack of trust – all hallmarks of Fox's reign – replaced by adult conversations with a down-to-earth copper who knew how to get the best out of Phillips and her team.

As Phillips entered the outer office, Carter's assistant, Diana Cook, offered a warm smile. 'Hello, Jane. How are you today?'

The welcome was a stark contrast to those previously dished out by Fox's assistant, Ms Blair, and just a month or so into the new regime, it still caught Phillips off guard. Consequently, she often found herself offering up far more information than was necessary. 'I'm good thanks, Di. A bit stressed about our caseload at the minute, but we'll keep plugging away.' Today was no different.

Cook stood. 'The chief super won't be a minute. He's just finishing up a call. Can I get you a coffee while you wait?'

'That would be lovely, thanks.'

Phillips watched on as Cook busied herself at the small coffee machine in the corner of the room. She was petite with dark, well-maintained hair, and smartly dressed with killer heels that seemed to go on forever. They were about the same age, but couldn't have looked more different. As Phillips cast her eyes down to her dark boots and charcoal grey trousers, she suddenly felt very scruffy.

Cook handed her her coffee and walked elegantly back round to resume her position behind her desk, where she checked the large phone console in front of her. 'He's free now. You can go in.'

Phillips took a sip of coffee, then opened the door to Carter's office and stepped inside.

Chief Superintendent Harry Carter cut a rugged figure, standing behind his desk in uniform with his back to her. He appeared to be gazing at a framed aerial photograph of St James's Park stadium, home to his beloved Newcastle United. She knew from their conversations over the last few months that he had a season ticket and had been attending games since he was a young boy. Carter was tall, at well over six feet, with an athletic, muscular frame. He had recently turned fifty, but aside from the salt and pepper flecks in his dark, wavy hair, you could easily have mistaken him for closer to forty.

'Do you miss it?' asked Phillips.

He turned, and a smile flashed across his handsome, chiselled face. 'What? St James's?' His voice was deep and rich, yet soft and unmistakably North East.

'Actually, I was thinking more about Newcastle as a whole.'

He nodded. 'I spent my entire career up there. To be honest, I never thought I'd leave.'

'But the lure of chief superintendent was too strong?'

'Something like that.'

Carter gestured for her to take a seat opposite his desk as he dropped into his own high-backed leather chair. 'It's Fran that's having the harder time adjusting, being stuck at home with the twins all day in a new city. Twins are hard, but twin boys? They're a nightmare at times. She keeps reminding me she's only forty and constantly exhausted, and that if she's not careful, the best years of her life will be behind her with nothing to show for them. And it doesn't help that she's also missing her mum and sisters, who she adores.' Carter shook his head. 'As you can imagine, it's not much fun at home at the minute.'

'No, I bet it's not,' said Phillips. 'Hopefully things will settle down for you soon, sir.'

Carter leaned forward and linked his fingers on the desk. 'Anyway, enough about my boring home life. How are you getting on with the care home poisoning?'

'Still a work in progress, sir. No updates as yet.'

Carter nodded. 'And how was the Galloway post

mortem this morning?'

Life really *had* changed for the better since Carter had replaced Fox. He seemed constantly aware of everything that was happening in the unit, but still managed to stay far enough out of the way to allow Phillips and her team to get on with their jobs without interruption. He was supportive in a way she had rarely seen in over two decades of policing, and there was little doubt he cared about his people – just as much as getting results, *maybe more*.

'The PM was as expected, really. Asphyxiation by strangulation. Chakrabortty reckons the killer used a man's belt or something similar.'

Carter nodded along.

Phillips continued. 'There were traces of rohypnol in her system, which could explain why the witnesses from the Pig and Whistle said she appeared to be drunk when she left after only a couple of drinks.'

'Was she raped, then?'

'No, she wasn't.'

'So why use the rohypnol?' asked Carter.

'Well, I guess to incapacitate her. Much easier to strangle someone if they can't fight back.'

'True.'

'And Chakrabortty believes the body was cleaned before it was dumped. So no fingerprints or DNA.'

'Damn it!'

Phillips smiled. 'That's exactly what I said.'

'So, what *do* we have?'

'The position of the body, sir. That appears significant.'

'The cruciform?'

'Yeah. When I first saw it, I thought it looked familiar but I couldn't put my finger on it. Then Chakrabortty mentioned something today, and it came back to me. The position of the body matches the victims of the Suffolk Strangler.'

Carter recoiled slightly. 'Steve Wright? But he's still inside, isn't he?'

'Yeah. He is, but that doesn't mean his crimes are.'

'What do you mean by that?'

'Well, could we be looking at a copycat?'

Carter frowned. 'It's a bit early for that, isn't it? It's only one victim.'

'Maybe, but it's worth throwing it out there. As we know, all serial killer cases start with one victim, sir.'

They both said nothing for a moment as they considered the possibility someone might be copying murders that had been committed over twelve years ago.

Carter was first to speak. 'How about CCTV? Anything from the pub or surrounding area?'

'Nothing, and it's potentially no accident that our killer picked the Pig and Whistle, for that very reason. The pub doesn't have any cameras, and the building itself sits in a total blind spot to all council cameras. We have no idea who went into that pub with her, *or* who helped her out again.'

'And what about the witnesses in the pub itself?'

Phillips shook her head. 'They describe her date as a man wearing a wig and thick glasses who, and I quote, "looked like a Thunderbird".'

Carter let out an ironic chuckle. 'Hardly something that will excite our friends in CPS.'

'Exactly.'

'How about the flatmate? Anything new from her? Any threats or violent relationships?'

'Nothing,' Phillips sighed.

'So, what's our next move?'

Phillips took a gulp of coffee before speaking. 'I've got the guys looking into Galloway's background, see if we can dig up anything of significance from her past. They're also going over the wider CCTV cameras across the town centre, plus ANPR. See if we can get a visual on her through any of those.'

'Did anything come back on the guy who found her – Cooper wasn't it?'

Phillips was impressed Carter remembered his name. 'Nothing. Clean record and an alibi. He was at home with his wife.'

Carter locked eyes with Phillips. 'Wives *lie* for their husbands, Jane.'

'I know that, sir.'

Carter's expression softened as he sat back in his chair. 'Unless, of course, they happen to be my *first* wife—' A wry smile spread across his face. '—who told nothing but lies *about* me to get custody of the kids and empty my bank account.'

Phillips chuckled. Carter's references to his demonic ex-wife had littered many of his conversations with her and the team. Always said in jest, and with razor-sharp comic timing, he used them to break the ice or relieve the tension. But, a few times so far, she had caught a flicker of sadness flash in his eyes when he mentioned her.

Carter changed tack. 'How about the Michael Yates poisoning? Any updates on that?'

'A total dead end, I'm afraid. We've been through the care home, questioned everyone working that night as well as his doctors and support workers, but found nothing. He'd sold his house to pay for his care, no savings, no relatives, and his will leaves what little money he had left to charity.'

'What about the doctor who treated him? Any chance of breaking her alibi?'

''fraid not, sir,' said Phillips. 'As much as I'd like to pin Yates's murder on that stroppy cow, she was nowhere near the care home that night.'

Carter tapped his right index finger on the arm of his chair. 'It's a bloody mystery, isn't it? Who would want to kill a sick old man like that?'

Phillips exhaled loudly. 'Did I tell you he was my teacher at sixth form?'

Carter's eyes widened as he sat forwards once more. 'No, you definitely didn't.'

'Yeah, Mr Yates. He was a great guy. Really helped me when I needed some advice that *wasn't* my mother's. In fact, he's one of the reasons I'm sat here today. He told me to follow my guts and do what I wanted with my life, and all I ever wanted was to be a copper. He helped me realise that dream.'

'Well, if that's the case, I have a lot to thank him for,' said Carter warmly.

Phillips felt herself blush, and was keen to change the subject. 'I'm hoping to go to the funeral in the next week or so. Would that be ok?'

'Of course. Whatever you need.'

'Thank you. My brother's gonna come too. He was taught by Mr Yates as well.' Phillips bit her bottom lip. 'It's funny, Mr Yates was such a massive influence on my life, and yet I never knew his first name until a few weeks ago.'

'Are you ok with all this, Jane?' Carter's voice was laced with concern. 'If it's too close to home, I can give the Yates case to someone else, you know. Let you focus on Galloway.'

Phillips straightened in her chair. 'I'm fine, sir. If

anything, I owe it to him to find his killer. Otherwise all his help back then will have been for nothing.'

Carter scoffed. 'Come on, Jane, that's not fair. You're one of the most successful detectives in the history of the GMP.'

Phillips nodded. 'Yeah, well. You're only as good as your last case, sir, so with that in mind, I'd better get back downstairs and see what the guys have come up with.'

'She warned me about you, you know?'

Phillips felt herself recoil. 'Sir?'

'Fox. When I was offered the job, she told me how you operate. "Relentless" I think was the word she used,' said Carter.

'And is that a bad thing for a murder detective?'

Carter shook his head. 'No, it's not, Jane. But take it from someone who's been there once and is in danger of making the same mistakes for a second time: make sure you make time for *you* and what's important outside of Ashton House. Burning yourself out won't help the victims or their families.'

Phillips nodded, but said nothing, the atmosphere suddenly awkward.

Carter glanced at his watch. 'Ok, well, I need to prepare for my weekly update with Fox.'

'How are you finding her?'

'*Relentless,*' he said, with a chuckle and a glint in his eye, which diffused the tension instantly.

A wry smile spread across Phillips's face. 'I have to say, I don't miss reporting directly to her.'

'No. I don't imagine you do,' said Carter.

Phillips stood. 'Right, well, I'll leave you to the joys of police politics,' she said, then made her way to the door.

13

Back downstairs on the third floor, Phillips entered the MCU offices carrying a cardboard tray containing hot drinks for herself and each of her core team, Jones, Bovalino and Entwistle, who all appeared focused on their tasks as she approached. She laid the tray down and began handing out the cardboard cups.

'How was Carter?' asked Jones, as he accepted his usual peppermint tea.

'Fine,' said Phillips, then took a seat at the spare desk. 'Keen to know how we're getting on with the Galloway and Yates cases. Any updates for me?'

'I'm going through the CCTV across the town centre, but so far nothing on Galloway,' said Jones.

Bovalino took a tentative sip of his steaming black coffee, then turned his computer monitor to face Phillips and activated a video on the screen. 'Me too. I've been looking at the footage the bus company sent over. Here we can see Galloway on the 245 bus heading into Altrincham just before 8 p.m. on the night she died.' He pressed play on another video. 'Ten minutes later, we see her walking across the bus terminal towards the Pig and Whistle, where she moves out of shot. That's the last footage of her we've got, so far.'

Jones cut back in. 'Because we have no idea which direction she went in when she left the pub, we've got close to fifty cameras to check, which is going to take time.'

Phillips took a mouthful of her tea, then placed the cup on the desk. 'Ok. Bov, if there's nothing else to review from the bus company, then you can help Jones with the rest of the council cameras.'

'Sure,' said Bovalino.

She focused on Entwistle next, hopeful that her digital tech specialist would have come up with a lead after spending the day searching the Automatic Number Plate Recognition Camera database. 'So, what about ANPR?'

Entwistle angled his laptop so Phillips could see his screen. 'Nothing of note regarding Galloway, I'm afraid...'

Phillips's heart sank.

'...and no stolen or cloned vehicles. But, there is something I thought you'd want to see.'

Phillips sat forward. 'Ok. What have you got?'

Entwistle double-clicked an image on his desktop so it filled the screen. On closer inspection, it looked like a grainy still from one of the cameras. 'This van was caught heading towards the Pig and Whistle just before 8 p.m., and then again, heading away, just after 9. What struck me about it was the fact the number plates didn't register with the database, and when I zoomed in – although the image quality is poor – it looks as if they've been covered over with something like mud, oil maybe, paint even. It's a Ford transit, and judging by the body shape, it's a first generation Mark-II.'

'What are you, a van geek or something?' teased Bovalino.

'No, Bov,' Entwistle shot back, 'I'm a detective with access to Wikipedia. You should try it sometime.'

'Never mind, Bov. Carry on,' urged Phillips.

'The Mark II was in circulation across the UK from 1977 to '96. I've checked the DVLA database for existing models in the Greater Manchester area, and there are just under a hundred still registered on the road, with a further thirteen off the road and certified as SORN.'

Phillips stared at the black and white image of the van on the screen. It looked dark and gloomy, sinister even. 'We need to find that van. Entwistle, draft in the wider team and coordinate the search. And make sure you use PC Lawford. She's got a keen eye for detail.'

'On it, Guv.'

'And what about Galloway's phone records? Anything of use there?' asked Phillips.

'I looked at those too, Guv,' said Bovalino, shaking his head, then checking his notes. 'It last connected with the mobile phone mast in Altrincham town centre at 8.43 p.m. Then it either ran out of juice or was switched off.'

'Well, that can't be a coincidence, can it?' said Phillips.

'No, Guv. That's what I thought.'

Phillips rose from the chair. 'Right, guys. Our priority is to find footage of Galloway, and we need to track down that van ASAP. Let's get on it.' She headed for her office. It was time she took another look at Steve Wright and the Suffolk Strangler murders.

14

SATURDAY, FEBRUARY 20TH

Gabe placed the small flat-screen TV onto the chest of drawers at the end of his father's bed, and inserted the HDMI cable that was connected at the other end to his open laptop. His hands were shaking slightly from the adrenaline coursing through his body in anticipation of what was to come.

'What the bloody hell are you doing to my TV?' Bert wheezed through his battered larynx from his bed.

Gabe ignored the question as he activated the camera feed on his phone, which was set up and recording next door, secreted on a shelf in the corner of the room. The footage appeared on the large screen, and his heart skipped a beat as he gazed at the young man seated on the sofa, sipping a glass of champagne. A chill of excitement run up his spine. With everything set, he stepped to the side, then turned to face his father.

'Who's that on the telly?' asked Bert. He was sitting at a 45-degree angle, propped up with pillows.

A broad smile spread across Gabe's face, but he remained silent.

His father's expression twisted as he focused on the screen. 'Is that our sitting room?'

Gabe angled his body so he could see the screen once more. 'Yes, it is, and that young man is called Sean. Adorable, isn't he?'

Bert locked wide eyes with Gabe's. 'What the fuck are you doing?'

'You'll see.'

'Turn it back to the proper telly!'

'What? And have you miss all the fun? No chance.'

'I'm telling you, turn my telly back on!'

'No.' Gabe chuckled. He was enjoying himself now.

'Do as you are told for once and stop this bloody nonsense right now. Do you hear me?'

'Oh, I hear you,' said Gabe, 'but I'm not listening. *Not anymore.*' He faced the screen fully now. Holding the remote in his hand, he increased the volume so they could hear the music that was playing in the other room: a compilation of 80s pop. He then placed the remote purposely out of his father's reach.

'Boy! I'm telling you, turn that shit off and stop this stupid fucking game right now.'

'I will not,' Gabe spat back, 'so just lie back and enjoy the show.'

A look of confusion spread across Bert's face. 'What are you talking about? What bloody show?'

Gabe grinned maniacally. 'You'll see,' he said, then made his way out of the room.

SEAN REMAINED SEATED as Gabe walked into the sitting room. He was twenty years old, and his slim, angular features were accentuated by the candlelight. The glass in his hand was empty.

'Sorry about that. I just had a few chores to get sorted, but I'm all yours now. Can I get you a refill?' Gabe asked.

Sean appeared nervous as he nodded. 'Yes please, that would be lovely.' The accent was thick Glaswegian, but with a tenderness that softened the hard edge.

Gabe took his glass and moved over to the small, kitsch, free-standing bar on the other side of the room, where he busied himself with the drinks. A classic Bronski Beat song played low on the stereo. 'I love this track!' he said, affecting a camp, high-pitched voice as he reached for the remote and turned it up.

A moment later, he flopped down on the couch and passed across the champagne. 'Bottoms up!' said Gabe with a wink, as he took a long drink.

'I've never had champagne before,' said Sean coyly.

Gabe flicked his head theatrically 'What? You've not lived, sweetheart.'

Sean took a sip. 'No. You're right there.' His head fell forwards slightly as his shoulders sagged.

'Well, you're with Gabriel now, darling. Your life will never be the same after tonight. That I can *promise*, you.'

An awkward smile flashed across Sean's face. 'How long have you been out?' he asked sheepishly.

Gabe blew his lips. 'God, it feels like forever. I was eighteen, so it probably is. What about you?'

'One week today.' Sadness filled his eyes.

'I take it it didn't go well, then?'

'You could say that.'

'So, who reacted the worst, your mum or your dad?'

'Dad.' Sean took a big gulp from the champagne. 'He kicked me out. Said I was a poof and no son of his.'

Gabe nodded. 'Sounds familiar.'

Sean bit his bottom lip for a moment. 'He says he never wants to speak to me again. That I don't exist as far as he's concerned.'

Gabe's tone softened. 'Well, if he's anything like my old man, you're better off without him.'

'You don't get on with your dad either?' asked Sean.

'No, I don't. In fact, I bloody hate him, and I'll be glad when he's dead.' Gabe stared in the direction of the camera, hoping his father was watching, but knowing for sure he could definitely hear him.

Another 80s anthem started on the stereo, and Gabe jumped up off the sofa. 'Come on, let's dance!' He held out his hand.

Sean took it, and as Gabe pulled him up from the chair, he got a sense of how slight the young man's frame was.

As the song played, Gabe threw himself into a virtuoso performance as a 'life and soul of the party' gay man, something he knew – because of his gentle nature as a child – his bigoted, right-wing father had always feared he would become. Once more, his mind's eye was drawn to the image of Bert lying in bed, watching his son frolicking with another man in his own house. A sudden urge to kiss Sean came over him, and he pulled his date into a clinch without warning, kissing him with ferocious abandon before pulling away and staring into Sean's dark, expectant eyes.

'Was that ok?' whispered Gabe.

Sean nodded with a smile for a moment, before his face changed all of a sudden.

'Are you ok?' said Gabe, affecting concern.

Sean's mouth opened as he placed his hand against his chest. 'I feel a bit queasy...'

Gabe reached out and grabbed Sean's wrists to steady him.

'Maybe it's the champagne?' Sean's words were slurred.

Gabe stared at him for a long moment before replying, 'It's not the champagne, darling.' He pulled Sean closer. 'It's the rohypnol I put in it.'

Sean's eyes bulged. 'You...drugged...me?' he mumbled.

'Yes, I did,' said Gabe, without emotion, as he stared into Sean's wide, terrified eyes. 'Don't worry. You won't feel a thing.'

Sean's knees buckled slightly, and a few seconds later his body went limp and he fell backwards onto the sofa, unconscious.

Gabe stared at the young man sprawled out in front of him. His heart beat loudly in his ears. A rush of excitement surged through every fibre of his body, relishing the control he had over another human being. Then, for his father's benefit, he turned to face the camera once more. 'Did you see how easy that was? How much power I have now?' He leered.

He turned back and grabbed Sean's ankles, then dragged him off the couch and onto the floor. His limp body felt heavier now, but was still light enough to drag across the carpet with ease. A few minutes later, he opened the door to his father's room, and dragged Sean inside next to the bed. When the young man's feet were level with his father's head, he dropped his ankles to the floor, stood upright and locked eyes with Bert.

'Stop this madness,' demanded Bert. 'Please, son.'

'Stop? Don't be absurd. I'm just getting started,' Gabe chortled as he left the room.

Returning a few minutes later, he placed a large bucket of water on the floor next to Sean's head.

'You've proven your point, son. Please, leave the boy alone. No one else has to die.'

Gabe ignored his father as he got down on his knees, then rolled Sean over onto his stomach. Next, he grabbed the thick hair at the back of his skull and lifted the young man's head and shoulders up from the floor with ease. He turned to stare at his father now. He could feel his boiling hatred for the man who had caused him so much pain as a child as if it was a living thing inside him. 'This is on *you*, father,' he growled, before thrusting Sean's head deep into the bucket of water.

'Stop it!' cried Bert.

Completely incapacitated by the rohypnol, Sean didn't react.

Gabe locked eyes with his father, his jaw fixed in anger, his gaze unflinching as he held Sean's head under the water. Bubbles popped on the surface as the air in his lungs was forced out by the water rushing in. Gabe's entire body began to shake with rage as he pushed Sean's head against the bottom of the bucket, holding it there with all his weight. Finally, a minute later, the bubbles stopped.

The young man was dead.

15

TUESDAY, FEBRUARY 23RD

Jones steered the squad car down the rough track, driving at a steady pace over the frosty, uneven ground as he and Phillips made their way onto wasteland located in Knutsford, about a mile outside of the town centre. Whatever industry had once been located here had long since gone, and the land had been cleared. 'Coming Soon' signs featuring images of new homes were located at the site entrance as they turned off the main road. Up ahead, the flashing lights of a fire truck illuminated the dark early morning sky as a number of fire fighters tackled the blaze.

'So, what are we expecting, here?' asked Phillips.

'Apparently it's a rubbish fire that contains a body,' replied Jones.

Phillips blew her lips. 'What a way to start the day, hey?'

'Nothing wakes you up quite like seeing a body first thing in the morning.'

'Do we know who found it?' asked Phillips.

'Uniform said the call came in from a security guard who was looking after the site. I told them to keep him on-scene for us.'

A minute later, Jones pulled the car to a stop next to a parked patrol car.

'Here we go again,' said Phillips, as she opened the passenger door and stepped out.

Jones tucked in behind her as they made their way towards the flames. A fire fighter turned and stepped towards them, followed by a uniformed police officer.

Phillips flashed her ID as she looked at the fire behind them.

'I'm Leading Firefighter Banks.'

'Sergeant Noakes, Ma'am,' said the police officer.

Phillips nodded in the direction of the fire. 'I'm told we have a body in that?'

'Yes, Ma'am,' replied Noakes.

'Along with a lot of other stuff, including old car tyres,' added Firefighter Banks. 'It's proving quite difficult to extinguish.'

'Is the body male or female?' asked Phillips.

Banks glanced back towards his men. 'We can't say, I'm afraid. It's too badly burnt at this stage.'

'I see,' said Phillips.

Jones turned his attention to Noakes. 'You said on the phone that a security guard had called it in.'

'Yes. Julian Macintosh. He's in that van over there.' Noakes pointed to a large white van with blue and silver livery running down the side. It gave it the look of a police van, apart from the logo, which read 'iSecure Group.'

Phillips locked eyes with Jones and thrust her hands into her coat pocket to protect them from the cold. 'Well, we'd better go and have a chat, hadn't we?' She gestured for her 2IC to follow.

As they approached the van, the driver's door opened and a man in a hi vis jacket climbed out. He was about six feet tall and, Phillips guessed, somewhere in his mid- to late-forties.

'Mr Macintosh?' Phillips extended her hand.

'Please, call me Julian,' he said with a firm grip. His accent was unmistakably Yorkshire.

'Can you tell us how you came upon the body in the fire?'

'I was doing my rounds this morning and spotted the flames as soon as I arrived on site. I thought someone must have been fly-tipping, or some kids messing about. I keep a fire extinguisher in the van, so I parked up and went to see if it was small enough to put out myself, and that's when I smelt it.'

'Smelt what?' asked Jones.

'Burning human remains.'

'How did you know what it was?' asked Phillips

'Two tours of Afghanistan. I'm ex-Green Howards.'

'I see,' said Phillips.

Macintosh continued. 'To be fair, it was masked by whatever else was in the fire to start with, but once my nose got a whiff of it, I knew it was human. You never forget that smell.'

'What time was that?' said Jones

'It was my second job of the morning, so just after seven. I called your lot straight away.'

Phillips cut back in. 'Did you see or notice anything out of the ordinary when you arrived on site?'

'You mean apart from the burning body, like?' chuckled Macintosh, but immediately seemed to think twice about it.

Phillips glared at him. 'Apart from that.'

'Well, there was a van just over there that I've never noticed before.'

'A van?' He had Phillips's full attention.

'Yeah. It was parked up over on the lane, just past those trees over there,' Macintosh pointed to the farthest corner of the site. 'As soon as I arrived, it moved on.'

Phillips and Jones locked eyes for a split second. 'What kind of van was it?' she asked.

'An old transit,' Macintosh said with confidence.

'You're sure of that?' said Phillips.

'Oh aye. I did sniper training in the army. Plus, I'm a right nosey bastard, so I'm always looking at what's around me.'

'Did you notice the colour?' asked Jones.

'It was too far away for me to be totally sure, and it was still dark at that time, but it was either dark green, navy blue or brown. And it had some faded white lettering on the side. I think it said "& son" or something like that.'

'What about the registration?' said Phillips.

Macintosh shook his head. 'I'm afraid not. Like I say, it was too far away and dark for me to get a proper look.'

Phillips nodded. 'Who owns this site?'

'Marvel Homes. They're due to start construction in the next month.'

'It's a big spot,' said Jones.

'Yeah. A hundred new homes, so I'm told,' said Macintosh.

Jones continued. 'And how long have you been looking after the security here?'

'About three months. It's not an active site, so we just do patrols.'

'Is the site secure? Around the perimeter, I mean?' asked Phillips.

'Not at this stage. There's nowt here, so nothing to nick. I just check in and make sure no one's fly-tipping or using it as a temporary caravan park, if you know what I mean?'

'Travellers?' said Jones.

Macintosh nodded. 'So far so good on that score.'

'Well, thank you, Julian,' said Phillips. 'You've been very helpful, and I'm sure we've taken up enough of your time. We'd better let you get on.'

Macintosh checked his watch. 'Yeah, I'm running about an hour behind, now.'

'Well, if your next client gives you any grief, you point him in my direction,' said Phillips warmly.

'I'll hold you to that,' said Macintosh with a cheeky wink, then turned and walked back to his van.

Phillips and Jones set off back in the direction of the fire, which the fire crew finally seemed to be getting under control. She pulled out her phone and called Entwistle.

'Guv?' he answered.

'Where are we at with that transit van search?'

'We're working through them at the moment, speaking to the owners on the database, but so far there's nothing of note.'

'Well, a witness here said he saw a similar-looking van when he arrived on site this morning. Reckons it had some white writing on the side that may have said "...& son", but he can't be sure. Still, keep that in mind when you and the team are speaking to the owners.'

'Will do. I'll send an email to the guys now,' said Entwistle.

'We can't be sure there's any connection to the deaths, but we should keep an open mind to it.'

'*Of course, Guv.*'

Phillips hung up and turned to Jones. 'Give Evans a call. We need him to look at what's left of the fire, as well as the tyre tracks from that van, and get that lane cordoned off urgently. I don't want anything to disturb those tyre tracks.'

Jones nodded. 'I'm on it, Guv,' he said, and headed off in Sergeant Noakes's direction.

16

WEDNESDAY, FEBRUARY 24TH

The following afternoon, Phillips gathered Jones, Bovalino and Entwistle in the Major Crimes conference room to go over the crime scene photos that had been sent over by Evans earlier that morning. As ever, Entwistle had been tasked with looking after the technology for the meeting, and the laptop in front of him projected his screen onto the large-screen TV mounted on the wall opposite. The rest of the team were positioned around the large conference table.

'Right. We've got a hell of a lot of open cases at the minute, so let's crack on, shall we?' said Phillips.

Entwistle clicked on the folder from Evans, which opened to reveal a host of photo thumbnails. He selected them all and moved them into a slideshow app, which started automatically a few seconds later.

The first images were of the body and made for grim viewing, the arms and legs bent in the pugilistic pose, a common sight with bodies recovered from fires.

'Evans reckons the body was an adult male,' said

Phillips. 'No idea on age or race yet. We'll have to wait for Chakrabortty and the post mortem for that.'

A close-up of the charred face filled the big screen. 'Jesus, that's horrific,' said Bovalino as he shifted in his seat. 'Why would someone do that to another person?'

'I've been in Major Crimes for over fifteen years, and I'm still surprised every day by what human beings are capable of,' said Jones.

The macabre viewing continued for the next thirty minutes as they examined each individual shot in the hope of finding clues as to either the killer or the victim's identity. When they had looked through all the pictures of the body without success, they moved onto the other elements found in and around the fire.

'Did Evans identify what the chemical element of the fire was?' asked Jones.

'No,' replied Phillips. 'He said it was all too badly damaged by the time the fire brigade put it out, and the car tyre that was burnt along with the body didn't help, either. Again, that should be something Chakrabortty can tell us.'

'When's the PM scheduled for?' asked Entwistle.

'Not sure, yet. I was planning on calling Tan for an update this morning,' said Phillips.

The slideshow continued, and myriad images of the remnants of the fire came and went on the screen, including a totally charred Samsung mobile phone. The next image that appeared was of a hotel room key, complete with a partially charred key ring. The name of the hotel was still visible, Palatine, followed by the number 3. Whatever came after could no longer be made out.

Entwistle switched from the slideshow momentarily, pulled up Google in his web browser, then typed in Palatine

Hotel, Manchester. A second later, an image of the front of the hotel filled the screen.

'I know that place,' said Bovalino. 'It's just outside the city centre as you head out of Rusholme. The guests are mainly DSS bed and breakfast. It's dirt cheap and full of asylum seekers.'

'Well, that's where we need to look next,' said Phillips.

'I'll go,' offered Bov. 'I've seen enough pictures of dead bodies for one day.'

'I'll come with you,' said Jones. 'I could do with a change of scene, too.'

Phillips nodded. 'Do we have any more images from Evans to go through?'

Entwistle flipped the screen back to the slideshow. 'Looks like that was the last one, Guv.'

'Ok. In that case, print a copy of the room key off for Jones and Bov, will you? They'll need it to show the hotel,' Phillips said.

Entwistle nodded. 'It's coming out now.'

Phillips stood. 'Right. Whilst you're doing that, I'm gonna speak to Evans about the tyre tracks. See where he's at with those.' With that, she left the conference room and headed back to her office.

A few minutes later, Phillips was sitting at her desk, phone in hand ready to call Evans, when Entwistle knocked on her door.

'You got a minute, Guv?'

'Sure.' Phillips placed her phone down. 'What's on your mind?'

'The tyre in the fire.'

'What about it?'

'Do you remember Denis Nilsen?'

'The Muswell Hill killer?'

Entwistle nodded. 'I studied him as part of my degree. When we were discussing the fire in there, it occurred to me that Nilsen also used car tyres when he was disposing of his victims, young men he'd picked up in gay bars. In his confession, he admitted strangling them unconscious in his flat before drowning them in the bath or a bucket.'

'I remember he strangled them, but I'd forgotten he drowned them at the end,' said Phillips.

Entwistle continued. 'Yeah, and when he was done with the bodies, he'd burn them with a tyre; claimed it was to disguise the smell of the burning flesh. In the same way the cruciform position of Gillian Galloway's body resembled what Steve Wright did with his victims, the disposal of our burnt body has a lot of similarities with Nilsen's crimes.'

Phillips's brow furrowed. 'You think this latest murder could be another copycat?'

'Maybe, maybe not, but I thought it was worth flagging.'

Phillips considered the information for a long moment, then began typing into her laptop in search of Nilsen's criminal history. When she found what she was looking for, she began reading aloud. '"In late 1980, Nilsen removed and dissected the bodies of each victim killed since December 1979 and burned them upon a communal bonfire he had constructed on *waste ground* behind his flat. To disguise the smell of the burning flesh of the six dissected bodies placed upon this pyre, Nilsen crowned the bonfire with an old *car tyre*". Bloody hell, they're almost identical.'

'I know, right? At first I thought it could just be a coincidence...'

Phillips raised an eyebrow.

'...but you're always telling us you don't believe in

them.'

'No, I don't.' Phillips picked up her mobile and rang Chakrabortty.

'*Jane. You're lucky you caught me, I'm about to start my next PM.*'

'When is the burnt body scheduled, Tan?'

'*Based on the backlog, probably not 'til next week, now.*'

'No chance of bumping me up the queue?'

Chakrabortty let out a frustrated sigh. '*I'll see what I can do, but I can't promise anything. With Ashworth still out with the flu, we're stacked.*'

'Anything you can do to expedite it would really help me out.'

'*I'll try.*'

'You're a star. Just do me a favour, will you? If you find water in the lungs, I need to know immediately.'

'*Water? Are you saying you think the victim drowned before being burnt?*'

'It's a theory. A long shot, but something I need to know one way or the other, as soon as possible.'

'*Sure, Jane. If I find anything like that, I'll call you.*'

'Immediately?'

'*Yes. Immediately.*'

'Thanks, Tan.' Phillips hung up and locked eyes with Entwistle. 'I hope to God you're wrong.'

'Me too, Guv,' Entwistle stood. 'I'd best get back to tracking down that transit van.'

Phillips watched him as he headed back to his desk, her guts churning with anticipation. If her DC was right about the link to Nilsen, then they were dealing with something she'd never encountered before: two murders that copycatted two *different* historical killers.

17

When partnered together, Jones had no choice but to let Bovalino drive. As an amateur rally driver in his spare time, the big Italian had a love of cars – as well as driving them at a terrifying pace – beyond the scope of most people. Little brought him as much joy as being involved in a high-speed police pursuit, but sadly for him, the work of a detective rarely required such a thing. Still, Bov never failed to test whatever car he was driving to its limits, whenever possible. Thankfully for Jones, this evening's journey from Ashton House in Failsworth to Rusholme, just outside the city limits, had been very uneventful. The early evening traffic had ensured their journey had taken almost twice as long as the twenty-five minutes suggested by the car's Sat Nav.

As they arrived at the Palatine Hotel, Bovalino pulled the squad car off the main drag and into the car park positioned directly in front of the four-storey red-brick Victorian building. All but one of the eight parking bays was empty, the sole car a gold-coloured, dilapidated E-class

Mercedes Benz parked up in a disabled bay, both front tyres completely flat.

Jones pulled the printout of the charred room key from his jacket pocket and checked it was all in order. Satisfied, he opened the passenger door and got out. Bovalino followed him, and a moment later they climbed the steps up to the imposing double front doors. The building itself was in a state of disrepair. Large single-glazed metal windows gave the structure a dramatic air, but on closer inspection, everything needed repainting or, better still, replacing.

'Bit of a shit hole, isn't it?' said Bov, as they reached the front door.

Jones chuckled. 'You ever thought of a job in advertising? "Come to the Palatine Hotel... it's a bit of a shit hole!"'

Bovalino laughed too, as Jones took the lead and stepped through the front door.

Inside, they found themselves in a narrow hallway with a long staircase running up the righthand side. The unmistakable smell of damp filled the air, and Jones noted the nicotine-stained wood-chip wallpaper was peeling back from the walls where it connected with the ceiling. The threadbare carpet that ran the length of the hallway had also seen better days.

On the wall to their left was a doorbell with a sticker underneath that read 'Press for assistance'. Jones followed the instruction, then waited for at least a minute. When no one appeared, Jones pressed it again, over and over this time, until finally a door at the end of the hallway opened. A young woman, who appeared harassed, came into view.

'What you want?' she asked, sounding more than a little irritated – exacerbated by her Eastern European accent.

'Detective Sergeant Jones and Detective Constable

Bovalino,' Jones held out his ID. 'We'd like to speak to the manager, please.'

The woman walked towards them and inspected their credentials closely for a moment. 'I am manager. What you want?'

She was unusually tall for a woman, her long limbs covered in close-fitting, cheap-looking clothes. Tightly curled, shoulder-length bleached blonde hair framed her angular face, a stark contrast to her thick, dark eyebrows.

'I didn't get your name?' said Jones.

'Olga.'

'Olga, what?'

'Svoboda.'

Jones presented her with the photo of the charred key fob retrieved from the fire. 'Is this one of yours?'

Svoboda's eyes narrowed as she inspected the image, then nodded. 'I think so. Where you get this?'

'It was found in a rubbish fire yesterday. We're looking for one of your residents who might have misplaced it.'

Svoboda stared at the image again. 'That looks like a third-floor key. Wait here.' She turned on her heels and headed back through the door from which she'd first appeared. A moment later, she was back. 'All keys on floor three are out.'

'And what does that mean?' asked Jones.

Svoboda shrugged nonchalantly, 'The residents have them.'

'Can you tell us who's staying in the rooms on that floor?' asked Bovalino.

'Three-one is Mr Abebe. I saw him leave about an hour ago. Three-two is Mrs Balodis and her daughter.'

'And the other?'

'Young guy. Mr Hamilton. Moved in last week. Paid two weeks in advance.'

'Have you seen him today?' asked Bov.

Svoboda shook her head. 'Not seen him since the weekend.'

Jones shot Bov a look. 'Is that normal?'

'Is what normal?'

'Not seeing a guest for days?'

Svoboda scoffed. 'I am not their mother. They pay rent, they do what they want.'

'We're going to need to see inside room three-three, please?' said Jones.

'You have warrant?'

Jones sighed, already beginning to lose patience. 'No, love. We don't, but we can get one, along with a small army of uniformed police with flashing lights and sirens to help turn this place upside down. If you'd prefer that option?'

A snarl appeared on Svoboda's lips. It was evident she had no affection for the police. 'Wait here. I get key.' She disappeared once again into the back room, returning soon after, a bunch of keys jangling in her hand. 'Follow me,' she said as she headed upstairs.

A few minutes later, they arrived on the cramped, dingy third floor landing, where they were presented with three dark brown, windowless doors. Each was emblazoned with a number, 3/1, 3/2, 3/3. Svoboda knocked loudly on door 3/3. With no answer forthcoming, she unlocked it and stepped to the side.

'Thank you,' said Jones. 'We'll let you get back to work.'

Svoboda needed no encouragement, disappearing back down the stairs in a flash.

Jones stepped inside to find it empty. Bovalino followed him in. The room was small and unusually clean compared to the rest of the hotel. A petite suitcase stood upright next to the dilapidated single wardrobe. Looking inside the wardrobe, Jones found a few well-pressed T-shirts, jumpers and jeans hanging on a variety of coloured wire hangers. Sat on the bedside table was what appeared to be a self-help book entitled, *Live Your Truth!* On face value, everything seemed to be in place. Nothing of note stood out, and after checking all drawers and the suitcase, they could find no trace of Hamilton.

Jones blew his lips. 'Well, mate, it looks like Hamilton could well be our key owner.'

'As well as the body in the fire?'

'Either that, or the person that put it there. Let's see if we can find out a bit more about him from Mrs Happy downstairs, shall we?'

Bovalino grinned. 'I think I'll leave that one to you.'

As they returned to the ground floor, Bovalino waited by the front door and Jones made his way through to the back room. Sitting behind an old desk, Svoboda appeared startled as he opened the door to the small office.

'Sorry to interrupt,' he lied. 'I'm hoping you might have a bit more information on Mr Hamilton.'

'Like what?'

'Well. Did he leave any ID when he checked in?'

Svoboda begrudgingly opened a large ledger on the desk and rummaged through the back pages before pulling out a sheet. 'He gave me this.' She handed over a black and white copy of a photo driving licence.

'Can I take it?' asked Jones.

The woman nodded.

'Did he leave anything else? Credit card details or a home address, perhaps?'

'He paid cash, up front.'

'I see.' Jones handed her his business card. 'If, by chance, Mr Hamilton comes back to the hotel, can you ask him to call me, please?'

Svoboda stared at the card but said nothing.

'Well, I'd better be going,' said Jones. 'You have yourself a happy day,' he added sarcastically as he left the office.

'If you see him first, tell him he owes me new key!' Svoboda shouted as the door closed behind him.

Jones ignored her as he strode back towards his partner.

Whether Hamilton *was* the body in the fire or the person who put it there, Jones was sure of one thing: providing his landlady with a new key to his poxy room was the least of his worries.

18

Bert was asleep as Gabe entered his father's quiet room, the only sound the hiss of the oxygen running into the tubes positioned in Bert's nose. He noted the clock on the side of the bed, it was just after 11 p.m. Gabe looked at his father's withered body for a long moment before coughing loudly. The noise was enough to wake Bert from his slumber, blinking his eyes into focus.

'What do *you* want?' the old man wheezed.

'To let you know it's done. I got rid of the body.'

Bert closed his eyes and shook his head.

'Do you want to know what I've done with it?'

Bert didn't answer. His eyes remained shut.

Gabe continued. 'Sean Hamilton's body is now nothing more than a pile of ashes.'

Bert's eyes opened now. 'Ashes? How did you do that?'

'I burnt it on a fire.'

'Where?'

'Some wasteland where they're looking to build houses,' Gabe said.

'What did you use to burn it?'

'Petrol, of course.'

'What else?' asked Bert.

'A car tyre, to hide the smell.' Gabe beamed with pride.

'Is that all?' Bert scoffed.

Gabe felt his stomach tighten. How could his father mock him after what he'd done? 'What do you mean, "Is that all?" What else were you expecting?'

Bert chuckled through his rattling larynx, which caused him to cough up a large ball of phlegm.

'What's so funny?' Gabe demanded.

Bert took a moment to clear his throat into an old tissue. 'Did you stay with the fire until it went out?'

'No, of course not. That could take hours. And besides, I had to get away – a security guard turned up at the other end of the site.'

Bert shook his head. 'Have you ever tried to burn a body before?'

'No! Have you?'

The old man's chest rattled with laughter again, which only added to Gabe's hatred for him.

Bert continued. 'No, but I've seen many people who tried. And unless you stick them in an oven at over a thousand degrees C – like you'd get in a crematorium – there's no bloody way that body will ever turn into a pile of ash. *Far from it.*'

'What does that mean?'

'It means, you bloody simpleton, that the body you so readily left behind for the security guard to stumble across will most likely be a curled-up mess of charred flesh. But – and here's the important bit – there'll still be plenty of stuff left for the cops to identify the body, like his teeth, piercings, jewellery even.'

'Jewellery wouldn't survive a fire. It would melt in the heat,' insisted Gabe.

'I wouldn't be so sure.'

Gabe clenched his fists by his side as he attempted to control his anger. 'Well, there's nothing left they can use to trace me, and that's what's important.'

Bert closed his eyes and shook his head once more. 'Oh, I wouldn't be so sure, boy. Even the *smartest* of killers have been convicted on evidence pulled from fires.'

'Well, I'll just have to go back and check to make sure, won't I?'

Bert let out another wheezy cackle. 'If you do that, then you bloody will get arrested! It's most likely a crime scene. You can't just walk up to it and start sifting through the remains. Plus, if it *is* a crime scene, SOCO will have been all over it with a fine-toothed comb by now, anyway. If that's the case, you can bet your bottom dollar they've already found anything and everything you left behind.'

Gabe knew that what his father was saying was correct, but it didn't make it any easier to hear. He cursed himself for not thinking through the disposal of Sean's body in more detail, and he vowed to be more diligent next time. At least that way, his father would have no recourse to mock him again.

Bert winced with pain. 'Get me a shot of morphine,' he said curtly. 'Quickly, boy!'

Reluctantly, Gabe moved across to the chest of drawers at the end of the bed and opened the top drawer, staring down at the myriad syringes and bottles of morphine in front of him. For a moment he considered just how easy it would be to give his father an extra-large dose and be rid of his cruel taunts and jibes forever. But doing that would likely come back to him, as well as take away the pleasure of seeing Bert's mounting horror as the body count grew and his precious reputation as a heroic copper was systematically destroyed, *forever*.

'My morphine, boy!'

Bert's rattling voice crystallised Gabe's focus, and he picked up a syringe and one of the small vials. Moving back to the side of the bed, he plunged the needle into the catheter attached to his father's hand and released the morphine into his system. A few seconds later, the old man's head lopped to the side and his mouth fell open. The man was in a deep sleep.

19

THURSDAY, FEBRUARY 25TH

Phillips sat in the car and waited for her brother to arrive for Michael Yates's funeral service at St John's Church in Didsbury, just a short walk from where her former mentor had lived for most of his adult life. She was early, so sat in silence, sipping a hot coffee. The time was approaching 11 a.m.

Her phone began to ring through the in-car system. It was Jones.

'Morning.'

'Morning, Guv. Are you free to talk?'

'Yeah, I've got a couple of minutes before I need to go in. The coffin's not arrived yet. What's up?'

'I've just got off the phone to Sean's Hamilton's older sister, Louise.'

'How did she take it?'

'Badly, as expected. She initially told me she'd not spoken to Sean since Saturday morning, which wasn't like him at all. So once I mentioned that we'd found a body

linked to Sean's hotel room, she broke down. Kept saying that her little brother was dead, that it had to be him.'

'Sounds like a tough call to make,' said Phillips.

'I've gotta be honest, it was.'

'Did she know why Sean was in Manchester?'

'She did, and that in itself is quite sad, as well.'

'Go on.'

'It seems Sean had recently come out to his parents, and it didn't go well. In fact, his father – a religious guy by all accounts – threw him out of the house and told him never to come back.'

'This is the twenty-first century, for pity's sake! The poor kid.'

'According to his sister, Sean decided Manchester was somewhere he could be openly gay, so he moved down a couple of weeks ago, hoping to start a new life.'

Phillips stayed silent as images of the charred remains they'd found on the tyre fire flashed into her mind's eye.

Jones continued. *'She asked if she could see the body, to make sure it's Sean, but I explained that wouldn't be possible due to the injuries.'*

'Did you get the details of his dentist?'

'I did, Guv. I'm calling them next, see if we can get Sean's records over to Chakrabortty ASAP.'

'Ok, Jonesy. Sorry you had to start your day with a call like that, and I appreciate the update.'

'It's all part of the job, Guv.'

At that moment, Phillips spotted the black hearse up ahead, crawling slowly down the road towards the church. 'I'm gonna have to go, Jonesy. Looks like it's about to start.'

'I'll see you later, boss.'

Phillips hung up and placed her coffee cup in the

central console before straightening her ponytail in the rearview mirror. There was a tap at her window; her brother Damien.

'You're cutting it fine, aren't you?' she said as she jumped out.

'Sorry, sis. You know me.'

She smiled. 'Yeah, you'll be late for your own funeral one day.'

'I bloody hope so!' chuckled Damien.

Once inside – given the fact Yates had had little or no visitors during his time in the care home – the church was surprisingly full. However, considering most of those in attendance were likely in their late seventies or eighties, Phillips reasoned that for many of them, it was simply something to do and somewhere warm to have a chat with their fellow parishioners.

The priest giving the service was an elderly man himself. He appeared uncomfortable with eye contact, having delivered most of the proceedings with his eyes shut, and showed little understanding of how to use a microphone without causing it to distort and feedback.

After an unnecessarily long service due to the painfully long eulogy, Phillips and Damien made the short car journey to the crematorium in Chorlton, where they could say a final goodbye to Mr Yates.

Inside the main crematorium building, they found themselves amongst just a handful of mourners, none of which Phillips recognised from their school days. The old priest from St John's reappeared and, sadly, picked up where he had left off at the church, delivering yet another verbose blessing to no one in particular. At length, the priest finished and disappeared through a door marked private, and Frank Sinatra's *My Way* began to seep at a low level through the speakers on the walls. Listening to the lyrics brought a smile to Phillips's face, and she turned to see Damien smiling too. 'That's so Mr Yates.'

'Yeah, it is. Shall we go, sis?' asked Damien.

Phillips nodded, and followed as he stepped up and headed towards the coffin where, in turn, they each touched the lid and said their own silent farewell.

A moment later, as they stepped outside into the cold winter air, Phillips linked her arm through Damien's and drew him in close. He was tall at over six feet two, and well-built with broad shoulders. Just as she had as a child, she felt safe holding onto her big brother.

'It's hard to think anyone would want to kill Mr Yates,' said Damien as they continued walking towards the car.

'Yeah, it really is.'

'Are you any closer to finding out what happened to him?'

'No,' said Phillips with a sigh. 'No, I'm not.'

They walked in silence for a moment.

'It's no way to end up, is it?' said Damien. 'Alone with no one to give a shit.'

Phillips's chin dropped to her chest. 'No, it isn't. He deserved more than that. He really was a great man, and like the song said, "he did it his way".'

'You really liked him, didn't you?'

'Yeah, I did,' said Phillips. 'But not in any kind of romantic way or anything like that. I mean, I had crushes on some of the teachers at school, but never on Mr Yates. In fact, I'm pretty sure he was gay.'

'That was the rumour going round the sixth form common room,' said Damien.

Phillips continued. 'No, with him I had a total sense of respect and a genuine fondness. In fact, without his advice and support, I'd never have had the guts to go against Mum's wishes and join the police.'

Damien nodded. 'It's all you've ever wanted, isn't it? To be like Dad.'

Phillips took a moment to answer. 'It used to be.'

'How do you mean?'

'Well, I've been a copper for over twenty years now, and in that time, I've sacrificed a lot for my career.'

'Like what, specifically?' asked Damien.

'Like a family.'

Her brother scoffed. 'Janey, being a parent isn't always everything it's cracked up to be, believe me. The lack of sleep, the tantrums, the mess everywhere...and that's just Grace.'

Phillips chuckled. Grace, her sixteen-year-old niece, was currently proving to be a handful for her parents. 'Yeah, but Charlie's still at that fun age, isn't he?' she said, referring to her five-year-old nephew.

'True, but Charlie wasn't planned. He was the result of our first night of freedom in years – and too many mojitos. Trust me, having a sixteen- *and* a five-year-old in the same house is no picnic.'

'Look, don't get me wrong,' Phillips countered. 'I'm not desperate to be a mum or anything, but seeing Mr Yates end up in a care home with no one to visit him, and just a handful of people at his funeral – even after dedicating his *whole life* to the service of others – well, it runs a little close to home for my liking. Do you know what I mean?'

Damien pulled his arm close to his body, squeezing Phillips's arm affectionately. 'I hear what you're saying, sis, but you're not Yates. You're our Janey, and there'll be no shortage of people at your funeral.'

'Yeah, they'll bus in the inmates from Hawk Green Prison, just to make sure I'm dead,' joked Phillips.

They reached Phillips's car and stopped.

'You should come over for dinner soon,' said Damien. 'The kids would love to see you, and so would Vanessa.'

Phillips smiled. 'I'd like that.'

'And you need to go and see Mum and Dad.'

Phillips felt her eyes roll.

'I know, I know, but Mum's always asking after you when she's round at ours, which at the moment seems like every second day.'

'Well, *you* were the one that wanted free childcare,' said Phillips.

Damien scoffed. 'I may not be paying her cash, but I'm certainly paying the price for grannie daycare.'

'Is it that bad?'

'I really appreciate the help, I do, but you know what she's like: "Do this…don't do that…you're too *soft* on Grace…you're too *hard* on Charlie…".'

Phillips nodded. 'She always *did* prefer boys.'

'Seriously, Janey, she's driving me mad. I honestly don't know how Dad copes.'

'He copes because he's deaf in one ear,' chuckled Phillips, 'and he always makes sure that that's the ear closest to Mum's mouth.'

Damien chuckled along. 'Seriously, though, go and see them. I think it'd do you good.'

Phillips exhaled loudly. 'I will, I promise. I just need to get a few cases off my desk.'

'You *always* need a few cases off your desk, Jane, and therein lies the problem.'

Phillips said nothing for a moment as she considered her brother's words. He was right, of course, but she was in no mood to start that age-old debate again. She decided to change the subject. 'Can I give you a lift to the hospital?'

Damien shook his head. 'No need. I can walk up to the Parkway and get a bus. With the bus lanes, I'll be there in half the time it'll take you.'

Phillips feigned shock. 'Dr Damien Phillips is getting a bus? Are you feeling all right?' she pressed her fingers to his forehead, pretending to take his temperature.

'Ha, ha, very funny.'

Phillips pulled him into a tight hug for a long moment before stepping back and rubbing his arms affectionately. 'Give my love to the kids and Vanessa, won't you?'

'No, I won't, actually. *You* can do that yourself when you come round for dinner,' said Damien, playfully.

A smile spread across Phillips's face and she raised her arms in surrender. 'Ok, ok, I get the hint.'

Damien leaned in and kissed her on the forehead. 'Look after yourself, sis, and be safe, ok?'

'I will,' said Phillips.

'Right, well, I'd better get to that bus. Those patients won't get better on their own,' said Damien as he set off walking towards Princess Parkway, just five hundred yards farther up the road.

Phillips watched him for a long moment before turning back to face the large, imposing crematorium building. Smoke had begun to rise into the morning sky. 'Goodbye, Mr Yates,' she said softly as she turned back to her car. 'I'm going to find the bastard that did this to you,' she added as she opened the driver's door and got in. 'No matter how long it takes.'

20

FRIDAY, FEBRUARY 26TH

Just after 1 p.m., the team gathered in the MCU's private meeting room to go over their findings, so far, on the burnt body case. Entwistle was once again at the controls of all things tech, with his laptop screen projected onto the wall opposite. Bovalino had just returned from the canteen with hot drinks and a selection of sandwiches, which each of them now tucked in to.

Phillips swallowed a mouthful of cheese and tomato before she spoke. 'So, to recap where we are: after Jones's conversation with Louise Hamilton, we now think it's likely that the body in the fire belongs to her brother, Sean. After being disowned by his father when he admitted he was gay, Sean decided to come Manchester to start his new life as an openly gay man. He booked and paid in advance for a two-week stay in the Palatine Hotel in Rusholme.'

'Aka, a bit of a shit hole,' interjected Bovalino through a mouthful of food.

'Quite,' Phillips continued. 'We're still waiting on the

results of the post mortem, but there was enough evidence at the scene to suggest that the manner in which his body was disposed of carried the hallmarks of Denis Nilsen, aka the Muswell Hill Killer.'

'Have you mentioned that to Carter yet?' asked Jones. 'The fact it could also be a copycat?'

'Yes.'

'How did he take it?'

'Naturally concerned, but he wants to wait until Chakrabortty comes back with the PM results before he takes that theory to Fox.'

'God only knows what the iron lady will say when she finds out about it,' said Bovalino.

'Yeah, well, that's not our issue anymore,' replied Phillips. 'Thankfully that's down to Carter these days.'

'Her head will explode if this gets out to the press.' said the big Italian. 'Rather him than me.'

'Rather him than any of us,' said Entwistle.

Phillips leant forwards on the desk. 'Well, it's a good job it's not getting out to the press anytime soon. This theory stays between us and Carter for now. No one else in the wider team can know. Understood?'

Each of the team nodded in unison.

'Based on what Sean Hamilton's sister said,' Phillips continued, 'we believe his stomping ground was in and around the village, and he'd been out there as recently as Friday evening. Entwistle, you were in charge of checking CCTV in that area. What did you find?'

Entwistle activated the screen on his laptop and double-clicked a window so it filled the wall opposite. He narrated the scene as the silent video footage played. 'This is Sean Hamilton on Friday night, walking down Canal Street at 10 p.m. towards Venus Bar, where he queues for fifteen minutes before gaining entry.' Entwistle opened another video. 'And this is him leaving, alone, at 2 a.m., where he heads towards Portland Street.' Switching to yet another window, he continued. 'We pick him up at Piccadilly Gardens ten minutes later, where he waits for another twenty minutes, then boards the 147 night-bus home.'

'Any footage from the bus company?' asked Phillips.

'The request's in, but it'll take a few days as usual.'

'What about CCTV at the other end?'

Entwistle nodded and opened the final window on the screen. 'I pulled this off one of the traffic cameras on Wilmslow Road by the bus stop. We can see he's very much alive and well at 3 a.m. Saturday morning, walking towards his hotel, which is about a hundred yards away.'

'Can we see if he made it home?'

Entwistle shook his head, 'No, sorry. The next camera's out of range, I'm afraid.'

'Bugger. Ok. Anything else?' asked Phillips.

'That's it for now, Guv.'

'Bov, anything from your phone sweep of the bars and clubs in the area?'

'Not really. Most of them don't open until the late afternoon, and even then, the managers usually start work in the early evening. So, we're gonna need to go down in person.'

Phillips grinned. 'Well, guess what you and Jonesy are doing tonight?'

The big Italian groaned like a petulant teenager. 'Oh do we have to? Can't Entwistle do it? It's far more his scene.'

Entwistle appeared affronted. 'What do you mean, "it's *my* scene"? I'm not gay.'

'No, but you look it, don't you?' replied Bov.

'What the hell are you talking about?'

'You know, all chiselled and over-dressed.'

'Piss off,' laughed Entwistle. 'Anyway, you've obviously never heard of a bear on the gay scene, have you?'

'What the bloody hell's a bear when it's at home?' asked Jones.

'I'll show you,' said Entwistle as he began typing into Google. A moment later, the slang-dictionary definition appeared on the wall ahead of them and he read the words aloud. '"Bear is a gay slang term. It describes a hairy, heavy-set gay or bisexual man. A bear typically projects an image of rugged masculinity. Some bears present a very masculine, over-the-top image of a ruggedly masculine man." Sounds just like you, Bov.'

Everybody laughed.

Bovalino threw his empty sandwich wrapper across the table at Entwistle. 'Cheeky bugger!'

'Right. Well, seeing as you and Jonesy have no idea about gay protocols, maybe Entwistle *should* go.'

'Result!' cheered Bovalino.

'I don't know what you're so pleased about, Bov,' said Phillips, smirking. 'He's taking Jones's place, not yours. *You're* still going with him.'

Entwistle affected a coy smile. 'Don't worry, papa-bear, I'll look after you,' he joked.

'And whilst you're at it, Entwistle,' said Phillips, 'bring Bov up to speed on everything LBGTQ, will you? We don't want him putting his size fourteen feet in it.'

'With pleasure, boss.'

Phillips locked eyes with Jones. 'Can you trace Hamilton's mobile phone movements before it went into the fire?'

'Of course. I'll get straight onto it.'

She turned back to Entwistle now. 'Where are we up to on the van spotted at the fire?'

'We're still working our way through them. I handed it

over to Lawford whilst I was looking into the Hamilton CCTV.'

'Anything of note?

'Sorry, Guv, nothing as yet.'

Phillips tried her best to hide her frustration. 'Well, keep at it. It can't have just disappeared. Identifying that van could be the key to finding our killer,' she stood. 'Right. You know your tasks. Let's get to it.'

21

SATURDAY, FEBRUARY 27TH

With the arrival of the weekend, Phillips's frustrations always seemed to deepen, especially when she found herself in the middle of a heavy caseload. She hated the fact the world seemed to stop for two days when all *she* wanted to do was carry on working until she'd made the arrests she craved so much. Sitting at the breakfast bar in her open-plan kitchen, drinking coffee on Saturday morning, she found herself running the Hamilton investigation over in her mind. At her request, Entwistle had called late last night with an update on his and Bovalino's trawl of the village bars and clubs. Frustratingly, they'd drawn a blank. None of the doormen or bar staff had recalled seeing Hamilton; just one more face in a sea of people, it seemed. Hardly surprising, though, given Hamilton's demeanour on the CCTV. She played a copy of the footage from Friday night on her laptop. He was hardly a stand-out kind of guy—which was probably one of the reasons he was targeted, mused Phillips.

Blowing her lips loudly, she distracted herself by turning her attention to Floss, her cat, in the corner of the room, snoozing – as per usual – on the designer armchair. God, how she envied the look of absolute bliss that filled the animal's tiny face as she purred loudly. 'Lucky bitch,' Phillips whispered as she placed her coffee cup on the bench top next to her laptop and phone.

Her phone vibrated. It was Chakrabortty.

'Tan? To what do I owe the pleasure on a Saturday?'

'Hi, Jane. I'm actually working today, trying to catch up.'

'Bloody hell, you really are stacked, aren't you?'

Chakrabortty continued. *'I've just finished the post mortem for the fire body.'*

Phillips sat forward in her stool. 'And?'

'Well, it's definitely Sean Hamilton. The dental records match the victim's.'

'I thought they would.'

'And there was water in the lungs, just as you suggested.'

Phillips's heart raced. 'How much water?'

'Enough to kill him. He had emphysema aquosum, which means the thoracic cavity was waterlogged. There was a significant amount of water trapped in the lower airways, which blocked the passive collapse of the bronchi that normally occurs after death.'

'So Hamilton drowned?'

'Yep, and it happened in a domestic setting. The water in his lungs contained traces of fluoride, sodium zeolite and chlorine, plus a host of others.'

'And what does that prove?'

'That he was drowned in tap water,' said Chakrabortty.

'What, like a bath?'

'*Perhaps, or a sink or even a bucket. As long as the victim's head was submerged for long enough for him to inhale enough water to fill his lungs, that would be sufficient to kill him.*'

'Any idea on the time of death?'

'*Sorry. Due to the fire, it's impossible, I'm afraid.*'

'I understand. Was there anything else?'

'*Nothing major. You have the key highlights.*'

'Can you send me the full report?' asked Phillips.

'*Of course, but it'll have to be Monday. I'll get one of the assistants to type it up for you.*'

'Thanks, Tan.'

'*How did you know about the water in the lungs, Jane?*'

'Entwistle suggested the body on the tyre fire was similar to the victims of Denis Nilsen in the nineties. I looked him up, and it turned out he drowned his victims at his home before burning their bodies on wasteland.'

'*Are you thinking it could be another copycat?*'

'Yeah. I'm afraid so.'

'*Jesus. What a world we live in, hey? Makes me glad I only have to deal with the dead.*'

Phillips didn't respond, her mind awash with theories.

'*Right. No rest for the wicked, I'm afraid. I'd better crack on,*' said Chakrabortty. '*Enjoy your weekend, Jane,*' she added, and rang off.

Phillips's worst fears had been confirmed: they were dealing with a second copycat of a historical murder. The burning question was, were two separate killers performing copycat murders – or was it one killer? One thing was for sure—whichever it was, there were no obvious clues as to what would happen next.

22

MONDAY MARCH 1ST

Despite her best efforts, Phillips had not been able to sleep much over the weekend, her mind racing with details of both the Galloway and the Hamilton cases. She had considered calling Jones on Saturday with Chakrabortty's update, but since spending too much time at work had almost caused the end of his marriage less than six months ago, she had decided against risking Sarah's wrath. So, by the time Monday morning came round, all she could think about was getting back to the front line and briefing the team.

She arrived at her desk at 6 a.m., made herself a long black coffee, and jumped onto her laptop. By the time Jones, Bovalino and Entwistle arrived just after 8, she had collated the information she'd pulled together over the weekend on Steven Wright and Dennis Nilsen and compiled a detailed dossier on each killer.

Whilst the other guys made their way to their desks, Jones stepped through her office door and grinned. 'Have you moved in here, Guv?'

Phillips looked up from her laptop. 'I may as well have. I've worked all weekend as it is.'

'The Hamilton case?'

'Yeah. Chakrabortty called me with the results of the fire post mortem on Saturday—'

'Saturday?'

'Yeah. She was catching up on a backlog. She confirmed the body *is* Sean Hamilton.'

'No surprise, really,' said Jones. 'Do you want me to ring his sister?'

Phillips shook her head. 'No need. I called her on Saturday afternoon.'

'How did she take it?'

'As you'd expect, really. Devastated that her brother was confirmed dead, but relieved in a way that she could at least start to grieve. No one wants to spend their life not knowing if a loved one is dead or alive, do they?'

'I can't imagine anything worse, Guv.'

Phillips sat forward now. 'And Chakrabortty also confirmed that Hamilton *had* drowned in a domestic setting before he was put on the fire.'

'Just like Denis Nilsen's victims.'

'Yeah.' Phillips tapped her finger on the stack of papers on her desk. 'I've been researching him, as well as Steve Wright, and it makes grim reading for *us*. Round up the guys and some fresh coffee, and I'll bring you up to speed.'

Ten minutes later, Jones, Bovalino and Entwistle took seats around Phillips's desk as she handed out the files.

Entwistle immediately began flicking through the pages. 'Wow, Guv. Who put this together for you? It's really good.'

Phillips feigned being offended. 'Who do you think did it? Me, of course. I wasn't always a DCI, you know.'

Entwistle blushed. 'Sorry, Guv. I didn't mean to—'

'She's messing with you, you tart!' Jones cut him off. A wide smile spread across Phillips's face. Jones continued. 'The Guv won a commendation for her research when she was a DC, didn't you, boss?'

'I did. On the Chadderton Strangler case. In fact, that's how I made DS in 2005. God, that seems a long time ago now.'

'It was, Guv. Sixteen years,' said Jones.

Phillips waved him away. 'Anyway, enough about all that. You're making me feel old.' She held up her copy of the file. *'This* needs our complete attention now.'

'So, what are we looking at?' asked Bovalino.

'The case files for Steve Wright and Denis Nilsen. I pulled them off the central database this morning after speaking to Chakrabortty over the weekend. She confirmed that the body in the fire is Sean Hamilton's, and that he'd been drowned in tap water before being put on the fire – along with the car tyre. The similarities to Denis Nilsen are remarkable. Listen to this.' Phillips opened the file and read aloud. '"Nilsen invited Stephen Holmes to his house with the promise of the two drinking alcohol and listening to music. At Nilsen's home, both he and Holmes drank heavily before they fell asleep. In his subsequent written confessions, Nilsen stated that Holmes was to stay with him whether he wanted to or not. Reaching for a necktie, Nilsen straddled Holmes as he strangled him into unconsciousness, *before drowning the teenager in a bucket filled with water".'*

'So, Nilsen picked up gay men, got them pissed, drowned them, then burnt the bodies,' said Jones.

Phillips nodded. 'Gay men just like Sean Hamilton.'

Bovalino's thick brow furrowed. 'So we're definitely looking for another copycat killer?'

'Either that, or the same person emulating *different* killers,' said Phillips.

Jones exhaled loudly. 'Jesus. I don't know which is worse.'

'Those were my thoughts exactly.'

'So what's our next move, Guv?' asked Jones.

'I want each of you to read these files in detail and go back through everything we have so far on the Galloway and Hamilton murders. See if anything stands out. Whether it's one or two different killers, both murders took planning and a *lot* of effort. Based on what we know about ritual murders like these, the killers rarely stop at one, or even two, for that matter. So we need to do whatever it takes to find out who's behind them before they strike again.'

A chorus of 'Yes, Guv' filled the room.

'Right. Let's get to it,' said Phillips.

23

After an extended meeting updating Carter on the second copycat murder, Phillips returned to the MCU incident room.

'How did he take the news?' asked Jones, as she wandered over to where the guys were working.

'I think it's fair to say he wasn't exactly delighted with the confirmation we're now looking at two copycats. Especially considering he has to brief Fox this afternoon.'

'Yeah, I bet,' said Jones.

'Guv, I think I've found something that might be useful,' Entwistle interrupted.

Phillips raised her eyebrows. 'Oh?'

'Take a look at this,' he said, handing her a printout of a photograph. 'It's one of the SOCO shots from Hamilton's room at the Palatine.'

'A box of medication?'

'Yeah, for Azathioprine. I looked it up. It's mainly used in cases of ulcerative colitis, which is an inflammatory bowel disease. It's an immunosuppressant designed to stop the patient's immune system from attacking itself, which is what causes the disease in the first place.'

'And how does this help us?' asked Phillips.

'It was quite hard to see it at first, but when I blew up the image, I noticed the pharmacy where he got them from is Manchester-based, as opposed to Glasgow.'

Phillips nodded. 'So Hamilton got them *here*.'

'Yeah. I called the pharmacy, and they said the prescription had been issued at Manchester Central Surgery, where Dr Goodwin works.'

Phillips took a moment to process the information. 'Dr Goodwin? As in Michael Yates's doctor?'

'Yep. That's her.'

'Bloody hell, don't tell me the cases are linked?' said Jones.

'Could just be a coincidence, Guv?' ventured Bovalino.

Phillips fixed him with a lopsided grin. 'And what have I told you about coincidences, Bov?'

Bovalino chuckled.

'This is great work, Entwistle.' Phillips smacked the back of her hand on the printout. 'Right, Jones. Get your coat. We're off to visit the good Dr Goodwin, see what she has to say about this.'

Jones stood.

Phillips continued. 'Entwistle, have a look and see if you can find any connection between Galloway and Goodwin – or anyone else at the Manchester Central Surgery.'

'On it.'

Phillips headed for her office and grabbed her coat and car keys, feeling suddenly energised. It was a small lead, but right now, any lead was progress.

Dr Goodwin appeared as pleased to see Phillips and Jones as she had been on their first visit. This time she allowed them to meet in her consulting room, where she sat at her desk, checking the patient database on her PC. After a few moments, she found what she was looking for. 'Sean Hamilton. A walk-in patient. Came to see us on the 15th February.'

'Who treated him?' asked Phillips.

'Dr Anderson. But it appears there was no examination. He just needed a script for Azathioprine, which was issued after speaking to his own doctor in Glasgow.'

'Can we speak to Dr Anderson?'

Goodwin nodded. 'Yes, you're in luck, actually.'

'Why's that?'

'He's a locum, so not around that often, but he's in today, covering Dr Singh.'

Phillips's eyes narrowed. 'And where is Dr Singh?

'At home with the flu,' Goodwin stood. 'Give me a moment. I'll need to check if Dr Anderson is with a patient.'

A few minutes later, Goodwin returned with Anderson, a short, shy-looking man with a round face and small paunch that strained against his freshly pressed checked shirt.

'This is DCI Phillips and DS Jones,' said Goodwin. 'I'll leave you to it.'

Anderson took a seat in Goodwin's chair. 'Dr Goodwin says you want to talk to me about one of my patients?'

Phillips produced the image of Hamilton's medication and handed it across. 'Can you tell us anything you remember about Sean Hamilton? You prescribed him these.'

Anderson pulled spectacles from his pocket and placed them on the end of his nose before scrutinising the picture.

'If it helps, Dr Goodwin was just looking at his files on her computer,' said Jones.

Anderson nodded, then looked at the screen for a long moment. 'Ah yes. Looks like he needed Azathioprine for his colitis. I remember it now, because I had to call through to his doctor's in Glasgow. He'd run out of tablets and they confirmed he was due his next batch.'

'And do you remember Sean?' asked Phillips.

'Not especially, no. I see so many patients as a locum, it's hard to recall much detail.'

Phillips produced a picture of Hamilton taken from his Facebook page earlier. 'Maybe this'll help jog your memory?'

Anderson stared at the photo and nodded. 'I think I do remember him, actually. He was quite quiet and well-spoken, compared to the receptionist at his doctor's. I struggled to understand what she was saying, her accent was so thick, but not his.'

'How did he seem in himself?' asked Phillips.

'How d'you mean?'

'Well. Was he happy, down, scared?'

Anderson shrugged. 'Normal, I guess. Nothing stood out. Well, at least it didn't to me, but then I wasn't looking. That's one of the challenges of being a locum—I don't get to know the patients, so I have no real reference point regarding their state of mind unless something is very obviously upsetting them.'

Phillips could feel her frustration building in her gut.

Her only lead was turning out to be a dead end. 'Did he say anything at all that might help us?'

Anderson frowned. 'Help you with what exactly? What has he done?'

'He's dead,' said Phillips flatly.

'Dead?' Anderson recoiled. 'How?'

'He was murdered.'

'Oh my God. When?'

'About a week after visiting here.'

Anderson shook his head. 'That's terrible.'

Phillips continued. 'So, if there's anything you can think of that might help us trace his movements in that week, it'd really help.'

'I'm sorry, but he never really said much at all. I didn't even need to examine him. He must have only been in here for the time it took me to ring Glasgow, then issue his script.'

'I see,' said Phillips, barely able to hide her frustration. She pulled a business card from her coat pocket and passed it across. 'Well, if anything comes back to you, give me a call, day or night, ok?'

'I will, of course.'

'Well, we better let you get back to your patients.' Phillips stood, and Jones followed suit. 'Thank you for your time, doctor.'

Anderson nodded. 'Sorry I wasn't more help.'

Outside, Phillips and Jones walked at pace back to the car.

'Well, that was a bloody waste of time,' growled Phillips.

'What is it they say about witnesses, Guv? No memory and bad eyesight.'

Phillips pulled out her phone and called Entwistle.

'Hi, Guv.'

'Do me a favour, will you?' said Phillips. 'Go through Galloway's and Hamilton's social media. See if you can find any posts or messages that might give us an idea of who they met in the days leading up to the nights they died.'

'I'll get straight onto it.'

'Thanks,' Phillips ended the call.

'So we're no further forward?' said Jones.

'No, we're not, and I've got a horrible feeling our killer – *or killers* – is already stalking their next victim.'

24

TUESDAY, MARCH 2ND

Just over an hour ago, Phillips had taken the call from Jones that she had been dreading; uniformed police had reported another dead body. Initial information suggested the victim was a young woman who had been found on a building site in Moston, approximately six miles north-east of the city centre, partially covered by building materials. As the time approached 9 a.m., she passed through the metal gates of the site and parked the car up in front of a row of Portakabins.

Jones was waiting alongside Bovalino as she stepped out of the driver's seat. 'Morning, Guv,' Jones said, pulling his collar up as protection against the raging wind blowing across the site. Bov, as usual, wore his fur-lined puffer jacket and seemed impervious to the cold.

'Morning.' Phillips wrapped her scarf tightly around her neck. 'Is it as bad as you described on the phone, Jonesy?'

'Worse, Guv. Much worse.'

Phillips felt her brow furrow. 'Why?'

'Whoever did it bit a chunk out of her.'

'Jesus,' muttered Phillips as she moved to the rear of the car and opened the boot. She pulled out her Wellington boots and slipped them on, along with a pair of latex gloves. 'Show me.'

Jones took the lead, with Phillips tucked in behind and Bovalino bringing up the rear, as they made their way over the uneven, muddy ground. It didn't take long to reach an area that had already been taped off by uniformed officers. Jones lifted the tape so Phillips could step under, then he and Bov followed her through. The dead girl lay on her back, her wide, almost black eyes staring into space. She had no coat, and her white, blood-stained blouse was unbuttoned down to her navel. Her skirt was pulled up around her thighs, but her knickers remained intact.

'He hit her on the back of the head with something blunt and heavy, by all accounts, Guv,' said Jones, leaning forward and pointing at the back of the woman's skull.

It was hard to see the damage from her position, so Phillips squatted down to get a better look. Fragments of pink, bloody brain hung loosely from a large hole in the back of her head. 'Jesus, that's brutal,' she mumbled.

'That's not the worst of it,' said Bovalino as he stepped forward and, using a gloved finger, carefully pulled the blouse aside to reveal the girl's right breast. 'He bit her nipple clean off.'

A spike of adrenaline surged through Phillips's body as the words landed. She has seen this exact thing before in a case from the seventies. 'The Beast of Manchester,' she said as she stared at the open wound, which had partially frozen overnight.

'You what, Guv?' asked Jones.

Phillips stood. 'I've seen similar mutilation before, in the case of Trevor Hardy. He killed three women around this area of Manchester in the mid-seventies. Raped them, then battered them to death and mutilated the bodies, biting the nipple off one of the victims. The press nicknamed him "The Beast of Manchester".'

Bovalino's eyes widened. '*Another* copycat killer?'

'Another killer? I'd seriously doubt it, but another copycat murder? It certainly looks that way.' Phillips removed her glasses and rubbed her face with one hand as she shook her head. 'Oh God. This is getting out of control.'

Jones and Bovalino stared at her with wide eyes and raised eyebrows.

'We need Evans and the team here ASAP,' she said finally, as she replaced her glasses.

'They're already on their way,' said Jones.

Phillips nodded and scanned the site for a moment. 'Ok. So, who called in uniform?'

'The site manager, Ben Dench.' Jones thrust his hands deep into his coat pockets for warmth. 'He opened up just after seven and noticed the pile of building materials had been moved from their usual location next to the offices. He came to inspect them, and spotted her feet sticking out.'

'Did he touch the body or the materials?'

'Reckons not,' said Jones.

'Well, we'll need his prints just in case. Have you spoken to him yet?'

'No. We thought we'd wait for you.' Jones nodded in the direction of the site huts. 'He's in the main Portakabin.'

'Right. Well, let's see what he has to say.' Phillips ducked under the tape and set off towards the temporary office.

Dench looked up from his desk as Phillips entered a few minutes later, with Jones and Bovalino in tow. She placed him in his late fifties, a portly man with a ruddy complexion and thick grey hair. The office was mercifully warm, the unmistakable smell of gas heaters hanging in the air.

'Mr Dench? I'm DCI Phillips. Can I have a word?'

Dench nodded and offered her one of the two plastic chairs opposite his desk. She took it, and Jones sat down in the chair next to her. Bovalino remained standing.

At that moment, Jones's phone rang. He fished it from his coat pocket. 'Do you mind if I take this, Guv? It's Evans.'

'Go ahead,' said Phillips.

Jones answered it and listened for a moment. 'Ok, I'll come out now,' he said eventually, then finished the call. 'SOCO have arrived.'

'You and Bov can go and brief them. I can deal with this,' said Phillips.

Jones nodded, stood, and left in a hurry, along with his partner.

As the door closed behind them, Phillips offered Dench a thin smile. 'Our Scene of Crimes officers are here,' she explained. 'They'll need to examine the body and the area around it for any forensic evidence.'

Dench's brow furrowed. 'What does that mean for the site?'

'I'm afraid you're shut down until they've finished.'

'How long will that take?'

Phillips shrugged. 'It really depends on what they find; a day, a week? It's hard to say for sure.'

A grave look spread across Dench's face. 'I'll need to call all my sub-contractors and tell them not to come in—and my boss. He won't be happy about this. We're already way behind schedule.'

Phillips didn't respond. She couldn't care less about his deadlines. She had much more pressing matters of her own to deal with. 'Who has access to the site overnight?'

'Just me and my assistant, George. We're the only ones with keys.'

'My sergeant said that you locked up last night?'

'That's right. George is on holiday in Florida at the moment. He's taken the kids to Disney World, the lucky bugger.'

'George who?'

'Darby.'

'And what time did *you* leave last night?' asked Phillips.

'Well, it gets dark about half four at the moment, so the lads will have left around then. I normally stay on for another hour or so, finishing up paperwork and catching up on emails. So I'm usually away between half-five and six.'

'Did you notice anyone hanging around by the gates when you locked up?'

Dench shook his head. 'Can't say I did, no.'

'I see from the signs on the gate that your site is monitored by a security firm. Would they have been on site last night?'

'They'll have parked up and checked through the gates a couple of times, but they only come on site if they see anything out of place. If that happens, then they're required to call me for permission. So I'd have known about it if they'd seen anything, and I didn't get any calls last night.'

'My sergeant mentioned you saw the building materials were out of place this morning, and that's what drew your attention to the body?'

'That's right,' said Dench.

'So were the gates still locked when you arrived?'

'Yes. I opened them myself, just after seven.'

Phillips took a moment to process the information. 'If the person who did this didn't have a key to the gate, how would they get a body onto the site?'

Dench shook his head. 'I have no idea, unless there's an issue with some of the fencing.'

'Have you checked it this morning?'

'No. I haven't had a chance. I called you lot as soon as I found her.'

'And what were you doing last night after work, Mr Dench?'

Dench flinched. '*Me?*'

Phillips nodded. 'Yes.'

'Er, well, I was at home. Same as every night.'

'And can someone vouch for you?' Phillips studied his face, looking for signs he was lying.

'Yeah, my wife and son. Mind you, my boy's only a baby, so I'm not sure his testimony would stand up in court.' Dench chortled nervously.

He seemed genuine enough, thought Phillips. She changed tack. 'Did you touch the body at all?'

Dench shook his head vigorously. 'No. No. As soon as I saw that lassie's feet sticking out, I came straight in here and called you.'

Phillips nodded. 'Well, we need to take your prints in any case. Purely for elimination purposes, you understand.'

Dench swallowed hard. His mouth opened, but no words were forthcoming.

Phillips allowed the silence to linger for longer than was comfortable. 'Is there something wrong, Mr Dench?'

'Erm... well, look...I *may* have touched her.'

'I see. And why would you do that?'

'Well. I wasn't sure if she was real, or a dummy or

something,' said Dench. 'You know, like a practical joke from one of the lads. So I moved a couple of the boards covering her to one side and pulled at her foot.'

'So why lie and say you hadn't touched her?'

Dench rubbed the back of his neck. 'I dunno. When your sergeant asked me, I guess I panicked. I thought I might get into trouble.'

'Not as much trouble as lying to the police during a murder investigation, Mr Dench.'

'I know. I'm sorry. I'm an idiot.'

Phillips held his gaze for a long moment, then stood. She'd heard enough for now. 'Like I say, one of the team will take your prints. In the meantime, you'd better get onto your contractors and close the site. No one comes in or out without our approval.'

Once outside, she retraced her steps to the location of the body, where the SOCO team had begun erecting their protective white tent. Jones and Bovalino were deep in conversation with Senior CSI Andy Evans, who had his back to her as she approached.

'Any ideas what caused the damage to her skull and how long she's been here?' Phillips said, interrupting their conversation.

Evans, dressed in his customary white overalls, spun round to face her. 'Steady on, Jane, I've only been here ten minutes,' he said.

Phillips was in no mood for levity. 'I'm not looking for details at this stage, Andy, just some idea of what happened and when.'

Evans blew his lips and shrugged. 'Well, from what I've seen so far, she suffered blunt force trauma to the head, something flat and heavy—'

'Like a breeze block, maybe?' Phillips cut in.

'Potentially, yes, especially given the surroundings. And based on the rigor, I'd say she's been dead approximately twelve hours, although the temperature overnight will have contributed to that as well.'

'The site manager wants to know how long he has to shut the operation down for. Any thoughts?' asked Phillips.

'At this stage, all I can say is it will take as long as it takes.'

'Fair enough. Just keep us posted.'

'Of course.'

'And you'll need to take his prints. He's changed his initial story and said he did touch the body.'

Jones let out an ironic chuckle. 'Of course he bloody did.'

Phillips continued. 'Says he wasn't sure the body was real or a practical joke from the lads on site, so he pulled her foot to see if it was a dummy.'

'Dickhead,' mumbled Jones under his breath.

'Yep,' added Phillips. 'Let's make sure that's all he touched, ok?'

Evans nodded, and pulled on his protective mask as he turned back to face the body.

Phillips focused her attention on Jones and Bovalino. 'Dench reckons the gate was locked when he left last night, and stayed that way until he turned up again this morning. There are only two sets of keys to the site and the other belongs to his deputy, who's supposed to be in Florida. His name's George Darby. Bov, check him out and see if he is where he's supposed to be.'

'Sure thing,' said Bovalino.

Phillips continued. 'So if he's saying the killer *didn't* come in through the gate, then he must have found another way onto the site. Let's check the perimeter fences, see if there's any signs of entry.' With that, she pulled her collar up against the bitter wind and set off towards the boundary.

Fifteen minutes later, they found what they were looking for in the far corner of the site. The temporary metal fencing that surrounded the building work had been forced open at one of the links. A heavy metal bracket that held the two fence pieces together had been shorn in half and, based on the precision of the cut, the culprit had likely used some kind of automatic machinery. Phillips bent down, picked up one half of the broken bracket, and inspected it. 'Whoever did this wasn't taking any chances.'

'Looks like it was well planned again, Guv,' said Jones.

Phillips turned and stared back at the site. They were at least a hundred yards from where the body had been found, their view of the location obscured by the partially built walls of a number of houses standing between them and the main entrance on the opposite side of the site. She stared at the ground for a long moment. 'There's no drag marks in the mud, and only one set of footprints.'

'Which means he probably carried the body,' said Bovalino.

Jones nodded. 'She didn't look particularly heavy to me, but that's still a long way to carry a dead weight.'

'Yes, it is.' Phillips's mind raced. The time between murders was getting shorter with each kill, a classic trait of a serial killer growing in confidence. Her gut was rarely wrong, and right now it was screaming at her; whoever was committing these murders was just getting started.

25

APPROACHING MIDDAY, WEDNESDAY, MARCH 3RD

Phillips stood in the incident room in front of the three large whiteboards secured to the wall, studying the evidence they had gathered so far. Various high-res images of the bodies of Gillian Galloway, Sean Hamilton and their latest victim were fixed against the plastic alongside grainy images of their potential historical counterparts. So far, the only link between any of the modern-day victims was the Ford transit van, which had left its mark near where Galloway and Hamilton had been dumped. Evans and the team had taken myriad casts of tyre tracks from the building site and surrounding area, and his team was working their way through them for a potential match at that very moment. They were also still examining the building site where the latest victim had been found, much to the irritation of Ben Dench.

'What you thinking, Guv?' asked Entwistle.

Phillips turned to face him, Jones and Bovalino, each busily working at their desks. 'Are we chasing one, two or three killers? A team, even?'

Jones folded his arms and leant back in his chair. 'Serial killers normally work alone, don't they?'

'Do you see anything *normal* in these cases?' she shot back.

Jones shrugged. 'Fair point.'

'Plus, let's not forget, some of the most vicious killers in British history worked in pairs, Myra Hindley and Ian Brady…Fred and Rosemary West.'

'A murdering couple, maybe?' ventured Bovalino.

'Maybe, Bov. Maybe. It would certainly explain how the body was carried a hundred yards across the building site.'

At that moment, Phillips's phone began to ring in her trouser pocket. She pulled it out. Chakrabortty. 'Tan?' she said, and walked towards her office.

'Hi, Jane. I'm working on the building site body PM. One of the guys has found a match on her fingerprints. I know this is urgent, so I wanted you to know immediately.'

'Who is she?'

'Her name's Wiktoria Szymańska. She's a Polish national.'

'How are you spelling that?'

Chakrabortty dictated the letters.

'Do you know why she's on the system?' asked Phillips, when she was finished writing it down.

'A theft of some kind. I didn't ask my assistant the details, just the name.'

'I really appreciate this, Tan. It's a massive help.'

'Look, I'll be finished in a couple of hours, so I can give you the full picture then, but what I can tell you so far is that she was hit with considerable force to the back of the head with a lump of breeze block, and that the killer left some DNA on the bite mark. We're testing it as a priority.'

A ripple of excitement surged through Phillips's body. If the killer was in the system, they'd have him. 'Thank you, Tan. When will you have the results?'

'Twenty-four to forty-eight hours. I've explained how urgent it is,' said Chakrabortty. 'We're also taking a cast of the bite marks. That should help in identifying the killer, too.'

'Amazing,' said Phillips.

'I'd better go.'

'Yeah, of course. Speak to you later.'

After the call ended, Phillips took a moment, daring to hope they would soon have a DNA profile and maybe even the name of the killer. Re-energised, she strode back to the team, unable to hide the wide grin on her face as she approached. 'The building site victim's real name is Wiktoria Szymańska, a Polish national already in the system.'

Jones's eyes widened. 'Wow, that was fast.'

'That's why it pays to be nice to the chief pathologist,' Phillips handed her spelling of Szymańska to Entwistle. 'Can you pull up her details?'

Entwistle carefully typed the name into his laptop.

Phillips continued. 'And even better, the killer left behind their DNA on the bite mark and enough of an imprint to get a cast from their teeth. We should have the results in the next couple of days.'

Bovalino clapped his hands together. 'Result!'

Just then, Jones's desk phone rang. 'DS Jones,' he said, picking up the receiver. Then, 'Hello Andy.' He listened intently for about a minute before speaking again. 'So it's a definite match?'

Phillips and the rest of the team watched him expectantly until he finished the call and replaced the receiver.

'That was Evans. We have a match on the van tyres from the previous two murders,' he said triumphantly.

'Get in!' shouted Bovalino.

For Phillips, the relief was palpable. 'And he's *sure*?'

'One hundred per cent, Guv. It's the same vehicle.'

'Which means it looks like the same killer,' said Phillips.

'Or *killers*,' Jones countered.

Entwistle cut in. 'I've found Szymańska.'

Phillips moved to his shoulder.

'Wiktoria Szymańska. Arrested in 2015 for shoplifting. She was given a fine and community service. Her address is 39 Haverley Way, Benchill. Says here she was reported missing by her husband, Petr Szymański, on Friday.'

Staring at the mugshot on the screen brought home the urgency of the case. It was easy to see the victims as simply bodies after death, but this was a young girl, couldn't have been much more than a teenager at the time, smiling at the camera. If they didn't catch her killer soon, they would almost certainly strike again. 'Jones. Come with me. Let's go and break the news to her husband,' said Phillips.

'Ok, Guv.'

She turned to Bovalino and Entwistle. 'You two, find out whatever you can about Wiktoria Szymańska. Family, friends, ex-boyfriends, girlfriends, work, bank accounts, social media posts, the lot.'

Both men nodded as Jones stood and pulled his coat from the back of his chair.

'You're driving,' said Phillips, throwing him the car keys, which he caught expertly in one hand. 'Come on, there's no time to waste.'

26

Petr Szymański's eyes were red and puffy as he answered the door an hour later. He couldn't have been more than thirty years old, but seemed almost twice his age, his face ravaged by fear.

Phillips spoke softly. 'Mr Szymański?'

He nodded.

'DCI Phillips and DS Jones,' she said, presenting her credentials.

'Is it about Wiktoria? Have you found her?' His voice trembled. The accent was Polish, the English perfect.

'May we come in? It'll be better if we talk inside,' said Phillips.

Terror oozed from Szymański's tear-stained eyes. Leaving the door open behind him, he turned and made his way into the small lounge and took a seat on the edge of an armchair.

Phillips and Jones had been in this position so many times she had lost count, but it still didn't make it any easier as they took seats opposite him. From experience, she knew the best thing to do was to get to the point quickly. 'I'm sorry to tell you this, Mr Szymański, but your wife has passed away.'

Like so many before, Petr Szymański appeared to crumble in front of them as the news he had been dreading for days was delivered. Dropping his head into his hands, he began to wail like a small child overwhelmed by distress.

Phillips and Jones's eyes met. Neither of them wanted to be here right now, but they had a job to do. A job that could potentially save more families from having to go through such an horrific ordeal.

Szymański lifted his head eventually. 'How did she die?'

'I'm afraid she was murdered,' said Phillips as gently as she could.

Szymański's bloodshot eyes bulged. 'Murdered? Why would someone want to kill Wiktoria?'

'We don't know, at this stage.'

'Where did it happen?'

Phillips released a long, silent breath. 'It's still early days in the investigation, but her body was found on a building site in Moston.'

'Moston? What was she doing in Moston?' asked Szymański.

'We were hoping you might be able to tell us,' Phillips replied.

'She's never even been to Moston. It's on the other side of the city. There is nothing there for her.'

Despite Szymański's obvious distress, Phillips pressed on. 'When did you last see your wife?'

'Thursday morning, when I left for work. She was in bed.'

'And what time was that?'

'Around 7 a.m.'

'And where do you work?' Phillips asked.

'Wythenshawe Hospital. Most people round here work there.'

'You last saw your wife on Thursday morning, but only reported her missing on Friday. Why did you wait so long?'

'Because she was working late Thursday night and I went to bed before she was due home. I woke up Friday morning and she wasn't there. I tried ringing her, but her phone was going to voicemail. I called the police straight away.'

'Could you talk us through what you did on Thursday night?

'I came home from work just after five. Cooked dinner, watched TV, then went to bed about eleven.'

Jones scribbled the details in his pad.

'Did you see or speak to anyone that night?' asked Phillips.

'No. Nobody.'

'What did your wife do for work?' Jones cut in.

'She was a cleaner,' Szymański nodded.

'Business, or private?'

'Business. Always business, through an agency. They're local, called A1 Domestics.'

Jones made a note in his pad. 'And what types of businesses did she clean?'

'Sometimes offices, but care homes, mainly. No one wants to clean up old people's piss and shit, so she always had lots of work.'

Phillips's interest was piqued. Fishing her notepad from her pocket, she flicked through the pages until she found what she was looking for. 'Did Wiktoria ever clean at the Cedar Pines Residential Care Home in Longsight?'

Szymański said nothing for a long moment, appearing deep in thought. 'Maybe,' he said eventually. 'She did have work in Longsight from time to time. Her boss Stefan will know. The office is just round the corner, on the main road.'

Phillips chose her words carefully now. 'Mr Szymański, your wife was convicted of shoplifting in 2015...'

Szymański nodded. 'She made a mistake. She was young and broke.'

'...did she have any other brushes with the law?'

'No. Never.'

'And you're sure of that?'

'Positive.'

Phillips changed tack. 'Did she mention anybody new in her life, recently?'

Szymański's eyes narrowed. 'What do you mean?'

'Anyone at work who she talked about? Any unwanted attention from a man, perhaps?'

'Do you mean was she having an affair?' snarled Szymański.

Phillips shook her head gently. 'No. That's not what I'm saying. I'm thinking more of anyone who might have shown an interest that she could have rebuked, potentially upset.'

'Wiktoria worked alone most nights, and Stefan only hires women. He says men are too lazy to do cleaning.'

'I see,' said Phillips. 'And how was your relationship with your wife?'

'I loved my wife, very much.'

'I don't doubt that, but did you perhaps have any serious problems or arguments, lately?'

'No. We never argued. We loved each other.' Szymański began to sob again.

Phillips glanced at Jones. His expression matched the feeling in her gut; Szymański was unlikely to be involved. He needed time to process what had happened, and they'd already pushed a grieving husband hard enough.

Szymański swallowed hard as he averted his eyes.

'Do you have any family, or friends, who can come and stay for a few days?' asked Phillips.

'My brother, Maric. He lives close by.'

'That's good,' said Phillips. 'We'll arrange for a family liaison officer to come and see you too. They'll be able to support you through the investigation.'

Szymański didn't respond as he stared into the distance.

Phillips stood, and Jones followed suit. 'We're very sorry, Mr Szymański. We really are,' she said, then made her way to the front door, along with Jones.

'Will you catch this man?' Szymański shouted after her.

Phillips turned and held his gaze. 'We'll do everything we can. I promise you that, Mr Szymański.'

Szymański nodded, then turned away as Phillips and Jones stepped outside.

After a quick Google search, Phillips and Jones located the offices of A1 Domestic Cleaners, just a five-minute walk from the Szymański family home. Frustratingly, the office was closed for the night.

'Call them first thing,' said Phillips as they walked back to the car. 'I've got a horrible feeling Wiktoria was a cleaner at Cedar Pines, and if she was, her death could well be connected to Michael Yates's. That's four murders in just over a week.'

'Jesus, Guv. What have we stumbled into?'

'I dunno, Jonesy, I really don't. But we need to get a

handle on these cases ASAP, or more people are gonna die.'

Jones nodded sagely as he deactivated the central locking on the car, causing the lights to flash.

Phillips opened the passenger door. 'Can you drop me off at home?'

'Sure,' said Jones.

'And I need you to pick me up in the morning at 8. It's time to take another look at Cedar Pines.'

'No problem,' replied Jones. He opened the driver's door and jumped in.

27

FRIDAY, MARCH 5TH

The following morning, despite Jones arriving on time to pick up Phillips at 8, they arrived at Cedar Pines just after 9 a.m. thanks to a glut of rush hour traffic. Before heading inside, Phillips called Stefan at A1 Domestics, who – after taking a moment to process the fact that Wiktoria was dead –confirmed she had indeed worked at Cedar Pines one evening each week. Usually a Wednesday – including the 3rd of February, the night Michael Yates had been poisoned. Armed with this information, they had made their way inside and requested a list of contractors the care home employed from Dianna Kirby.

Kirby retook her seat behind her desk and handed the list of names across. 'That's everyone we have on the books at the minute.'

Phillips cast her eyes down the page in silence.

'Is this about Michael Yates's death?' asked Kirby.

'In a way, yes,' said Phillips, without looking up.

'Do you know how he died, yet?'

'Poisoned,' said Jones, flatly.

Kirby's jaw dropped. 'Poisoned? What with? How?'

'I'm afraid we can't tell you that,' said Jones.

Phillips returned her gaze to Kirby. 'Do you know if any of the contractors drive a Ford transit van?'

Kirby let out a nervous chuckle. 'I'm afraid I don't. I'm hopeless with cars. I could just about tell you the colour of my own, but not much else.'

'Ok, how about a dark green or blue van? Any of them use one of those?'

Kirby's brow wrinkled for a moment. 'I don't think so, but then I don't get out to the delivery area much. I'm either in here or out there.' She pointed behind their heads towards the residents' rooms. 'Your best bet is to speak to Mark Holloway, our caretaker. He looks after deliveries and services, etc.'

Phillips pulled her phone from her pocket and opened up a photo of Wiktoria, taken from her Facebook profile. She presented it to Kirby. 'Do you recognise this woman?'

Kirby nodded. 'That's Tori, she's one of the cleaners here. Nice girl.'

'We understand she worked for you on a Wednesday evening each week.'

'That's right, yes.'

'Did she have access to the residents' private rooms?'

'Of course. That's where most of the cleaning gets done. Why do you ask?'

'I'm afraid she's dead, Miss Kirby.'

Kirby was incredulous. 'Dead?'

'Yes.'

'How?'

'We believe she was murdered,' said Phillips.

'Oh my God. When?'

'Last Thursday.'

Kirby shook her head. 'I can't believe it. I only saw her last week.'

Phillips pressed on. 'We've spoken to her boss and he confirmed she was working on the 3rd of February – the night Michael Yates died. Do you recall seeing her in his room at all?'

'Er, no, but then I usually leave about 6.30, and her shift ran until 10. You don't think she had anything to do with Mr Yates's death, do you?'

'That's what we're trying to find out,' said Jones.

'Do you know if Wiktoria was close to any of the men working here?' asked Phillips.

'I know she was a smoker and a sociable girl. I can imagine she would chat to whoever was outside when she went for a cigarette, but I couldn't say one way or another whether she was particularly close to anyone. Like I say, I only ever saw her in passing each week.'

Phillips nodded. 'You mentioned the caretaker, Mark Holloway. Is he in this morning?'

'Yes, he started at 7.' She checked her watch. 'He's probably on his break in his room out back. I'll take you over there.'

A few minutes later, Kirby knocked on the open door marked *Caretaker* and stood in the doorway. 'Mark, the police would like to talk to you.'

Holloway was sitting in a battered old armchair inside what appeared to be a large cupboard. He looked up from his morning paper, a steaming mug in his right hand. He seemed non-plussed at having his break interrupted. He had close-cropped ginger hair and wore a grey hoodie and black workwear trousers. Phillips put him in his forties.

'Well. I'll leave you to it,' said Kirby, before hurrying away.

Phillips stepped inside the small room. 'Mr Holloway. I'm DCI Phillips and this is DS Jones from the Major Crimes Unit.'

Holloway, remaining seated, put down his drink and folded his newspaper. 'What can I do for you?'

Phillips handed him the list of contractors. 'Do you know if any of your suppliers use a dark green, or perhaps blue, Ford transit van?'

Holloway glanced at the names for a moment, then shook his head. 'Not that I recall.'

Jones pulled up an image of an old Mark II transit on his phone and passed it across. 'It would look like this.'

Holloway examined the image. 'Doesn't look familiar, but then we get a lot of vans in and out of here. That said, most of our guys are bringing in sterile or specialist kit, and that looks a bit old to be handling stuff like that.'

'I see,' Phillips presented the photo of Wiktoria. 'Do you recognise her?'

'Of course. That's Tori, one of our cleaners.'

'When did you last see her?' asked Jones.

'Why? Has she done something wrong?'

'No.'

'Well, why do you want to know?'

'Because she's dead.' Phillips studied Holloway's face to gauge his reaction.

His eyes widened and he said nothing for a long moment. 'How?'

'We think she was murdered last Thursday night. I'm afraid we can't tell you any more than that,' said Phillips.

'The poor thing,' Holloway mumbled. 'Her husband will be devastated.'

'Do you know him?' asked Jones.

'No, no. But she talked about him a lot. Childhood sweethearts, apparently.'

'How well did you know her?' Phillips asked.

Holloway shrugged. 'Not very well to be honest. Just someone to talk to over a fag, but I always thought she was lovely. Really lovely. Just a nice person with a big smile for someone doing such shitty work.'

Phillips continued. 'Do you know if any of the other staff spent much time with her?'

'I don't. She was only in once a week, so I'm guessing not.'

'Did you notice any of the male staff showing an interest in her on the nights she was working?' said Jones.

Holloway scoffed. 'What male staff? I'm the only bloke in here. I'm not sure if you've noticed, but there aren't many blokes in the care home business.'

'Where were you last Thursday night?' Phillips cut in.

Holloway frowned. 'What? You think I had something to do with it?'

'Just trying to rule out anyone with an alibi,' said Phillips. 'Standard procedure. I'm sure you understand.'

Holloway folded his arms across his chest. 'I play five-a-side with the lads on a Thursday, then we go for beers and a curry.'

Jones made a note in his pad. 'And your mates will vouch for you, will they?'

'Yeah,' said Holloway, stony-faced.

Phillips didn't respond, allowing an uncomfortable silence to linger. 'Could I have that list of contractors back, please?' she asked finally, with an outstretched hand.

Holloway obliged, but remained silent.

'Thank you,' said Phillips. 'You've been very helpful. We'll be in touch if we need to speak to you further.'

'What about?'
'Just whatever comes up, Mr Holloway,' said Phillips, as Jones made for the door.
Back in the car, they debriefed. 'Do you think he's telling the truth, Guv?' Jones asked.
'He seemed genuine enough, and appeared shocked when he found out she was dead—'
'*But?*'
'But there's something about him I don't like. I don't know what it is, but I get a sense he's hiding something,' said Phillips.
'I know what you mean. I thought that too.'
Phillips pulled up Entwistle's number on the in-car system and dialled.
'*Guv?*' he said, answering after a few rings.
'It looks like our Moston victim, Wiktoria Szymańska, *was* a cleaner at the Cedar Pines Care Home, where Michael Yates was poisoned—'
'*No way!*'
'Yes way. Not only that, but she was also working the night he was killed.'
'*Do you think the deaths are connected?*' asked Entwistle.
'Potentially. It's too much of a coincidence otherwise, so I want you to look into historical cases involving serial killers who used poison, specifically strychnine.'
'*Ok, Guv.*'
'And tell Bovalino I want a full background check on Mark Holloway, who works as a caretaker at Cedar Pines.'
Entwistle scribbled on a pad at the other end. '*Will do.*'
'We're heading back to base now, so I want that info as quick as you can, ok?'
'*Consider it done, boss.*'

With that, Phillips rang off. 'Is it too early for a drink?' she asked.

'Well, it's five o'clock somewhere,' chuckled Jones.

Phillips chortled. 'I wish it was bloody five o'clock here.'

Jones started the engine. 'Come on, Guv. Let's get back. I'll treat you to a coffee from the canteen instead.'

'You spoil me, you do,' said Phillips sarcastically.

'I do my best.' Jones slipped the car into reverse and pulled out of the parking spot. After slowing nudging forward and out into the mid-morning traffic, he gunned the engine and set off back to Ashton House.

28

'So, what have you found?' said Phillips, as Jones passed round hot drinks for the team.

Bovalino jumped in first. 'I've run a quick background on Holloway and he's got form.'

'Really? What for?' Phillips took a mouthful of coffee.

'ABH, back in 1991 when he was a teenager. Seems he was a member of the Red Army, Man. United's hooligan firm. He and a load of his mates beat up a bunch of locals in Leeds after a game. He did six months of a twelve-month sentence in Armley. Nothing else since then.'

'How long's he been working at Cedar Pines?' asked Phillips.

'About five years. Prior to that, he was a hospital porter for ten years at Wythenshawe Hospital.'

'Is he married?' Jones asked.

'Yeah. For the third time, and he's got four kids. One with his current wife, who's quite a bit younger than him, one with the previous, and two with the first Mrs Holloway.'

'Any known associates?' said Phillips.

'Nothing on file, and looking at his social media, he doesn't appear to have many mates outside of the five-a-side team – the Red Devils.' Bovalino handed over a printout of various Facebook photos of Holloway. 'It's just pictures of him and the football team.'

Phillips examined the photos for a long moment before looking back up. 'I don't know what it is about this guy, but something doesn't sit right.'

'Well, as far as I can see, Guv, so far, so clean,' said Bov.

Phillips passed the printout back. 'Ok, well, let's not discount him just yet. See what else you can find.'

Bovalino nodded.

Phillips turned her attention to Entwistle. 'How you getting on with the historical poisonings?'

'Have you ever heard of Graham Young?'

'Can't say I have,' said Phillips.

'He was nicknamed *The Teacup Poisoner*, and is probably the most recent British serial killer to use strychnine, back in the sixties and seventies. After that, forensics got more sophisticated, so it was easier to trace. He ended up in Broadmoor Hospital in 1962 after poisoning several members of his family and killing his stepmother when he was just fifteen. He was released in 1971 and, believe it or not, got a job working as quartermaster at John Hadland Laboratories, where he was given complete access to a whole host of chemicals each day. He went on to poison seven more people at work, killing two. He was eventually caught and sent to Parkhurst Prison, where he died of a heart attack in 1990.'

'Sounds like a total nut-job,' said Jones.

Entwistle produced an A4 black and white printout and held it up for everyone to see. 'Look familiar?'

Phillips stared at the image of a contorted, twisted dead body on the page.

'It's exactly the same as Michael Yates's body.'

'Young's first victim, his step-mother,' said Entwistle. 'This was taken at the crime scene.'

'Oh, shit,' said Phillips, dropping her head into her hands.

'Looks like copycat number four,' said Entwistle.

Phillips took a moment before looking up again. 'Jesus. How come we get all the easy cases, hey?'

'How on earth are an elderly ex-teacher, a nurse, a runaway gay teenager, and a Polish cleaner all connected?' asked Jones. 'It just doesn't make sense.'

Phillips sighed heavily. 'Bov, you said Mark Holloway was a porter at Wythenshawe Hospital before Cedar Pines?'

'That's right.'

'Gillian Galloway was a nurse there,' Phillips said. 'Maybe that's a connection?'

'Plus Wiktoria's husband, Petr, works there, too,' added Jones.

Phillips continued. 'And Wiktoria is connected to Michael Yates through Cedar Pines.'

'So where does Sean Hamilton fit into all this?' asked Entwistle.

'He used the same doctors' surgery as Yates,' said Jones.

'But *not* the same doctor,' Phillips added.

The team fell silent for a moment as they considered the latest information.

'We're onto something here, I can feel it,' said Phillips,

'Exactly what, though, I'm not sure.' Phillips pulled out her phone and called Chakrabortty.

'Hello, Jane. You've just caught me. I was about to start my next PM.'

'It's just a quick one.'

'Ok.'

'Could Michael Yates have been poisoned with strychnine over a period of time? Days, or weeks, even.'

'No, not with strychnine. It's way too corrosive. Even the smallest amount would have a serious impact within a few hours.'

'Right. So it had to have been administered the night he died?'

'Absolutely, and most likely within two to three hours of the time of death.'

Phillips took a moment to think. 'I don't suppose you've got anything back on the DNA found on Szymańska, have you?'

'Not yet, but I'm expecting the results back within the next twenty-four hours.'

'Let me know as soon as you get them, won't you?'

'Of course.' There was a pause on the line. 'Is that it, Jane?'

'For now, yeah. Thanks, Tan,' said Phillips, and ended the call. 'Chakrabortty reckons Yates was given a single dose of strychnine, just a few hours before he died. His killer had to be someone who knew what it would do *and* had access to his room around the time he died.'

'We know Wiktoria Szymańska was working at Cedar Pines that night. Could she have administered the poison?' asked Jones.

Phillips felt her face wrinkle. 'Maybe, but why? Aside from shoplifting in her teens, her record is clean, and everyone who knew her liked her. I just don't see her suddenly turning into Harold Shipman all of a sudden.'

'Maybe *she* saw the killer do it, and that's why she was targeted?' suggested Entwistle.

'That's plausible,' Jones said.

Phillips tapped her pen against her teeth. 'So the big question is, who had access to Yates's room that night?'

'Dr Goodwin?' said Bovalino.

Jones shook his head. 'Cast-iron alibi, Bov. She was on stage in front of a hundred or more doctors, with time-stamped video of the event to prove it.'

'The caretaker, Holloway?' said Entwistle.

'He certainly would have access, but why would he want to kill a dying man in care?' mused Phillips.

At that moment, the door to MCU opened. Phillips and the team turned to see Chief Superintendent Carter striding towards Phillip's office, a rolled-up newspaper in his right hand. 'Can I have a word, Jane?' he said, before stepping inside.

'Of course, sir,' Phillips got up from her chair, followed him in and closed the door, They both remained standing. 'Everything all right, sir?'

'Have you seen this?' He handed her the newspaper. 'They've got wind of the body on the building site.'

Phillips scanned the story for a moment. 'It's to be expected. They did a small piece on Galloway's body being found at Dunham Massey, but somehow missed Hamilton on the fire. At least they've not connected the murders, sir.'

'Maybe not, but if he keeps going, it's only a matter of time.'

'I doubt it, sir. Each of the victims died in a totally different way, and without the kind of information we're getting from forensics and pathology, it'd take one hell of an eagle eye to make the connection.'

'Even so, this many murders in such a short space of time does not look good, Jane,' said Carter firmly.

'I understand, sir, and I can promise you, we're working flat out to get a breakthrough.'

Carter seemed to soften slightly. 'How did you get on at the care home this morning? Anything on the building site victim?'

Phillips had debriefed him on her way home the previous evening. 'We can't say for sure, but we suspect our killer may have also poisoned Michael Yates at Cedar Pines.'

'You're kidding?'

'I wish I was. His case is very reminiscent of Graham Young in the sixties and seventies, aka The Teacup Poisoner, who was jailed for three murders over a ten-year period. In fact, Yates's distorted body looks identical to that of Young's first victim, his stepmother.'

The colour seemed to drain from Carter's face. 'The press can't get hold of this. Fox will go mental.'

Phillips knew only too well how the rising body count, and the possibility of a copycat serial killer, would be received by the chief constable, who only ever wanted good news.

'We have to stop this guy, Jane. *Right now!*' said Carter, his soft Geordie tone replaced by almost primal panic.

'We're working on it, sir, I promise you, but from what we can see, there's no discernible pattern. We should have DNA from the bite mark on Szymańska in the next twenty-four hours, which will hopefully give us a name.'

Carter remained quiet for a moment, apparently deep in thought. 'Have you ever used psychological profiling?'

'Not really. DCI Brown claimed to be an expert in it, but the only profiling I ever saw him do was looking at himself in the mirror.' Phillips allowed herself a chuckle.

The joke seemed to be lost on Carter. Either that, or he wasn't listening. 'I used a profiler a few times in Newcastle and it really helped. I'd like to bring one into MCU to help us figure out what we're up against.'

'Sure,' said Phillips. 'Anyone I know?'

'I doubt it. She only practices in the North East. Her name's Dr Siobhan Harris. She can start straight away.'

'You've already spoken to her?'

'Yes, about ten minutes ago.'

Phillips was taken aback. Bringing in outsiders without consulting her was the kind of stunt Fox would pull, not Carter. She had been sure he trusted her – until now.

'Is that ok with you?'

Phillips adopted her best poker face. 'Yes. Of course, sir.'

'Good. She'll be here at ten, Monday morning,' said Carter, then left the room.

With her back to the team, Phillips moved across to the window and stared down at the car park as she bit her top lip. Her head awash with theories, her gut twisted with fear of what the killer might do next. But most of all, she was thoroughly pissed off at being undermined by Carter. She knew bringing in a profiler was probably a good idea, and she welcomed all the help she could get, but it was *her* investigation, *her* team out there on the ground doing the grunt work, and *her* job to catch this guy. Which was exactly what she was going to do. Turning on her heels, she headed back out to the team. The stakes had just got higher.

29

MONDAY, MARCH 8TH

Phillips had been at her desk for almost three hours by the time Carter led Dr Harris into MCU and made a beeline for her office. The door was open, so they walked straight in.

'Jane, this is Dr Harris.'

Petite and strikingly beautiful, Harris had thick brown hair and sparkling green eyes, and was smartly dressed in a pencil skirt, white blouse and killer heels. She smiled and offered her hand, which Phillips shook firmly. 'Please, call me Siobhan. It's good to meet you.' Her voice was soft and refined, with just a hint of a Newcastle accent. 'I've heard so much about you from Harry.'

Harry? thought Phillips. *All very cosy.*

Carter, slightly uncomfortable for the first time since Phillips had started working with him, resembled a bashful teenager. 'Shall we meet the team,' he mumbled awkwardly.

'Sure. Come through.' Phillips stepped out from behind her desk and led them out into the incident room.

'Guys, I'd like you to meet Dr Harris. She's the profiler I mentioned to you last night.'

A chorus of 'hello's followed.

'Please, call me Siobhan, or Doc if you prefer.'

Phillips continued with the introductions, gesturing to Jones. 'This is my 2IC, DS Jones. The man-mountain in the corner is DC Bovalino—'

'Wow, that's an unusual name,' said Harris.

Bov smiled widely. 'Yeah, Doc, it's Italian.'

'No shit, Sherlock!' chuckled Jones, drawing laughter from the room.

Bovalino flicked the Vs, pretending to be offended, then chuckled. 'Bloody Cockney.'

'And this, here…' She placed her hand on his shoulder. '…is our research and tech expert, DC Entwistle.'

'He's Irish-Caribbean, aren't you mate?' teased Bovalino.

It was Entwistle's turn to laugh and flick the Vs.

'I've allocated you the spare desk here with the guys, but if it's too noisy, I can organise an office farther down the corridor,' said Phillips.

'This will be fine,' said Harris, setting her large leather bag down on the desk.

Carter clapped his hands together. 'Right, well, I'll leave you guys to get acquainted. I have a meeting with the chief constable.'

'Give her our love, sir,' joked Bovalino.

Carter smiled politely before leaving the room.

'Shall we get started?' asked Harris.

Phillips forced a smile. 'Absolutely.'

'Great. Chief Superintendent Carter tells me you believe each of your current murders is a copycat of a historical case.'

'That's correct,' said Phillips, wondering what else Carter had shared with the doctor as she handed over a copy of her dossier.

Harris flicked through the pages slowly, the team watching on. She nodded. 'Impressive, very detailed work indeed. I know time is of the essence in this case, so why don't you guys bring me up to speed on the similarities between the old cases and the current murders.'

Phillips nodded. 'It makes sense to run through them in chronological order.' She turned to Entwistle. 'If we assume for now that Michael Yates *was* the first victim, then why don't you start with him?'

Harris took a seat.

Entwistle opened his file at the relevant section. 'The method of Yates's murder – the use of strychnine – is a dead-ringer for the first committed in 1962 by Graham Young, aka The Teacup Poisoner. He was convicted of murdering his stepmother the same year, and was committed to Broadmoor Mental Hospital. The judge ruled that he should serve a minimum of fifteen years, but he was released after just eight.'

'Some soft-hearted bureaucrat thought it would be a good idea to let him out early,' added Phillips.

Bovalino scoffed. 'Typical.'

Entwistle continued. 'In 1970, he got a job working with chemicals in Bovingdon. His employers *were* aware that he had served time at Broadmoor, but not the reason *why* he was there. And it wasn't long before he was up to his old tricks, poisoning seven more people by spiking their hot drinks at break times. Interestingly, it was Young himself who inadvertently brought the police to his door by asking his bosses if they'd considered thallium poisoning. They reported it to the police, who discovered his past crimes and raided his house. They found all the evidence they needed to convict him, and in 1972 he was sentenced to life.'

'And this time there was no cushy time at Broadmoor,' Phillips cut in.

'Indeed,' said Entwistle. 'He was sent to Parkhurst on the Isle of Wight, where he died of a heart attack in his cell, aged forty-three.'

Harris smiled. 'Very thorough.'

Entwistle blushed slightly.

Phillips turned to Bovalino. 'Let's see if you were paying attention, big man. Fill the doc in on Gillian Galloway and Steve Wright.

Bovalino nodded, tapping his copy of the file on his desk. 'As you say, Guv, Galloway's killer appears to be mimicking the murders of Steve Wright, also known as The Suffolk Strangler. *His* killing spree began in October of 2006, and lasted only a couple of months. He was arrested in December of the same year, but still managed to kill five women in under two months. Galloway, like Wright's third and fourth victims, was found naked in woodland, laid out in a cruciform position, and – again, like Wright's victims – she'd been strangled. There was no sexual assault, which also matches the historical victims.'

'And where is Wright now?' asked Harris.

Bovalino scanned his file for a moment. 'Er, says here he's currently serving a full life tariff in HMP Long Larton, Worcester. It's maximum security and he'll never be released.'

'He looks bloody dangerous,' said Jones, pointing to Wright's mugshot in the file.

Phillips nodded. 'The judge thought so too, which is why he's never getting out. Thanks, Bov.' She turned back to Entwistle. 'You know Denis Nilsen better than anybody. Talk us through his connection to our third victim, Sean Hamilton.'

Entwistle wasted no time. 'Like all of Nilsen's victims, Hamilton was a young gay man, living alone in a new city. And, like in a number of the Nilsen cases, his body was found burning on a fire on remote wasteland. The post mortem revealed Hamilton had been drowned in a domestic setting, such as a bath, sink or maybe even a bucket, then set on fire along with a car tyre. Exactly like Nilsen's at least twelve victims, who were murdered in London between 1978 and 1983, each of them gay, and each of them loners or estranged from their families. He got the nickname "The Muswell Hill Murderer", and was eventually sentenced to a whole life tariff. He died in HMP Full Sutton in 2018, aged seventy-two, of a pulmonary embolism.'

'Good riddance,' said Jones.

Phillips took the lead now. 'As for our latest victim, Wiktoria Szymańska, I remember hearing tales about The Beast of Manchester, aka Terry Hardy, when I was a young PC. Whoever killed her copied the murder of Wanda Skala in 1974 in almost forensic detail. Both women were battered about the head with a concrete block, mutilated, and left on a building site in the Moston area of Manchester. And both of them had a single nipple bitten off.'

'I still don't know how anyone could do that,' muttered Bovalino.

Phillips continued. 'Hardy loved violence of any kind. It was said that when he walked into a pub, people would immediately walk out, such were the odds of him delivering a horrific beating to innocent bystanders for absolutely no reason. He even tried to kill his own brother for reporting him to the police. A real piece of work, who was sentenced to life in 1978. He died of a heart attack in Wakefield Maximum Security Prison in 2012, aged sixty-seven, after thirty-seven years inside.

'Very impressive, guys, and quite the rogues' gallery,' said Harris. 'Any thoughts on what motivated them to kill?'

'We were hoping you could tell us,' said Phillips.

Harris sat forward in her chair. 'Ok. From a psychological standpoint, there are certain common traits that we see in the make-up of a serial killer, such as childhood abuse – sexual or physical, sometimes *both* – or being separated from their families at a young age. Childhood trauma, like losing a parent or close grandparent – as was the case with Denis Nilsen, who adored his grandfather and was heartbroken when he died at just sixty-eight. After he was caught, he admitted that it was seeing his grandfather in the funeral home that prompted him to keep his victims' bodies in his flat for days and weeks after death. He felt close to their corpses and didn't want them to leave – as with his grandfather.'

'That's so messed up,' said Bovalino.

'Yes, it is. But sadly, childhood trauma is the biggest cause of mental health issues in adults that we know of, and each of the historical killers suffered from one or more of these – apart from Hardy, that is. There's no clear early-life reason for his behaviour other than he was unstable and violent. His crimes started with fighting in pubs, progressed on to beating women, and culminated in him raping and battering them to death.'

'So do you think our killer – or killers – suffered from childhood trauma?' asked Phillips.

'Statistically speaking, I'd say it's highly likely, yes.'

'Knowing that doesn't help us catch them any quicker though, does it?' added Jones.

'Maybe not, but it can certainly help build a profile of the killer and narrow down your suspects.'

'If we had any suspects,' said Bovalino.

Harris ignored the remark. 'Chief Superintendent Carter mentioned you weren't sure whether you were looking for one killer for all of them, four single killers, or two killers working together.'

'That's right,' said Phillips. She couldn't help feeling more and more undermined as the details of Carter's private briefing with Harris unfolded.

'Well, based on the evidence so far, it's my belief that you're looking for *one* killer for all four murders, working alone: a *man* who has been emasculated all his life and grown up around abuse.'

Phillips folded her arms across her chest. 'Oh? Why do you think that?'

'Well.' Harris cleared her throat. 'I'd say it's a man because it's so rare for women to strangle, batter or mutilate, and the chances of coming across a single copycat killer are quite remote. Most serial killers are driven by their past, which is individual to them, and manifests itself in their method of murder. For example, it would be highly unlikely that, say, two people shared the exact same early life issues and motivations and, as such, subsequent killing methods. I mean, it's not *impossible,* but it's highly, highly unlikely. But for *four* individual people to have the exact same issues and motivations as previous killers, and then act out their rage in the same way? Well, in my experience, that would be pretty much *impossible.* Especially within a period of just a few weeks and within the same city.'

'So, if it is one man, why is he copying different

killers?' asked Phillips. 'Why not just repeat the method that matches his own issues over and over?'

'Well. I think your killer's issues and motivations are actually being served by him copying murders committed by different people – in this case, the crème de la crème of British serial killers, some of the most infamous, high-profile killers ever witnessed in this country.'

'What about Peter Sutcliffe, the Yorkshire Ripper?' said Entwistle. 'He's probably the most famous of all, and he's not been copied.'

'Not yet, but I fear he's on the list,' said Harris.

'Why do you think that?' Phillips asked.

Harris tapped the file with her finger. 'Look at the crimes. In chronological order, he starts with a poisoning, moves on to strangulation, then drowning, and finally, he beats Szymańska with a brick. He's getting more and more violent – probably increasingly confident too. I'm sorry to say this, but I fear his next victim will suffer an even more violent death than Szymańska's. Sutcliffe's crimes were horrifically violent – one of the most brutal killers ever seen. So, he could well be on our killer's list to be copied as he escalates.'

'God, that's all we need.' Phillips exhaled loudly. 'You say his motivations are actually being served by him emulating previous murderers, but how?'

'Like I said, the men he's copying are some of the most infamous killers ever seen, god-like in some people's twisted fantasies. If I'm right and he *was* abused and emasculated as a child, then by copying them, he's saying to the world that he's as infamous as they were, as powerful, as fearsome, as evil. I suspect he was never allowed to think for himself or to make up his own mind, so he has little frame of reference for what constitutes success other than to look at historical cases and the terror they inflicted, then copy them. If he does it right, then he's achieved his goal.'

'Which is?' said Phillips.

Harris locked eyes with her. 'To strike fear into the hearts of the people of Manchester. To know for sure that they are as scared of him as people of the past were of Graham Young, Steve Wright, Denis Nilsen and Terry Hardy. Plus, by changing his MO each time, there's less risk of creating a pattern that could help you stop him.'

Silence descended on the incident room once more as the realisation of what they were up against began to sink in.

Phillips stared at the dossier of killers with a heavy heart. Everything Harris had said made sense, and if she was right, then their killer would soon strike again, with even greater violence. Though she resented how Harris had been brought on board, she had to give the woman credit. She now had a better picture of what they were looking at, when previously all there had been was an apparent mess and confusion. She wasn't sure, yet, if she was willing to forgive Carter, though. As for their solo killer, where, when, and who were the questions. In twenty years of policing, she had never felt more powerless.

Her phone rang. It was Chakrabortty. Phillips excused herself and stepped away from the group. 'Tan. Please tell me you have the DNA results.'

'I do.'

'And?'

'Nothing in the system, I'm afraid,' said Chakrabortty.

'Damn it!'

'But I can tell you, you're looking for a white male.'

'Well, that narrows it down to just twenty million or so suspects.' Phillips's tone was sarcastic.

'*Don't shoot the messenger, Jane,*' Chakrabortty hit back.

'I'm sorry, Tan. I was just so hoping we would get a hit on this guy.'

'*I know. I'm sorry we haven't got better news for you.*'

'Well, thanks for the update. Look, I'd better go.' She rang off, and walked back to the team. 'No match on the DNA. But we know he's a white male.'

The guys groaned in unison.

'So, we're gonna have to do this the old-fashioned way. I want a list of all the violent serial killers convicted in the UK, ASAP.'

'How far back do you wanna go?' asked Jones.

'Let's assume his starting point is Graham Young. So, anyone who was convicted after he was put away for the second and final time. So, 1972 onwards.' Phillips looked at Harris. 'Do you agree?'

'Yes. That makes sense.'

'Good,' said Phillips. 'Let's see if we can figure out who he's gonna try and copy next.'

30

Gabe watched from the darkened cab of the van, parked up in the shadows of the city-centre back street. Outside, the temperature had dropped below freezing. The heavy snow that had started in the afternoon was set to continue well into the early hours, so he had the heater running at full blast. He wanted the van nice and cosy, welcoming, even. Twenty minutes later, he spotted her as she stepped out of the service entrance of the hotel and into the alley. She wore a thick coat, woolly hat and scarf against the weather, and carried a large handbag over her shoulder. She strode off towards the main road and her bus home. He knew that last part because he'd watched her do it for the last three nights in a row, as she finished her late shift. He waited for her to turn right at the end of the alley and disappear out of sight before making his move. He checked his watch. It was 11.03 p.m., and he had just eight minutes to execute his plan before her bus arrived. He quickly reversed back down the alley to the next junction, pulled the van left onto the adjacent road, then left again and finally another left onto the main drag. Stopping at the red light, he could see her up ahead, sitting alone at the bus stop. Perfect. As the light turned green, he moved forward at a steady pace, then indicated and gently pulled the van towards the kerb. The old brakes squeaked as he came to a stop. Leaning across the seat, he wound down the window. 'Hello Wendy, do you wanna lift?'

Wendy flinched, appearing startled as she stared into the dark cab. She clearly didn't recognise him, so he flicked on the light above his head. 'Wendy, it's *me*.'

Wendy's face softened suddenly, and she let out an audible sigh of relief. 'Oh hello. Sorry, I didn't realise who it was. I thought it was some weirdo.'

Gabe chuckled. 'Yeah, sorry about that. Seriously though, do you want a lift?'

Wendy checked her watch. 'No, you're all right. My bus will be here in five minutes. I'll be fine.'

'You live in Moss Side, right?'

'Wow. You've got a good memory.'

'My wife doesn't think so,' he joked. 'I'm going that way and the weather's awful. Come on, jump in. I'll drop you off.'

Wendy glanced up the street, then up at the snow falling in big white clumps. 'Oh, go on then,' she said, and stood.

He opened the door, and a moment later she was in the cab.

'Oooh, it's lovely and warm in here,' she said as she pulled the door shut.

'Better than a bus,' he replied with a smile, before switching off the light and pulling away.

'I didn't mean to be rude back there, but I never expected you to be driving a van,' she said as they headed towards Mancunian Way.

'Especially not one as old and knackered as this, hey?'

Wendy smiled coyly. 'No, I guess not.'

'It's my dad's. I've been dropping off some old furniture to a friend of his in Failsworth. I should have been home an hour ago, but she's a little old lady and a bit lonely. She wouldn't let me leave and kept plying me with cake. I feel a bit sick now.' He patted his stomach.

'Sounds like my grandma. I put on a stone every time I go to visit her.'

He smiled.

For the next few minutes, they drove in silence as he savoured her scent. He had been mesmerised by it the first time they had met, and it was just as intoxicating as he had remembered; a mixture of the oil she used to straighten her Afro-Caribbean hair, and the moisturiser on her dark, perfect black skin.

'Busy day?' he asked.

'Long,' she said, looking out of the window. 'Twelve hours dealing with whinging hotel guests, moaning about hairs in their bathtubs, not enough towels or too many towels, the price of the mini-bar and anything else they can think of.'

Gabe chortled. 'You have more patience than me.'

'Sometimes.'

He indicated and took the exit signposted for Hulme. 'You're on Kenside Street, aren't you?'

Wendy smiled. 'Wow, you really do have a good memory. I'm impressed.'

'I do my best,' he said with a chuckle.

A few minutes later, they drove under the Hulme Arch, then passed between the ASDA superstore on the right and the Heineken Brewery on the left.

'You want to take the second road on your right,' she said, pointing ahead.

Gabe nodded, but didn't reply.

'You'll need to get onto the right lane or you'll miss it,' she added urgently.

Again he said nothing and continued driving on past the road.

'You've missed the turning!' she said, swivelling in her seat to look back.

He nodded.

'Are you gonna turn round?'

He shook his head.

'What's going on?' Her voice cracked slightly.

'We're taking a small detour,' he said, without looking at her.

'What kind of detour? Where?'

'You'll see,' he said, and began to accelerate.

'Seriously. This isn't funny. You're scaring me.'

He glanced sideways at her for a moment, then turned his attention back to the road.

'Can you stop the van, please? I want to get out.'

He continued to stare at the road ahead in silence.

She pulled at the door handle next to her. 'Stop the van. I want to get out!'

'Soon.'

'Stop it now!'

Gabe laughed. 'I'll stop when I'm good and fucking ready, Wendy.'

She began to cry. 'Please stop the van. I want to go home.'

He remained silent and continued driving at speed up the Parkway.

Fishing in her bag, she pulled out her mobile phone. 'If you don't let me out, I'm calling the police.'

Without looking, he snatched it from her hand and threw it to the floor. 'No, you won't,' he growled, then moved the van into the right-hand lane before stopping at the intersection, then turning right down Mauldeth Road West.

'Where are you taking me?' she cried through her tears.

'Somewhere we won't be disturbed,' he said with a wicked grin.

'Why are you doing this?'

A few hundred yards farther down the road, he turned left and drove straight onto the Hough End playing fields, and a minute later brought the van to a stop. He switched off the engine and turned to face her.

She stared back at him with wide, terrified eyes, then started screaming as she yanked wildly at the door handle. It wouldn't budge. He had made sure of that, fixing it so only he had the knowhow to release it.

The area around them was cloaked in darkness, with a slight white hue from the falling snow. It was perfect. Just as he'd imagined. As she continued to fight with the door handle, he reached down into the door well and found what he was looking for.

'Do you know what this is?' he said, lifting it up so she could see it.

She turned to face him. 'No,' she whimpered, as tears streaked down her cheeks.

'It's a hammer. But not just any hammer, you understand,' he said gleefully. 'It's a ball-peen hammer.'

She said nothing as she continued to cry.

He relished the sound of her breathing – rapid, and oozing with fear.

He leaned his body across her chest, which caused her to flinch and cry out. Stopping for a moment, he took a loud, audible sniff, and basked in her luxuriant scent once more before jiggling the handle until the door popped open and cold air rushed into the cab. Still holding the hammer in his right hand, he slid back across to the driver's seat.

'Now you can get out.'

Wendy stared at him for a moment, as if lost.

'Get out, you fucking whore!' he shouted.

Pushing the door open wide, she jumped down onto the rough ground into the snow and began running for her life. Exactly what he wanted her to do.

Opening the driver's door, he jumped down and, gripping the hammer tightly in his right hand and a screwdriver in his left, set off after her.

She was surprisingly agile as she raced across the snow towards the lights of the main road just a few hundred yards up ahead, but he was taller and quicker, and soon he was right behind her, matching her step for step as the lights drew nearer. Lifting the hammer into the air, he held it there for a long moment, savouring her cries for mercy, before slamming it down with a sickening thud into the back of her skull.

31

Gabe parked the van up behind the dilapidated old out-house and switched off the engine. He sat in silence for a long moment, replaying the events of the evening in his mind. He felt exhilarated, but as the adrenaline began to fade, he sensed the onset of exhaustion. It was close to 2 a.m., and he really should be getting home, but he couldn't resist going inside the house to see his father and share the details of his latest kill. Plus, he needed to clean himself up. A few minutes later, he walked through the filthy old kitchen, where he deposited his bag on the table, then strode into his father's room. His father appeared to be asleep, the only sound in the small space the low hiss coming from the oxygen tubes inserted in his nose. But as Gabe approached the side of the bed, Bert's eyes shot open.

'You've decided to grace me with your presence, have you?' he rasped, then began coughing. 'I could die in here and you'd never know!'

As ever, his father knew exactly how to bring him

crashing back down to earth. 'Oh, shut up!' Gabe sneered.

Bert's eyes dropped slowly to Gabe's coat sleeves, which were spattered with blood. 'What's that on your coat?'

'Exactly what it looks like.'

'Blood?'

'Yes.'

'Human blood?'

Gabe smiled wickedly, and nodded.

'Why, boy?'

'You know why. To hurt *you* like you hurt me.'

'This has to stop, boy. Now.'

'It stops when I say it stops,' said Gabe.

Bert shook his head and tears welled in his eyes. 'To think the good Lord took my Maggie and left me with *you*. A pitiful excuse of a man and a human being.'

'Oh, don't start with all that again. I've heard it a million times before.'

'And you'll never stop hearing it, will you?' Bert coughed violently. 'Because even when I'm dead, you'll still hear my voice, reminding you what a total waste of life you are. A useless, pathetic child who grew up into an even more pathetic man. I didn't think it was possible, but you finally exceeded my expectations.'

Gabe breathed heavily through his nose, his jaw clenching as he tried desperately to contain his rage. 'Say what you want, you spiteful old bastard, but I'll be the one laughing when this is done. When I reveal to the world that you, the great Detective Sonny, spawned a brutal killer, then sat and watched while he murdered, over and over again.'

'Sat and watched? What am I supposed to do when you've locked me up in here, like a prisoner in my own home? No phone or contact with the outside world. I don't even have a window, for God's sake!'

'Well, now you know how *I* felt as a kid, trapped in this god-forsaken shit hole in the middle of nowhere. No friends to play with nearby, no visitors ever allowed to come to the house. Just you, a drunken old man, bringing whores home to fuck in *my* mother's bed, then beating the shit out of me because I had the audacity to cry myself to sleep.'

'You were always bloody crying.'

'I was a young boy whose mother had died, for Christ's sake!' yelled Gabe. 'Why couldn't you understand that? I needed love and compassion, not hatred and beatings.'

'Love? How could I have loved *you*? You weren't even mine!'

Gabe froze. 'What did you say?'

Bert's lip curled into a snarl. 'You heard me.'

'Say it again.'

Bert paused for a long moment before continuing. 'I *said* that you, boy, are the bastard son of someone other fella. Your mother had an affair.'

'That's not true. It can't be.'

'It is.'

'When?'

'I'd guess about nine months before you were born, wouldn't you?' Bert said sarcastically.

'You're lying,' said Gabe.

'I wish I was. I only found out after she died and I realised I was stuck with you, someone else's pitiful excuse for a son. I did my best, but every time I looked at you, all I saw was betrayal from the woman I loved.'

'I don't understand. If you knew she had an affair, how come you've spent my whole life telling me what a saint she was? That you wished God had taken me and not her.'

Bert coughed. 'I meant it. I *do* wish she was still here, because I could forgive an affair. It happened a lot with coppers and their wives back in the day. Especially with detectives and the hours we worked. I wasn't such a saint myself, to be fair, but then she died and I was stuck on my own with *you*.'

He stared at Bert in silence, hatred clawing at his throat.

'Well now you finally know. You boy, are a dirty, illegitimate, unwanted, unloved, useless little bastard.'

Gabe's chest heaved as rage threatened to overwhelm him. All he wanted to do was to strangle the old man right here, right now. But he had a job to finish. A series of events that would deliver his ultimate revenge and hurt his father far beyond physical pain.

'Fuck you, old man,' he growled, and stormed out of the room, slamming the door behind him.

THE HEAVY DOOR connected with the ancient timber frame, the vibrations disturbing the room. A thick cloud of dust rose into the acrid air. The hum of thousands of flies buzzing echoed around the room, their bodies flickering in the low light like dark embers above a raging fire. The television placed on the cabinet at the end of the bed blared at full volume, playing nothing in particular. Oxygen tanks hissed as they pumped air into redundant tubes fixed into the decaying nostrils of what remained of the corpse laid out flat on the bed. The eyeballs had long since been devoured by the maggots that now crawled from the eye sockets into the fleshless, open mouth. In a matter of weeks, nothing would remain of the old man but a twisted, rotting skeleton.

32

9.33 A.M. TUESDAY, MARCH 9TH

Phillips stared down at the frozen body of the pretty young black woman, partially covered by the blood-stained snow that surrounded it. Her coat had been pulled open, her torso and breasts exposed to the elements. The killer had struck again sometime overnight and, judging by the mutilation of the body, Harris's theory – that he was growing more violent with each murder – was confirmed. This time, judging by the twin trail of footprints leading up to this point, he had chased her down, then killed her where she lay in the snow.

Senior CSI Andy Evans was already on scene with his team. Their white tent had been in place for almost an hour now. 'Not a morning I'd choose to be outside,' he said as one of his assistants crouched and took close-up photos of the body. 'At least it's stopped snowing at last,' he added.

Jones blew his lips. 'Jesus, Guv. This guy is out of control.'

Phillips nodded.

'Look lively,' said Bovalino. 'Here comes the doc.'

Phillip and Jones followed his line of sight.

Dr Harris was making her way across the snowy ground. 'He's struck again, I believe?' she said as she reached the police cordon a few feet away from them.

Phillips stepped out of the tent and moved towards her, tapping her own white forensic suit. 'You'll need to put on one of these if you want to see inside the tent.'

'Thanks, but I think I'm good out here, to be honest. I'm not great with blood.'

'Based on the footprints, SOCO think she was chased across the field, hit on the back of the head, then stabbed repeatedly,' said Phillips.

'All the hallmarks of Peter Sutcliffe,' Harris said.

'That's what we were thinking. So, you were right about him getting more violent with each murder.'

'You sound surprised, Chief Inspector?'

'Perhaps I am. Just a little bit.'

'Believe me, I really wish I wasn't,' said Harris. 'Any ideas who she is?'

'Photo ID around her neck says her name's Wendy Marsh,' Phillips replied. 'Worked at the Marlow Hotel in the city centre. Entwistle is gathering her full details as we speak.'

Harris paused and looked around. 'What is this place?'

'Hough End playing fields. Last used last night by a five-a-side football league, until the snow came down heavy and they had to call off the games. The caretaker was the last to leave, at nine, and reckons everything was in order when he closed up for the night.'

'Any ideas around time of death?'

'Too early to say. We'll need the post mortem for that, but looking at the frozen state of the body, she must have been out here for most of the night,' said Phillips.

'Who found her?'

'The caretaker. He's in a right state. Poor bugger must be knocking on eighty years old.'

'Well, I think it's safe to rule him out, in that case,' Harris ventured. 'Whoever did this is most likely fit and athletic.'

At that moment, Jones joined them. 'Morning, Doc,' he said, nodding to Harris before continuing. 'Guv, Entwistle has been on. He's found the girl's address. Apparently she's local, 42 Kenside Street, Moss Side. Lives with her parents. Do you want me and Bov to go and break the news?'

'No. I'll do it. You and Bov speak to the neighbours round here, see if anyone saw or heard anything.'

'Sure thing.'

'And find out where Mark Holloway was last night,' said Phillips.

'The caretaker from Cedar Pines?'

'Yeah. He's big into five-a-side football. Find out if his team ever played here. We know our guy loves to plan his kills, so he must be familiar with this place and the fact it would be empty at the time he brought her here. And tell Entwistle to speak to the Marlow Hotel, find out what time Marsh finished work, check their CCTV as well as any cameras in the area. See if we can find out how she ended up out here with the killer.'

Jones nodded and headed back into the tent to get his partner.

One of the SOCO team approached, holding a large digital camera. 'Excuse me, Ma'am.'

Phillips turned to face her. 'What have you got?'

'I specialise in tyre track analysis.'

'Yes?'

'Well, I'll need to do a final check at the lab, but I'm

almost certain the tyre tracks here are a match for the ones we found in Dunham Massey, the body fire, *and* the building site.'

Jones emerged from the tent alongside Bovalino, and they began removing their overalls.

'Looks like he used the same van as all the others, Jonesy,' said Phillips. 'Tell Entwistle to check ANPR as well. We need to find that bloody van.'

'You got it, Guv,' said Jones.

Bov nodded.

Phillips turned back to Harris. 'I don't suppose you want to come with me to see Wendy's parents?'

Harris smiled weakly. 'Er, no. I don't think I'd be any help in that kind of situation.'

'Fair enough,' said Phillips as she unzipped her forensic suit. 'Well, in that case, I'll see you back at the office this afternoon.'

'Great,' said Harris. She glanced one last time at the tent before turning and trudging off through the snow towards her car.

33

It was just after 1 p.m. when Phillips walked back into MCU. Entwistle was at his desk, his head buried in his laptop. Harris sat at the spare desk next to him, working away.

As Phillips approached, Entwistle looked up. 'How did it go with the parents?'

Phillips dropped into Jones's empty chair. 'Bloody awful.'

Harris offered a sympathetic smile. 'I really don't know how you can deliver such awful news to someone.'

'I'd like to say it gets easier the more times you do it, but it doesn't,' said Phillips with a sigh. 'It was just as bad today as it was my very first time. But it's part of the job, and all you can do is explain the situation as simply and as kindly as possible.'

Harris shook her head. 'I couldn't do it.'

Phillips said nothing for a moment as her mind flashed back to Wendy Marsh's parents' faces as she broke the news that their youngest daughter was dead, murdered overnight. She closed her eyes and tried to bury the awful image.

'You ok, Guv?' asked Entwistle.

Phillips opened her eyes and offered a faint smile. 'Yeah, I'm fine. Anything from CCTV, yet?'

'Yeah,' he tapped the screen. 'I've found video of her getting into a Mark II transit van.'

Phillips's eyes widened. She jumped up from the chair and moved to where she could see over his shoulder. Harris craned her neck to get a look too.

Entwistle hit the keyboard and the silent video began to play.

They watched as Marsh appeared from under the camera, walking along the snowy pavement towards a bus shelter, a bag over her shoulder. Reaching it, she sat down, then waited. A few minutes later, the van appeared and stopped in the road in front of her.

'The plate's been covered again, Guv.'

After a brief exchange, Marsh got up and climbed into the van, which then moved off in the direction of Mancunian Way before turning right and disappearing from shot.

'Tell me you have ANPR footage of where the van went next,' said Phillips.

'I do.' Switching windows, he pulled up footage from a number of different ANPR cameras and hit play. 'He drives up onto the Mancunian Way, but not for long, pulling off at the next junction for Hulme. He follows the underpass, then takes a left onto the Parkway heading towards Moss Side—'

'Which is where Marsh lived,' Phillips cut in.

'Yeah, but he drives right past the junction for Kenside Street, at which point he begins to speed up.' Entwistle switched to another ANPR feed, which faced the oncoming traffic. 'We pick him up here as he passes Hulme Grammar School.'

'Pause it, there,' said Phillips.

Entwistle obliged, and a frozen image of the van, viewed from the front, filled the screen.

Squinting, Phillips leaned closer to the laptop. 'The windscreen looks almost reflective.'

'Yeah. It must be some kind of coating or film that's been applied that somehow reflects light back at the camera. I'm guessing he's done that so we can't see into the cab.'

'Clever bugger. He knows that some of the cameras can capture the faces of drivers.'

'He's certainly meticulous,' said Harris.

Entwistle continued to narrate the video. 'Finally, he turns right at Mauldeth Road West, towards the playing fields, at which point we lose him and he kills her.'

'What about when he leaves afterwards?' asked Phillips.

'No sign of him. He must have taken the back roads.'

'So, say he does know about the cameras, why drive through the city centre and then along the Parkway?' Phillips said. 'CCTV and ANPR are all over those routes. Why not use the back roads all night?'

'Because he *wanted* you to see him,' Harris interjected. 'He's showing you how good he is. That he knows all your tricks. That you use cameras to track suspects, and he knows how to bypass them and beat you. It's classic cat and mouse.'

Phillips's eyes narrowed. 'Are you saying this is just a game to him?'

'Yes, I'm afraid it is. But then, life is a game to people

in all walks of life. I'm sure you'll have heard the phrase "play the game" during your time on the force. It refers to understanding the politics of business and using it to your advantage. Well, it's the same in *his* world. His goal is to outsmart you, and his victims, for as long as possible. But for people with psychopathic tendencies, there's no fun in being smarter than the next man and not being able to tell anyone about it. Being blatant like this is his way of boasting about how clever he is. Then, to rub salt into the wounds, he disappears into the back roads because he knows how to disappear without trace. He's reminding you he's one step ahead of you.'

'He certainly is at the minute,' replied Phillips. 'So, why did Wendy get in the van with him? Talking to her parents, they said she was a street-smart girl who knew the risks of being out alone at night.'

'If that's true, then we can probably assume she knew him,' said Harris.

'That would make sense,' added Entwistle. 'It really didn't take long for him to persuade her to get into a sinister-looking, clapped-out old banger.'

Phillips nodded. 'True. Let's take a look at Marsh's social media. See who she's been interacting with recently; any messages that could have potentially come from this guy.'

'Sure, Guv,' said Entwistle.

'And go back through the other victims' social media too. It's a long shot, but look for any mutual friends.' Phillips's phone began to ring. 'Jonesy?'

'Hi, Guv. How did it go with Marsh's parents?'

'Don't ask. What about you? Anything from the neighbours?'

'Seems nobody heard a thing.'

'That can't be true? The poor girl was battered and mutilated. Surely someone had to have heard something?'

'Well, if they did, they're not saying anything, Guv.'

Phillips ran a hand through her hair. 'Jesus. When are we gonna catch a break on this case?'

Jones continued. '*What about the CCTV and ANPR cameras? Any luck?*'

'Yes and no. We know he used the same transit van as the others, and we've got footage of Marsh getting into it of her own volition, but once again the plates are unclear. And, based on ANPR footage captured on the Parkway, we also think he's put some kind of film on the windscreen that means the cameras can't see into the cab.'

'*Sneaky bastard.*'

'Yeah. Not only that. After the kill, there's no sign of the van anywhere on any of the surrounding cameras. It's like he just disappeared,' Phillips added.

'*This guy's like a ghost,*' said Jones.

'You can say that again,' replied Phillips. 'Anyway, where are you?'

'*On our way back to the office.*'

'Ok. We'll see you when you get here.'

'*No worries. We shouldn't be more than half an hour.*'

With that, Phillips rang off.

Harris angled her laptop so Phillips and Entwistle could see her screen. 'I hope you don't mind, but I wanted to try and do my bit. So, I've been looking at British serial killers considered by society to be in the same league as Wright, Nilsen and Sutcliffe, etc. People he might look to emulate next.'

'So, who've you've got?'

'Well. Following his pattern of copycats, so far I've narrowed it down to single men who worked alone. That eliminates killers who worked in couples such as Ian Brady, Fred West and Ian Huntley, for example.'

'And who does that leave us with?' said Phillips.

'Well, the most prolific serial killer the UK has ever seen was Dr Harold Shipman, who murdered over two hundred of his elderly patients. But, one could argue, our man has already had his poisoning and pensioner fix with the murder of Michael Yates. In fact, each method of murder has been unique so far: poisoning, strangulation, drowning, battery and now stabbing. If this guy is as meticulous as we believe, then that was no accident and he intends to use a different method with each kill.'

'So, what and who's left?'

Harris opened a mugshot on screen. 'An obvious one would be Levi Bellfield, aka the Bus Stop Killer.'

'I remember him,' said Entwistle.

'Me too,' said Phillips.

'Again, I'm not sure he's on our guy's list, because Bellfield's methods were very similar to Trevor Hardy's and Peter Sutcliffe's – beating his victims to death. Plus, our guy picked up his last victim at a bus stop. You can never discount him, of course, but the pattern suggests it'll be something very high profile, incredibly violent, and different to the other murders.'

'Anyone fit the profile?'

'Of those I've researched so far, two stand out: Stephen Griffiths, also known as the Crossbow Cannibal. He was convicted of murdering three street workers in 2009 and 2010.'

'God, it just gets better,' said Phillips sarcastically.

'I'm afraid that none of what I've found is good news for the case, Chief Inspector. The other potential, is Bruce Lee—'

Entwistle flinched. 'The kung fu guy?'

Harris shook her head. 'No. His real name was Peter George Dinsdale, but as a kid he was obsessed with the martial arts star, Bruce Lee. So when he was old enough, he changed his name to Bruce George Peter Lee.'

'And what was *his* method of murder?'

'Arson,' said Harris. 'And it's worth noting, the jury ruled he was actually guilty of multiple manslaughters as opposed to murder. Thirteen in total.'

Phillips took a moment to process the information. 'Based on what we've seen so far, I think the Crossbow Cannibal has more the kind of profile that would appeal to our guy.'

'I'd have to agree with you,' said Harris.

Phillips turned to Entwistle. 'He's a stickler for detail. Find out what type of crossbow Griffiths used, then get in touch with all the sporting goods stores in the Greater Manchester area. I want the names and addresses of anyone who bought the same crossbow within the last twelve months.'

Entwistle nodded and began typing into his laptop.

'Would you like me to continue looking for other potentials?' asked Harris.

'That would be great. Thank you,' said Phillips, and stood. 'I better go and update Carter. We'll need to make some kind of statement to the press.'

Harris leaned forward on her elbows. 'Would you like me to come with you? Maybe I can help?'

Phillips flashed a thin smile. 'No, thanks. I've got this.' She headed for the door.

34

WEDNESDAY, MARCH 10TH

'You look tired, Jane,' said Chakrabortty as she passed across the Wendy Marsh post-mortem report.

Phillips took the file. 'I'm not sleeping much at the moment.'

'I'm not surprised, with a case like this. I've never seen anything like it.'

Phillips began scanning the overview at the front of the document.

Chakrabortty explained her findings. 'It appears she was hit twice over the head with great force by a small round object. Her injuries are consistent with something like a ball-peen hammer—'

'Which is what Peter Sutcliffe used, right?'

'Yes. It's likely she would have been unconscious after the first blow, and her brain was almost certainly dead after the second. Mercifully, she'd have felt nothing after that, at which point he used a very sharp, narrow metal spike of some kind to stab her.'

'Fifteen times?' said Phillips, reading from the report.

'Wound placement suggests a frenzied attack.'

To protect her own sanity, Phillips pushed the image of Marsh's last moments on earth to the back of her mind. 'Sutcliffe used a sharpened screwdriver, didn't he?'

Chakrabortty nodded. 'I took the liberty of looking at a couple of files on the ripper. The injuries to his victims are consistent with Marsh's, and I'm fairly confident your killer used the same sort of weapon in this attack.'

'When she was struck on the head, would she have made a noise, do you think?'

'I very much doubt it. As the hammer connected with her skull, the damage to the brain would have caused instant limitations to her reactions.'

'That's why none of the neighbours living around the playing fields heard anything,' said Phillips.

'And that's why Sutcliffe used the same method. The victim was instantly incapacitated with limited noise and fuss, and as his intention was always to kill, it really didn't matter if they were brain dead by the time they hit the ground or not. Their hearts and lungs would still function for a time, which meant plenty of blood loss as a result of the stabbing. Something, it would appear, Sutcliffe revelled in.'

'Those poor women.'

'There was something else too,' added Chakrabortty. 'We found traces of semen on her abdomen.'

'Another Sutcliffe trait?' said Phillips.

'Yes. I'm afraid so.'

'Where are you at with the DNA?'

'It's with the lab. We'll know in the next couple of days.'

Phillips closed the file and laid it on the desk in front of her, sighing. 'Five dead and all I've got is an old van that I can't trace, and DNA without a match. I'm running out of ideas to catch this guy.'

'What does Carter think?'

'Your guess is as good as mine, Tan.'

Chakrabortty's brow furrowed. 'I thought you guys were close?'

'Up until a few days ago, so did I. Then out of the blue he tells me he's bringing in a criminal psychologist from his old patch in Newcastle.'

'Siobhan Harris?'

'You know her?' asked Phillips.

'Not really, but I've seen her speak at a few medical conventions. I had heard she was in town.'

'News travels fast in the GMP.'

'You know coppers. Anything new or different stands out. Anyway, I'd have thought having someone like her on board would help. She seems very smart.'

'She is, and to be honest, I don't have an issue with her so much. It's more the fact Carter didn't talk to me about it first. He just announced she was coming and that was that. Plus, there's something a bit odd about how they are around each other.'

'Oh? How so?'

Phillips could feel her face wrinkling. 'I dunno. It was the way he blushed when she called him Harry the other day. He got all awkward and tongue-tied.'

'Do you think there's something going on between them?'

'I honestly couldn't say, Tan. Harris is gorgeous, so I could see why he might want to, but he's married with twins. I guess I hoped someone like Carter was beyond that kind of thing.'

'I hear what you're saying, but it happens a lot in our line of work. People thrown together, working long hours. Partners stuck at home who don't understand. Feelings develop.'

Phillips let out an ironic chuckle. 'Well, in that case, I'm glad my team resembles the customers at the Star Wars bar.'

Chakrabortty chuckled. 'That's a bit harsh...well, on Entwistle, at least.'

Phillips tilted her head to the side. 'Oh, aye? Has the newly married chief pathologist got designs on my young detective?'

Chakrabortty waved her away. 'Not at all,' she grinned. 'I can just appreciate a man who looks after himself.'

'Well, I can honestly say, I've never looked at him in that way, but if you'd like me to put a word in for you?'

'Oh, give over. So anyway, getting back to Carter...' Chakrabortty appeared keen to change the subject. 'What are you going to do about the situation?'

'I honestly don't know, Tan. At the minute my head's all over the place. I feel like I'm drowning. Maybe I'm imagining it, but I'm starting to wonder if Carter thinks I'm not up to the task.'

'I'm sure that's not the case. He's only been here a couple of months and your conviction rate is the highest in the force.'

'Maybe so, but you're only as good as your last case, and right now I'm failing, Tan. Seriously failing.'

'That's not true, Jane.'

'Well, it's how I feel at the moment.'

'Why don't you talk to him. Tell him how you're feeling?'

'What good will that do? If he is having doubts, I'll just look even weaker to him,' Phillips said.

'Whether he is or he isn't, at least you'll know and can do something about it. Wasting time and energy second-guessing him is just going to make things worse. And right now, you've got enough on your plate trying to catch this guy without worrying about what your boss may or may not be thinking.'

'I guess you're right.'

'Trust me. You'll feel better if you do,' said Chakrabortty.

Phillips nodded, then picked up the file and stood. 'It's time I got back. You'll call me as soon as the DNA results are in, won't you?'

'The moment they land, I promise.'

'Thanks,' said Phillips making for the door.

'Talk to Carter, Jane,' Chakrabortty called after her.

Phillips turned back. 'I'll think about it,' she said, then left the room.

35

Phillips returned to MCU to find Carter and Harris in conference, in her office, with the door closed.

'Sorry. I'm not interrupting, am I?' she asked, opening the door.

'Jane? No, no, not at all.' Carter mumbled. Harris shook her head.

'How was Chakrabortty? Anything new on Marsh's murder?' asked Carter.

'No. Pretty much as we expected. Her wounds are carbon copies of Peter Sutcliffe's victims. Two heavy blows to the back of the head from something like a ball-peen hammer, then a frenzied attack with a sharp metal spike—'

'Sutcliffe used a sharpened screwdriver,' said Harris.

'Exactly. Chakrabortty reckons she was brain-dead before she hit the ground, so we can assume she felt nothing after that,' Phillips said.

Carter ran his hand through his thick grey hair. 'The poor girl.'

Phillips held up Chakrabortty's post-mortem report. 'I'm just about to brief the team if you'd like to join us?'

Carter glanced at Harris, who nodded. 'If you think we could be of help.'

'Well, based on what little information we have so far to track this guy, I'd say the more the merrier.'

Phillips led the way. Due to the sensitivity regarding the copycat theory, the briefing would take place in the private conference room and be limited to the core team of Jones, Bovalino and Entwistle, plus Carter and Harris.

With the door firmly shut and the blinds shielding them from the extended team outside, Phillips took a seat at the conference table and opened the report. Ten minutes later, everyone had the same amount of information as she did on the Marsh post mortem. 'So, as we suspected, it's another copycat murder – this time of Peter Sutcliffe.'

As usual, Entwistle had brought his laptop to the meeting, and a loud ping indicated he had received a new email. 'It's from Evans,' he said as he opened it.

Phillips stared at him. 'Anything useful?'

Entwistle nodded. 'The tyre tracks found at Hough End playing fields are a definite match for those found at the other copycat murders.'

'We expected that, though,' said Phillips.

Entwistle continued. 'And they've got clear footprints from the snow.'

Phillips raised her eyebrows. 'Go on.'

'A size seven Doc Martin boot. Based on that, Evans estimates the killer is between five foot seven and five foot nine.'

'We're chasing a bloody midget!' said Bovalino.

'So was Sutcliffe,' said Harris. 'Well, not a midget, but he was a lot shorter than people imagined a cold-hearted killer would be. In fact, when he first appeared in court, that was what stood out about him. He was short, with a slight frame and a very soft voice. People couldn't quite believe he was the ripper.'

'I really wasn't expecting that,' said Phillips, turning to Jones. 'How tall is the caretaker at Cedar Pines?'

'Mark Holloway? Well over six foot, Guv.'

Phillips let out a frustrated sigh. 'Well, that's another one we can probably rule out, then.'

The room fell silent for a moment.

Carter was the first to speak. 'I don't get it. Why go to the trouble of copycatting different murderers? Why not just kill them all the same way?'

'I mentioned this the other day,' said Harris. 'Our guy was probably abused as a child and not allowed to think for himself – to ever make up his own mind. So, he's looked at historical cases and the terror they inflicted, and is copying them. He wants to strike fear into the hearts of the people of Manchester, and by changing his method of murder each time, he's limiting our chances of spotting a pattern. Each of the previous killers got caught, and I suspect he feels he is competing with them. He's determined that won't happen to him.'

'So, what are you saying? He's never going to stop?' said Carter.

'Not unless you catch him, or he decides he's had enough of the game. Which is what it is to him,' Harris replied.

'Try telling that to Wendy Marsh's parents,' said Jones.

At that moment, there was a knock on the conference room door and PC Lawford stepped inside, a grave look on her face. 'Sorry to interrupt, Ma'am, but the chief constable is in your office and would like to see you and Chief Superintendent Carter right away.'

Phillips glanced at Carter, who rolled his eyes.

'Thanks for letting us know,' said Phillips, as she and Carter stood in unison. '

'Right, back to work guys. There's no time to waste,' she said as she left the room, Carter in tow.

'Any idea what this is about?' said Carter out of the corner of his mouth as they walked side by side towards Phillips's office, where Fox waited for them.

'No idea,' mumbled Phillips.

'Close the door,' said Fox gruffly as they entered the room.

Phillips obliged.

As the door clicked shut, Fox wasted no time. 'What the fuck is going on down here?'

'Ma'am?' said Carter.

'In less than a month, we've had four brutal copycat murders and yet, not a single arrest.'

Carter obviously hasn't updated her on the fact Yates was likely the first victim, thought Phillips.

Fox continued, her voice louder than necessary in such a small, badly insulated room. 'We've been lucky so far, but it's only a matter of time before the press get a hold of the copycat angle and this blows up in our face!'

Carter attempted to placate her, 'Ma'am, this is a very complex case—'

'I'm well aware of that, Chief Superintendent,' Fox spat back, 'but this wouldn't have happened on my watch!'

Carter opened his mouth to speak, but seemed to think better of it.

Fox focused her full attention on Phillips now, her black eyes narrow and cold. 'I don't care how you do it, Phillips, but you'd better catch this guy, and quickly. Because if you don't, I'll bring in people who can. Do I make myself clear?'

'Crystal,' said Phillips, barely able to hide her contempt for her old boss.

'Of course, Ma'am,' added Carter.

Fox stormed passed them both, yanked open the door, and slammed it loudly behind her.

'Always nice to get a visit from the boss,' said Phillips sarcastically.

Carter stared out of the office window at the team. 'Do you think they heard that?'

Phillips shrugged her shoulders. 'I wouldn't worry. They've heard worse.'

'Was she always this difficult?' asked Carter.

Phillips shook her head. 'Not at all. In fact, I'd say she's mellowed since she got the top job,' she said with a thin smile.

Carter allowed himself a chortle before his expression turned grave. 'We will catch him, won't we, Jane?'

Phillips dropped down into her chair. 'I hope so, sir. I really hope so.'

'So do I,' said Carter, then left the room.

36

Lachlan Sims was packing up for the night when his desk extension began to ring. Looking at the clock on the wall, he realised that if he left right now, he still stood a chance of catching the 7 p.m. train home. If he took the call, he would almost certainly have to wait for the next one, at 8. He decided to let it ring out and continued packing his laptop into his bag. Eventually, the ringing stopped.

As was usually the case, he was the last one in the team of journalists at the *Manchester Evening News* to leave for the day. But as the most inexperienced, he felt he had a lot to prove, so didn't mind putting in the extra hours. Standing, he switched off the desk lamp, then slung his bag over his shoulder. He checked that his travel card was in his pocket, along with his house keys, then headed towards the door. As he did, his desk extension began to ring again, stopping him in his tracks. He checked his watch: 6.42 p.m. If he kept going and maybe jogged a little, he could still get from the MEN offices on Deansgate to Victoria Station in time to catch the next train. But something in his gut – his journalistic instincts – told him that by not answering this persistent caller, he could potentially miss out. As his university tutor had never tired of telling him, news was not a nine to five job, and the best journalists were never off duty. Moving to the nearest desk, he picked up the phone and answered from there. 'The MEN news desk, how can I help?'

'Is this Lachlan Sims?' The voice sounded muffled and distorted.

'It is. Who's this?'

'That's not important just now. I have a story for you.'

It wasn't the first time Sims had dealt with what sounded like a prank caller, and for a moment he chastised himself for picking up the phone to yet another one and missing his train. 'And what's so important it means you can't tell me your name?' asked Sims impatiently.

'A serial killer is on the loose in Manchester,' said the voice, 'and the police are keeping it secret from the public.'

A cold shiver ran down Sims's spine, and his mouth suddenly felt very dry. 'What are you talking about?' he said, barely managing to hide his cracking voice.

'Do you have a pen?'

'Yes.' Sims pulled one from the plastic holder on the desk, along with a Post-it Note.

'*Take a look at the recent deaths of Michael Yates, Gillian Galloway, Sean Hamilton, Wiktoria Szymańska and Wendy Marsh. They all look like random murders, but it's the same guy who killed them all.*'

'Why do you think that?'

'*I don't think.* I know,' the voice sounded smug.

'How are you spelling Szymańska?'

The voice spelled out the letters as Sims scribbled furiously on the note.

The voice continued. *'It seems Detective Chief Inspector Phillips and her Major Crimes Team aren't being honest with the public. They're trying to play down the murders as random acts, but believe me, there's nothing random about them at all. Each of them is a replica of historical murders committed by Graham Young, Steve Wright, Denis Nilsen, Terry Hardy and Peter Sutcliffe. Check out the files, you'll see it for yourself. They're identical, Lachlan.'*

'If this is true, this is national news. Why give it to me, specifically?'

'Because you're young and trying to make a name for yourself...'

How did he know all this?

The voice continued. *'...but if you don't want the story—'*

'No. I didn't mean that. Look, if this is true...'

'It's true.'

'...if it is, then how come *you* know about it?'

'Because, Lachlan, I know who killed them,' said the voice, then hung up.

'Hello? Hello?' shouted Sims into the phone, but the voice was gone.

He tried dialling 1471 in the hopes of tracing the call, but a loud beeping noise made it clear that function was not possible through a phone connected to a switchboard. Taking a seat on the nearest chair, he replayed the conversation over in his mind. Was the man on the phone telling the truth, or was he just a nut-job with a conspiracy theory? The paper took prank calls every single day.

Tapping the pen against his teeth, he thought about what to do next. Realising he'd missed his train made up his mind for him, and he headed back to his desk. A few minutes later, he had restarted his laptop and got to work.

37

It had been Phillips's idea to go for a drink with Carter after work. Chakrabortty's words had been ringing in her ears since their morning meeting, and after another crappy day where she found herself no further forward with the copycat killer, she decided it was time to take Tan's advice. As Carter lived in Wilmslow and her house was in Chorlton, she suggested they go to The Metropolitan in West Didsbury, which was sort of on the way home for both of them.

It was Carter's first time at The Met', and he seemed momentarily taken aback as he stepped out of his silver Audi Q7 and took in the large red-brick Victorian building. 'Bloody hell, this is impressive,' he said.

'Yeah. Used to be rough as old boots back in the day, but gentrification soon changed that,' said Phillips.

'Nice place to live round here, is it?'

'If you've got a million for the mortgage, or like living in a shoebox, then yeah,' Phillips said, and ushered him inside. They quickly found seats near one of the large leaded windows. 'What do you fancy?'

'Just a pint of cooking lager for me. None of the strong stuff,' said Carter.

Phillips headed for the bar and returned a few minutes later with a pint of Amstel and a large glass of Pinot Grigio, which she set down on the sanded oak table before taking a seat opposite Carter. She swallowed a large mouthful of wine and immediately felt more relaxed than she had in a week.

'God, I need this,' said Carter, before draining half the pint.

Phillips smiled. 'You're not kidding.'

Carter wiped his mouth and sat back in his chair with a loud sigh.

'How's Fran and the kids?'

'Back in Newcastle,' said Carter flatly.

Phillips cocked her head slightly. 'What? How come?'

'She doesn't like it down here. Because I'm working so many hours, she says she never sees me. So last week I came home and found the house empty and a note on the kitchen bench.'

'She's left you?'

Carter shook his head and took another large mouthful. 'No. Not officially, anyway. She just needs to be around her mum and sisters at the moment, and wants some time to figure out *us*.'

'I'm sorry, boss.'

'Yeah, me too, but what can I do? Fox is on my case constantly, and I need to make this job work. This is my big chance to run an elite unit. So, I'm leaving her to it for the time being. To be honest, it's a bit of a relief. It's hard enough dealing with Fox all day without going home to an interrogation as well.'

Phillips nodded. 'And how are you finding Chief Constable Fox?'

Carter scoffed. 'Like a rabid dog with a bone. She's a bloody nightmare. Nothing's ever good enough, and woe betide if the news isn't good. I've never worked for anyone like her.'

'Yep. That's Fox.'

'You know her better than me. Do you think she meant what she said today, about replacing us?'

'Absolutely,' said Phillips. 'Trust me, the only thing that matters to Fox *is Fox*. So, if we can't crack the case, we'll be out.'

'She's off the scale.'

'Like I said, that's Fox.'

'How long did you work with her when she was chief super of MCU?' asked Carter.

Phillips cast her gaze to the ceiling as she worked out the dates in her head. 'About six years, I think.'

'God. How did you *not* kill her?'

'I've never carried a gun,' she joked.

Carter burst out laughing, then drained what remained of his pint. 'Another?'

Phillips had nowhere to be and no one waiting at home – aside from her cat, Floss, of course. 'Yeah, why not.'

The pub was beginning to fill up, so it took a little longer to get served this time. Carter returned to the table ten minutes later with the next round.

'Trouble getting served?' asked Phillips.

Carter blew his lips. 'Just a bit. It's packed, and it doesn't help that people are sat at the bar. There's no bloody room to get through.'

'Yeah. That's one of the downsides to this place, but the atmosphere makes up for it.'

Carter took his seat.

Tucking into their fresh drinks, they both remained silent for a moment.

Phillips replaced her drink on the table as she searched for the right words.

'Something on your mind, Jane?'

'Yeah, there is.'

'What's up?' said Carter.

'Why did you not talk to me before bringing Harris in on the copycat case?'

Carter's brow wrinkled. 'I thought I did? In your office, the night before she came down.'

'With respect, that was an update. I'm talking about us having a discussion about it *before* you reached out to her.'

'I didn't think you'd mind, and Siobhan has been a real help to me in the past.'

Phillips took another drink. 'I don't mind Harris so much, and I appreciate the insight on the killer, but I did feel undermined. Almost as if you didn't trust I could crack the case.'

'That's not what I meant at all—'

'Because if that's how you feel – that I'm not capable – then I'd rather know, sir,' she cut in.

Carter looked aghast. 'Seriously, Jane. How could you think that? You're the best detective on the force. Everybody knows that.'

'Then why not trust me to get the job done my way?'

Carter exhaled loudly. 'I've really fucked up here, haven't I? I thought Siobhan would be of benefit. I never intended for you to feel undermined. I know how lucky I am to have you as my DCI, Jane. I really do. In fact, you're one of the reasons I took the job in the first place.'

Phillips did a double take. 'What do you mean?'

Carter chuckled. 'I may look and sound like a daft Geordie, but I was once a pretty good detective myself, you know? When this job came up, I checked you out, and what I found impressed me greatly. Your conviction rate is second to none, and your dedication to the cause is evident for all to see. I mean, how many other coppers would come back from taking a bullet at point-blank range...or being attacked in your own home by the very killer you were trying to catch?'

Phillips was impressed. He had done his homework.

Carter continued. 'I knew this job was gonna be a big jump up for me, and I wanted to make sure I had a DCI and a team that were on point. And from what I've seen so far, my instincts about you, Jonesy, Bov and Entwistle were correct. You're the best there is, and I'm sorry if I made you feel anything other than that.'

A smile crept across Phillips's face. 'Wow. Well, I wasn't expecting that.'

Carter drained his remaining lager, and glanced towards the bar. 'I've got a taste for these now.'

'It's my round,' said Phillips, who downed the remnants of her own glass and stood.

'How much is a taxi from here to Wilmslow?' asked Carter.

'Thirty quid, probably,' replied Phillips.

'In that case, get us a couple of shots too.' He passed her a crisp twenty-pound note. 'I could do with letting off a bit of steam.'

Phillips took the money and made her way to the bar.

Two hours and several drinks each later, Phillips and Carter plotted their next move on the copycat killer.

'I bloody hate them, but if you think it'll help, I will do a press conference with you,' said Phillips. 'But *you* have to do all the talking. I'll answer questions if I have to, but the less I say, the better.'

Carter nodded. 'Not a problem. I'm happy with that. So tomorrow, then?'

'Let me speak to Rupert Dudley in the morning—'

'Is he our PR guy?'

'Yeah. He can set it up with the TV, radio and newspaper guys. It won't take him long. I'm guessing we can put something out in the afternoon before the weekend.'

'Great,' said Carter, appearing satisfied, then slipped off his seat in search of yet more drinks.

Phillips checked her watch. It was coming up to 10.30 p.m. and she knew she needed to eat soon or she'd regret it in the morning.

Returning with another round of beer, wine and shots, Carter resumed his position opposite her. He appeared quite tipsy as he licked the salt from his hand, downed the shot of tequila, then chomped on a large piece of lemon. He grimaced, then greedily gulped down a couple of mouthfuls of beer, shuddering as he replaced his pint on the table. 'Your turn,' he said enthusiastically.

Phillips matched the routine and, a minute later, guzzled her wine in an attempt to get rid of the foul taste of the tequila and the bitterness of the lemon.

Carter laughed and cheered her on.

'Well, I can honestly say, I never did shots with Fox!'

'No, I *bet* you didn't.'

Phillips chuckled. 'So, tell me about you and Harris.'

Carter flinched, suddenly appearing defensive. 'What do you mean, *me and Harris?*'

'Well, as you say, I am a pretty good detective, and from what I can see, I think she fancies you.'

Carter scoffed, 'Nonsense,' he said, as his cheeks flushed.

'You fancy her too, don't you?' said Phillips.

'God. Don't you start on that as well.' Carter took a swig of beer.

'Why? Who else has said that to you?'

'Fran. She was always saying it in Newcastle. Didn't like the fact I spent so much time with Siobhan on a case. Said that I talked about her too much. She was always mimicking me, saying, "Siobhan this, and Siobhan that", which was bad enough, but then she met her at a black tie dinner. Well, Fran went off it *big time*. She was heavily pregnant at the time and didn't like the fact I was spending so many hours working late with someone who looked like Harris.'

'She is beautiful,' said Phillips.

'She's stunning,' added Carter, before catching himself.

Phillips grinned. 'Did anything happen?'

Carter shook his head vigorously. 'No, no, no. I'll admit, Siobhan and I grew close through the investigation and she is very pleasing on the eye, but I love Fran. And besides, who has time for an affair in this job?' he added glibly.

Phillips nodded absentmindedly.

'So, what about you?'

'What about me?' Phillips asked.

'Anyone special in your life?'

'No. Just my Ragdoll cat, Floss. Like you say, who has time for relationships in this job?'

'No,' Carter replied. 'I said who has time for *affairs*. Relationships are different.'

Phillips forced a thin smile. 'Not for me, they're not.'

Carter eyed her in silence for a moment.

'Look. I'm starving,' she said, keen to change the subject. 'Fancy a curry?'

Carter nodded as he finished the remainder of his pint. 'Sounds perfect. Anywhere good nearby?'

'Take your pick. This is Manchester,' said Phillips, and pushed her empty glass into the middle of the table.

'Well. In that case, lead the way.' Carter stepped up and grabbed his jacket from the back of the chair.

Phillips matched him. 'I know just the place,' she said, pulling on her coat. 'Namaste Nepal. It's just round the corner, and the King Prawn Karahi is amazing.'

38

THURSDAY, MARCH 11TH

Phillips arrived at her desk the next morning nursing quite a hangover. After leaving The Metropolitan, and egged on by Carter, they'd continued drinking at the curry house and eventually ordered separate taxis home just after midnight. That in itself meant an early start and a tram ride from Chorlton to Burton Road to pick up her car. For the first time in weeks, she arrived in the office after everyone else, but still before 9 a.m.

In no mood for chit-chat, she headed straight into her office and fired up her laptop. Despite adopting her best resting bitch face in an attempt to ward off any unwanted company, she wasn't on her own for long before Jones knocked on the door and stepped in. 'Well, you look like shit,' he said playfully.

'I've often wondered how you ever managed to find a woman willing to sleep with you,' she replied acerbically.

'With great difficulty,' Jones said as he took a seat. 'Were you out last night, Guv?'

'Yes, with Carter.'

'Dirty Harry?' joked Jones. It hadn't taken the team long to come up with a nickname for their new boss. 'Where did you go?'

'The Met' in Didsbury. It was only supposed to be for one drink, but one turned into two bottles of pinot for me...'

'Bloody hell, Guv!'

'...and a constant supply of tequila shots.'

'Ouch,' said Jones, wincing.

Phillips opened her desk drawer and pulled out a box of aspirin. 'It's true what they say about Geordies; they know how to drink.'

Jones nodded. 'I went up to Newcastle on a stag do once. I think my liver's still recovering.'

'Anyway, I'll need to double check in case it was the beer talking last night, but Carter wants to do a press conference on the murders this afternoon.'

'What? Is he gonna talk about the copycat killer?'

'No,' said Phillips, putting two tablets in her mouth and gulping down a mouthful of water. 'He wants to focus on the fact the van has been seen in the vicinity of each of the crime scenes. See if we can flush out someone who recognises it. So, if Carter confirms he still wants to go ahead, I'll need you to brief the team to be prepared. We know how many loonies and attention junkies like to call up after a public appeal.'

'As soon as you've spoken to him, let me know and I'll talk to the guys.'

Phillips's mobile began to ring. It was Chakrabortty. 'I'd better take this.'

Jones made himself scarce.

'Morning, Tan. Any news on the DNA?'

'Yeah, that's why I'm calling. The sample taken from the semen on Marsh is a match for the saliva taken from the bite mark on Szymańska.'

'So no doubt about it. It's the same guy.'

'One hundred per cent, Jane.'

'Well, that's something, at least. It's a shame he didn't leave anything behind on the other three, but I'm certain it's the same guy.'

'I'd say it certainly looks like it,' said Chakrabortty.

'That's what my guts are telling me.'

'Knowing you, Jane, they're usually right.'

Phillips nodded into the phone.

'Right, well that's all I have for you.'

'Thanks, Tan,' said Phillips.

'That's what I'm here for.'

'And thanks for the chat yesterday. It helped a lot.'

'Good. So, are you going to speak to Carter?'

'I already did, last night.'

'Wow, that was quick.'

'Yeah, and I have the hangover from hell to prove it.'

Chakrabortty chuckled. *'It went well, then?'*

'Yeah it did, actually. We cleared the air and I got to know him a bit better, too. So, it was worth feeling like I've been dug up today.'

'Good. I'm pleased.'

Phillips's phone began to beep, indicating she had a call waiting. She checked the screen. It was the MEN's chief reporter, Don Townsend. 'I've got another call coming in, Tan.'

'No worries. I'll chat to you later.'

Phillips ended the call and accepted Townsend's. 'Don,

this is a surprise.' They hadn't spoken since the trial of his girlfriend's killer, three months ago.

'Yeah. Sorry I've not been in touch. It's been a difficult time,' said Townsend. It was evident from the ambient noise that he was outside.

'How have you been?'

'Good days and bad, to be honest. Burying myself in work helps.' He sounded like he was puffing on a cigarette.

'I can imagine. So, what can I do for you?' asked Phillips.

'This might be nothing, but I thought you'd want to know.'

'Know what?'

'One of my young journos took a call last night from someone who claimed that a bunch of recent murders were the work of one man.'

Phillips's heart jumped into her mouth. 'Who said that?'

'He wouldn't give his name, but he claimed the deaths of Michael Yates, Gillian Galloway, Sean Hamilton, Wiktoria Szymańska and the young woman murdered at Hough End playing fields, Wendy Marsh, were all copycats of previous serial killers.'

Phillips's stomach turned. 'That's nonsense,' she lied, trying to figure out how anyone outside of her team would have that information.

'I have to admit, it did seem a bit far-fetched.'

'Who's the journalist?' asked Phillips, attempting to sound casual.

'His name's Lachlam Sims,' replied Townsend. 'Been with us six months, straight out of college. He's young, but very, very bright. He's done his homework and he seems to think there could be something in it.'

'And what do *you* think, Don?'

There was a pause on the other end as Townsend took a long drag. *'That even if it was true, you wouldn't tell me.'*

Phillips knew better than to piss off the press, and Don Townsend in particular, but at the same time, she couldn't risk the copycat theory getting out into the public domain. Not yet, when they had so little to go on. 'Look, Don. Off the record, we *are* investigating the fact those deaths could be linked, and we're even considering going public with it. If that happens, you'll be the first to know. But as far as the copycat angle goes, I think it's way too early to start thinking like that. You'd be doing me a favour if you could sit on it as a story. At least for the time being.'

'So there is something in it?'

Townsend was experienced enough to read between the lines. 'Please, Don. If we get anything concrete on it, you'll get the exclusive, I promise.'

'Ok.' Townsend took another long drag on his cigarette. *'I'll sit on it for the time being, but I can't keep Sims muzzled forever. He's got the bit between his teeth and he can see his name in lights with this one.'*

'I understand,' said Phillips. 'You said that someone called Sims with the information.'

'That's right. Rang the office last night around 7 p.m.'

'Did your source give a name?'

'You know I can never reveal a source, Jane, but as it happens, no, he didn't,' Townsend said.

'So how did he claim to know about the murders?'

'Again, it's probably bullshit, but he told Sims he knew the killer.'

All the air seemed to rush from Phillips's lungs in an instant as a spike of adrenaline coursed through her veins.

'I don't suppose he left a number, did he?' she asked, trying, and failing, to sound nonchalant.

Townsend chuckled. *'No. He was too smart for that. He rang through the switchboard so there was no way to trace the call. Believe me, it was the first thing Sims tried after the guy hung up.'*

Phillips's mind raced. Did this guy really know who the killer was, or did they have a leak in the team? Gazing out on her team, she couldn't believe any of them would have disobeyed her direct order, so maybe he was telling the truth?

'Are you still there, Jane?' said Townsend.

'What?' Phillips's focus returned to the call. 'Sorry, Don. I was just thinking about something.'

'Anything you want to share?'

'No. Not right now.'

'Look, Jane. I can give you a few days, but I must warn you, Sims is furiously working on the copycat angle, and if he finds something he can use that will make a great story, I won't be standing in his way. Ok?'

'I understand,' said Phillips. 'Look, Don, I've got to go. I'm late for a meeting.'

'I'll be in touch, Jane.' Townsend's words sounded like a threat as he rang off.

Phillips stared out at her team and the incident room for a long moment. Could one of them have let something slip without realising, or was this the killer taking the game to the next level? Either scenario didn't bear thinking about. Picking up her desk phone, she called Carter's PA.

'Hello, Jane,' said Cook.

'Is the chief super available, Di?'

'Yes. He's just this minute finished his morning call with Chief Constable Fox.'

'Hold his meetings and calls. I need to speak to him urgently.'

'Can I ask what it's about?'

'I'm afraid I can't say on the phone, but I'm on my way up now.' Without waiting for a response, Phillips replaced the receiver, then jumped up from her desk and set off at pace for Carter's office.

39

After hearing the details of Townsend's call, Carter cancelled all his scheduled meetings for the day and hunkered down in his office with Phillips to plan the press conference. He seemed even more determined to get out in front of the media so they could try to manage the story. After a longer than expected trip along the fifth-floor corridor to Fox's office for final sign-off on their strategy, Carter returned to where Phillips sat, waiting patiently.

'She's signed off the plan,' said Carter as he walked back in.

'How did she take it when you told her about Yates's murder being connected?'

'Not well, but once she'd finished bollocking me for not telling her in the first place, she did offer some guidance which I think makes sense. She thinks we should keep Yates separate for the time being – doesn't want the public thinking we've got another Harold Shipman on the loose, plus there's no connection between that murder and the van. She was also very clear that the copycat theory is off limits.'

'Well, they won't be hearing it from me,' said Phillips.

Carter checked his watch, then began pulling on his black uniform jacket. 'We'd better get over to the press room. Dudley said he wanted us there at least twenty minutes before he opens the doors so we can brief him.'

Phillips stood, her stomach already churning at the prospect of having to speak in public, something she loathed and avoided at all costs.

Five minutes later, they stepped through the double doors and into the conference room on the ground floor of Ashton House. The cavernous space was empty, aside from row upon row of temporary chairs running from the back of the room all the way to the front, where a long, covered table was placed in front of a large GMP-branded media wall, flanked on each side by pull-up projector screens. The whole setup made Phillips feel nauseous, and her hangover wasn't helping.

The force's Marketing and PR Director, Rupert Dudley, stood by the media wall speaking loudly into his mobile – about what, Phillips couldn't decipher and frankly didn't care. In her experience, Dudley talked a lot but managed to say very little. As Phillips and Carter approached, he said his goodbyes and offered an outstretched hand to both of them in turn.

'Chief Superintendent Harris, DCI Phillips.'

'Who and what are we expecting today?' asked Carter.

'All of them: TV, radio, newspapers, online outlets,' said Dudley, with his ubiquitous enthusiasm. 'We haven't had a live-presser in a while, so there's a lot of interest.'

The butterflies in Phillips's stomach churned harder than ever, and for a moment she wondered if she would vomit. Taking a few deep breaths, she managed to keep it under control.

Dudley continued. 'In your brief, you mentioned you want to talk about the transit van and it's connection to the four murder scenes.'

'That's right,' said Carter.

'Is there anything else you want them to take away?'

'Not at the moment, no.'

'Anything off limits that you want me to shut down?'

Carter shot a glance at Phillips. 'No. I don't think so.'

Dudley checked his watch. 'Ok, well, I'll open the doors in ten minutes so they can set up the cameras and recording devices. In the meantime, you might want to head into the green room.' He pointed to a single door in the corner of the room behind the media board.

Carter nodded, and gestured for Phillips to lead the way. A moment later, they stepped through the door into the small space that resembled a storeroom far more than a back-stage waiting area.

'Why did you shut him down just now?' asked Phillips in a low voice. 'What if whoever spoke to Lachlan Sims has contacted other news outlets about the copycat murders? What if they start asking questions about it?'

'If that happens, then *I'll* shut it down. I don't know Dudley from Adam yet, and in my experience, the PR guys have bigger gobs than the journalists.'

'As long as it's *you* that shuts it down and you don't put it to my door,' said Phillips, almost trembling.

Carter's brow furrowed. 'Are you all right, Jane?'

Phillips swallowed hard. 'Yeah. I just hate speaking in public, and I had a boss once who used them to throw me and the team under the bus whenever he could.'

'Superintendent Brown?'

'You know Brown?' she asked, surprised.

'"Bollocking Brown"? *Everyone* knows him. He's a legend in the force. At least, in terms of being an arse-kissing wanker.' Carter chuckled. 'The man couldn't detect flames in a fire. Don't worry. I'm not like him. I told you, I'll handle the presser. I just need my star SIO up there with me to show we mean business.'

Relief washed over Phillips like a warm wave, and she couldn't stop the smile that spread across her face.

'I meant what I said last night. I've got your back, Jane, and you're the best copper I could wish for in my team.'

Phillips exhaled and chuckled. 'I know it's silly, but when I see all the cameras and faces, my heart feels like it'll explode, and I panic that my words won't come out right.'

Carter placed his thick hand on her shoulder. 'You'll be fine. You've got this.'

The door behind them opened, and Dudley poked his head inside. 'Are you guys ready? We're all set to go live.'

Carter looked at Phillips, who nodded.

'Show us the way,' he said.

'Right. I'll do the intro,' said Dudley.

Phillips followed Carter and Dudley as they made their way to their seats at the table in front of the media wall, trying her best to ignore the expectant faces of the assembled journalists.

Once they were seated, Dudley addressed the room. 'Thank you all for coming. As many of you already know, I'm Rupert Dudley, Marketing and PR Director for the Greater Manchester Police. I've asked you all here today for a briefing on a recent spate of crimes, and I'd like to hand you over now to Chief Superintendent Carter to give you the details.'

Carter jumped straight in. 'Thank you and good afternoon, everyone. As Rupert has already stated, I'm Chief Superintendent Carter and I head up the Major Crimes Unit. To my left is Detective Chief Inspector Phillips, who is the senior officer in charge of our investigations into a series of murders committed in the last month. Crimes that we believe could, in some way, be connected. We can now name each of the victims as Gillian Galloway, Sean Hamilton, Wiktoria Szymańska and Wendy Marsh. Although the cause of death was different in each case, we have found evidence linking this van—' Dudley hit his keyboard, and an image of the van appeared on the two screens. '—to each of the crime scenes.'

Carter continued. 'It's a dark blue or green Mark II Ford transit, a model that was in general circulation in the early eighties. As you can see, the registration plate has been masked in some way, but if we can move to the next image...'

Dudley obliged.

'...from this angle, we can see a segment of the side of the vehicle that carries some form of lettering. The next image is a close-up. We believe the letters may relate to a company name, ending with the words, "& son". We're appealing to anyone who may recognise this van, or who has perhaps seen one like it in the last few weeks, to come forward. Even if you don't recall the writing, any sightings of a van matching this description is of great interest to us. Naturally, all information will be treated with the strictest confidence, and could be of vital importance in helping us solve these crimes. That's all I have to say for the moment.'

Dudley took this as his cue. 'Are there any questions?'

A sea of hands shot into the air.

'John,' said Dudley, pointing at an older man in the front row.

'Chief Superintendent. You said in your statement that the four deaths are connected. Are you suggesting they may be the work of one person?' asked the older man.

Carter didn't miss a beat. 'At this stage of our investigation, it's too early to speculate as to *who* committed the crimes, but we are very interested in tracing the owner of this van, as we believe they may have vital information regarding the deaths of the four victims.'

Dudley was quick to move onto another question. For the ten minutes that followed, he expertly marshalled the room as Carter effortlessly managed the message: MCU was in control of the investigation, their team of experts was working night and day to deliver convictions for each murder, and it was only a matter of time before they delivered justice to the victims' families. Phillips marvelled at his slick delivery and effortless charm, bolstered by his soft Geordie accent, which she noticed he had laid on thicker than normal.

Just as it seemed all the questions had been answered, a young-looking man towards the rear of the room raised his hand. Once he was given the go-ahead from Dudley, he stood and fixed his eyes on Phillips. 'Is it true that the deaths of Galloway, Hamilton, Szymańska and Marsh are the work of one man, the "Copycat Killer"?'

Phillips's blood ran cold and she held her breath for a moment as she tried her best not to swallow, fearing the crack of her dry mouth would betray her shock.

Carter shook his head, evidently trying to appear as casual as possible. 'I...erm...don't know where you got *that* from,' he said, forcing a light chuckle, 'but that's not part of our investigation.'

The young man continued. 'Really? As I understand it, each of the deaths is a direct copy of historical crimes committed by the likes of Steve Wright, the Suffolk Strangler, Denis Nilsen, the Muswell Hill Murderer...'

Carter shifted in his seat as Phillips tried to calm her racing pulse.

'...Terry Hardy, also known as the Beast of Manchester, and Peter Sutcliffe, the Yorkshire Ripper.'

Carter sat forward in his chair and linked his fingers together. 'What's your name?' he asked.

'Lachlan Sims.'

'And where are you from?'

'The *Manchester Evening News*.'

'How long have you been a journalist?'

'Just over six months.'

'I see,' said Carter, nodding, as if that explained the young man's outlandish question. 'Well, as the more seasoned professionals in the room will know, in cases such as this, wild theories – without proper factual basis – may sell papers, but only serve to stir up the public and hamper our investigations. So I would urge you to be a little bit more responsible from a journalistic point of view when reporting this briefing. There is absolutely no evidence to support such a theory. My team and I are focused on uncovering the facts and using all our expertise and experience to deliver justice for the victims and ensure the people of Greater Manchester feel protected. Now, if there's no more questions, we'll finish there.'

Dudley's experience of managing such briefings was evident to see. He was on his feet in a flash, utilising his well-practiced closing statement. 'Thank you very much, everyone, for coming this afternoon. Any further questions should be directed to my team via email. For those of you that don't already have it, please take one of the PR team contact cards on your way out.'

Carter's eyes met Phillips's as he stood up from the chair. They both knew enough to mask any reaction or emotion to the questions until they were out of sight and earshot of the press pack. Carter led the way back to the so-called Green Room and closed the door behind them.

'Fuck!' he growled, keeping his voice low so as not to be heard. 'I thought Townsend was gonna sit on Sims?'

'He was! At least, that's what he bloody well said to me,' Phillips replied.

'He caught me off guard, the little shit.' Carter rubbed his face with his hands, causing it to redden. 'Fox is gonna go fucking mental when she sees this.'

'If she hasn't already seen it, sir.'

At that moment, Carter's phone began to ring. Pulling it from his pocket, he groaned, then closed his eyes as his shoulders sagged. Opening them again, he presented the screen to Phillips. Fox.

He cleared his throat, took a deep breath, then answered. 'Good afternoon, Ma'am…'

Despite the phone being pressed against Carter's ear, Phillips could hear the expletives as if Fox was in the room with them. Making her silent excuses, she opened the door and left Carter to it.

40

'What do you think about that then, hey?' said Gabe, barely able to hide his glee as he switched off the TV coverage of the live press conference.

'They're on to you boy,' Bert rasped, struggling for breath. 'Now they have the van...it's only a matter of time...,'

'What? Your manky old transit van caught on CCTV? They've got *nothing*. They even think the writing says "& Son", which you and I both know isn't what's written on it.'

'Mark my words...that woman detective is smarter than you'll *ever* be.'

'Really? Did you see the shock on her face when that journalist asked her about the Copycat Killer? She almost shit her pants.'

'So, I'm guessing you put him up to that?'

A satisfied smile spread across Gabe's face. 'Yes, but he came up with the nickname all by himself. I like it, though.

"The Copycat Killer"? It has a real ring to it, don't you think?'

Bert closed his eyes and turned his head away.

'What's the matter? Cat got your tongue?'

'Just let me die,' whispered Bert.

'And have you miss out on all the fun of my big reveal? Not a chance, old man. You're gonna watch on, from that rancid bed of yours, as *I* become a worldwide news story, part of modern-day history. And you, you horrible, evil, vicious old bastard, will go to your grave in unedifying shame.'

Bert opened his eyes and turned to face him.

'Damned for eternity,' said Gabe, checking his watch. 'But before I do that, I haven't finished with Peter Sutcliffe's legacy just yet, and I need to get my skates on. I have a few more surprises for DCI Phillips and her cronies. Seriously, you're gonna *love* what's coming next.'

Bert locked eyes with him, his breathing shallow. He beckoned Gabe forwards, then drew him in close.

'What?'

Bert was struggling to speak between breaths. 'I'll... I'll...'

'You'll what?'

'I'll see you in hell!'

41

Back in her office, Phillips closed the door and dialled Don Townsend's number.

He answered promptly. *'I've been expecting your call. I saw the presser.'*

'What the fuck was that all about, Don? You told me Sims was under control.'

'I thought he was, Jane, but the little shit went off-piste.'

'I hope you tore him a new arsehole?'

'Well, I was just about to when he came back to the office, but the editor beat me to him and had a very different view; loves the sound of the Copycat Killer and wants to know everything Sims has on the guy.'

'That story *cannot* happen, Don.'

'What are you not telling me, Jane?'

Phillips paused for a moment and contemplated coming clean with Townsend, something she would never have done in the past. But their relationship had changed. When the love of his life had been found hanged last year at someone else's hand, it was Phillips and her team who had found Vicky's killer and put him away for life. Since then, she and Townsend had developed a mutual respect for each other, but that still didn't mean she could trust him with the facts of this case. 'If I thought it would help, Don, I'd tell you, but it's just too complicated at the moment to explain. Please, I need some time – just a few days, even – to deal with the fallout from the press conference so I can track that van. If the Copycat Killer angle comes out now, it'll overshadow everything and stir up a public shit storm I won't be able to control. Please, Don.'

'If I could, I would,' said Townsend, *'but the editor's salivating. He has an exclusive and he wants to run with it before anyone else picks up on it.'*

Phillips rubbed her forehead with her fingers. 'I didn't want to do this, Don, but y*ou owe me*. We both know that.'

Townsend remained silent on the end of the phone.

'Think about how you felt when I was chasing after Zhang Shing. What he did to Jonesy, what he nearly did to me. Well, there's a guy out there who makes Shing look like a boy scout, and he won't stop unless I catch him. He's killed four that we know of so far, maybe even five—'

'So you are looking for a serial killer?'

'Yes,' Phillips said, reluctantly. 'And in the last month I've had to sit down with four of the victims' families and friends and tell them their loved ones have been murdered. Just like I had to with you when Vicky was killed. I know the exclusive is important, Don, but so is catching this guy before he kills again.'

There was a pause on the other end of the line. Phillips could hear Townsend's heavy breathing. *'Ok, Jane. I can't promise anything, but I'll see what I can do.'*

Phillips let out a sigh of relief. 'Thanks, Don.'

'But I want the exclusive on anything you can tell me about the case, as soon as it's available.'

'Deal.'

'Well, you'd better get your arse in gear, Jane, because Sims is not going to let this go and neither is the editor. Whatever time I can buy you will be short.'

'Don't worry, I hear you.'

'Right. Wish me luck,' said Townsend, then hung up.

Phillips blew her lips and stared out across the incident room. Even with the door closed, she could hear the phones ringing off the hook outside. This always happened after a TV appeal, as every attention-seeking wannabe and do-gooder in the city called in with 'information.' Almost every call led to a dead end, but each one needed to be dealt with and processed correctly, as vital clues could come from anyone. Jones caught her eye and gestured that he needed to see her. She nodded, and watched as he approached.

He opened the door. 'You ok, Guv?'

'Yeah, but Carter's taken a bit of a beating from Fox.'

'For what it's worth, I thought he handled himself really well. Especially the copycat question. I believed him.'

'Yeah, but the problem is, the journalist in question didn't. I've just spoken to Townsend, who's agreed to muzzle him for as long as he can, but it seems the editor of the MEN loves the copycat angle and wants to make a big splash with it.'

'Jesus, that's all we need. If the killer sees that, he could go underground.'

'Exactly,' said Phillips. 'And then we'll never find him.'

The room fell silent for a moment.

'Well, if it helps, Bov and I have a couple of promising leads on the van. One woman reckons she saw it near

Dunham Massey the night Galloway died, and another guy says he's seen it driving around near Brammall. They both seem pretty genuine and very certain, so we're gonna head out and see if there's anything in them.'

'Great. Keep me posted. And close the door on the way out, will you?'

Jones obliged and headed back out to the incident room.

Phillips spent the next few hours in her office, going over the case files for each of the murders, looking for any details they may have overlooked. The last file belonged to Michael Yates, and as she stared down at the crime scene photos of his twisted body, her overwhelming sense of failure returned. She had promised to catch his killer, but she was still no further forward than the day he died.

Her hangover had not yet receded, and she suddenly felt tired, her head foggy. Checking her watch, she saw it was approaching five o'clock. Having been camped at her desk for almost three hours, she decided to get some fresh air.

Once outside, she made her way to a spot she used regularly as a place to think. Out of sight of the main office block, she took shelter from the wind. Spring was on its way and the nights were getting lighter after a bleak winter. The setting sun cast a stunning orange hue across the horizon.

Taking a few deep breaths, she closed her eyes and allowed her mind to quieten. 'What are you missing, Jane?' she whispered to herself, as images of the five victims appeared in her mind's eye and she recalled the sad conversations with their families. Trying her best to block it all out, she breathed deeply for a few minutes in the hope it would bring clarity to her thinking. But it was no use. Her head was fried. Suddenly feeling cold, she decided to head back inside and see if there had been any further updates on the TV appeal. Walking back round the corner, she made her way across the car park to the main entrance before stopping and standing for a moment as the revolving door dispensed a uniformed courier. She nodded as he stepped out, then took his place in the door. Striding across the large double-height reception area, Sonia, behind the desk, called out to her. 'DCI Phillips? I have a package for you.'

Phillips walked over and collected the small padded envelope, then took the stairs up to the third floor. As she stepped into the MCU offices, she was hit by a wall of sound as phones rang, the wider team doing their best to keep up with the influx of information. Heading into her office, she closed the door and inspected the package. Her name had been handwritten on the front, but there were no sender's details. She pulled it open and peered inside, then pulled out the small pen drive contained within and held it in the palm of her hand for a moment. 'What's this?' she mumbled as she took a seat and plugged it into her laptop. The portable disk icon appeared on screen in her list of drives, but was greyed out. Clicking on it furiously, nothing happened. She shouted for Entwistle, who appeared at the door a moment later.

'What's up, Guv?'

'Can you have a look at this? I can't access this pen drive.'

Entwistle moved to where he could see the screen. 'Looks like it's locked,' he said, then ejected the drive. He fiddled with it for a brief moment, then reinserted it. 'It should work now,' he added, and clicked on it again.

An audio bar opened on the screen and began playing automatically. What Phillips heard made her blood run cold.

'*I'm Jack. I see you are still having no luck catching*

me.' The voice on the audio was distorted, but unmistakably North East. *'I have the greatest respect for you, Jane, but Lord! You are no nearer to catching me now than you were five weeks ago when I started with old Mr Yates. I reckon your boys are letting you down, Jane. They can't be much good, can they? You're having no luck finding me, are you?'*

Phillips paused the audio and stared, wide-eyed, at Entwistle. 'It sounds exactly the same as the guy who pretended to be Peter Sutcliffe back in the eighties. The hoaxer. What was his name?'

'Wearside Jack,' said Entwistle.

Phillips pressed play again.

'I hear you're the best detective there is, that if anyone can catch me, it's you, Jane. Well, if that's the case, you need to look a little closer to home. That way, you may find that what you've been looking for is right under your nose. Good luck, Jane. I'm looking forward to seeing how good you really are.'

The audio ended.

'Do you think that's really him, Guv, or just some nutter getting in on the drama?'

Phillips shook her head. 'It's him, I'm sure of it. No-one outside of this team, with the exception of Fox, knows that Yates is connected to the other four murders. It has to be him.'

'What do you think he meant about "looking closer to home?".'

'No idea,' she said, then pressed play again.

For the next ten minutes they played the audio file on repeat, trying desperately to decipher what it meant, but struggled to make sense of the message. Dropping her head into her hands in frustration, the padded envelope caught her eye and, in particular, the handwriting – a messy, almost frenzied scrawl. Then it hit her. 'It was hand delivered,' she said, jumping up from the chair and grabbing Entwistle by the shoulder. 'Come with me,' she added as she dragged him out of the office.

'SONIA, WHO DELIVERED THIS PACKAGE?' said Phillips.

The urgency of Phillip's tone seemed to catch the receptionist off guard. 'Erm, I don't know, Ma'am. I didn't really pay much attention.'

Phillips felt her jaw clench as she attempted to hide her frustration. 'Think, Sonia. It's important.'

Sonia was well and truly flustered. 'I'm not sure. I think he had a hat on, a beard or a moustache, maybe.'

'What about his accent? Did you notice where he was from?'

'No. I don't think he spoke.'

'Damn it!' Phillips growled.

Tears welled in Sonia's eyes. 'I'm sorry, Ma'am. I just see so many faces each day.'

Phillips realised she was taking her frustrations out on someone who didn't deserve them. It wasn't Sonia's fault the killer was now openly mocking their lack of progress on the case. 'Listen. I'm the one who should be sorry. You've done nothing wrong.'

Sonia flashed a soft smile and wiped a single tear from her cheek.

'Can you remember when it was delivered?' asked Phillips.

'Not long before I gave it to you.'

'Which was just after five, wasn't it?'

'I think so, yes,' said Sonia.

'We can check for sure on the CCTV, Guv,' suggested Entwistle.

'Good idea,' said Phillips. In no mood to hang around, she marched off in the direction of the security team's office.

It didn't take long to find the footage they were looking for and, having dismissed the security manager, Phillips and Entwistle watched alone as the video played on the screen in front of them. According to the timestamp, at just after 5 p.m. a man wearing glasses and a brown uniform, complete with baseball cap, entered Ashton House through the revolving door, where he proceeded to the reception desk carrying the small padded envelope.

'I'm sure that's the guy I saw coming out of the door when I was coming back in,' said Phillips.

The video continued. As Sonia had suggested, the man appeared not to speak as he handed the envelope over, then swiftly turned and made his way back to the door. Phillips paused the feed, capturing the man's face on screen. 'Look at that – the beard. He's a dead ringer for Peter Sutcliffe.'

'God, he is, isn't he?' said Entwistle.

Phillips allowed the feed to play once more. Just moments before the man reached the main door, he glanced up, looked straight into the camera, and offered a wicked grin.

'Holy shit,' Phillips muttered.

A split second later, Phillips appeared on screen as she walked into reception and over to the desk to speak to Sonia, before taking the package and heading upstairs.

Phillips clasped her hands to the side of her head. 'The killer was right under my nose... and I missed him!'

42

FRIDAY, MARCH 12TH

First thing the next morning, Phillips gathered the core team in the conference room, along with Dr Harris. She played them the audio file from the killer, followed by a YouTube clip from a Ripper documentary that contained the original message recorded by the man dubbed Wearside Jack.

'The first part is identical,' said Phillips. 'The second bit is his own words.'

Bovalino blew his lips and linked his fingers on top of his head. 'He must have some balls, mind. He took a huge risk walking in here with that package.'

'He's ramping up the game now, bringing it to your door,' said Harris.

'Why now? Why take the risk when so far he's revealed so little of himself?' asked Phillips.

'Like I said before, he's showing you just how clever he is,' said Harris. 'So clever, in fact, that *he* – the most wanted man in the country right now – can wander into the headquarters of the Greater Manchester Police, and when he's done, walk straight back out again.'

'Do you think he was waiting for you, Guv?' asked Jones.

'No. We checked the CCTV footage of the car park, which shows him parking up at the back of the building, then heading straight round to the front door. I was out of sight when he arrived, so he would have had no idea I was outside. It's just pure luck that he happened to be walking out as I was walking back in.'

'I'm sure he'd have enjoyed that, seeing you in the flesh,' said Harris.

Phillips sighed heavily. 'I even acknowledged the bastard as he came out of the door. How could I have been so fucking blind?'

'Come on, Guv,' implored Jones. 'Any of us would have done the same. Until now, we had no idea what the guy looked like.'

In no mood to let herself off the hook just yet, Phillips continued. 'Yeah, but the guy was a dead ringer for Peter Sutcliffe and I missed it.'

'I'd suggest the beard's a fake,' said Harris. 'Dressing up is all part of the fun for him.'

'We could try the fancy-dress shops. See if anyone recognises him?' Bov suggested.

'It'll take too long,' replied Phillips. 'And besides, it looked real, so it's more likely to have come from a professional costume company. None of which exist in Manchester – I've already checked – so he probably bought it online.'

Jones leaned forward on the conference table. 'What about the van? Anything new captured on our own CCTV?'

Phillips shook her head. 'We've checked ANPR and

CCTV footage from the surrounding roads but, like before, the plates are covered, and not long after he drives out of the gate, he disappears down a back road and we lose him. So once again, we've got nothing.'

'Does Carter know about all of this?' Jones asked.

'Yeah. I briefed him last night. As you can imagine, he wasn't happy.'

'And Fox?'

'He's telling her as we speak.'

'That's why he gets paid the big bucks,' said Jones.

Phillips let out a deep sigh. 'I'm sorry to say it guys, but as Jonesy and Bov's leads on the van sightings came to nothing last night, the killer is right: we really are no further forward with this case than we were five weeks ago.'

'What about the fact it was a North East accent on the message? Anything in that?' asked Bovalino.

'I'd say it's unlikely,' said Harris. 'Again, I think he's playing with us, copying Wearside Jack in the words and delivery. The distortion he used is probably just a bit of a gimmick.'

Phillips cut back in. 'The doc and I both believe our killer's not finished yet, and this latest stunt certainly backs that theory. As the doc said, he's enjoying the game. Our priority now has to be in trying to identify who he will copycat next.'

Harris nodded.

Phillips continued. 'As we've discussed previously, based on the killer's pattern so far, there is one serial killer who stands out above the rest, and who we believe could be next on his list of copycats.' She pointed at the historical mugshot on the board. 'Stephen Griffiths, also known as the Crossbow Cannibal.'

Harris jumped in. 'There's no concrete evidence to suggest that Griffiths did actually eat any of his victims. He was given the nickname after only partial remains were recovered from his last two victims, and the body of his first was never found. His crimes were high profile and very unusual, even for a serial killer. To my mind, Griffiths's crimes have all the elements that would appeal to our man. As his recent activity would suggest, he's growing in confidence and the level of violence is escalating. Plus, so far, each method has been entirely different. Killing with a crossbow and leaving no body for us to find could be the natural next step for him, complicating the puzzle even further.'

'Entwistle, how did you get on with tracing the make of crossbow Griffiths used?' asked Phillips.

'It was a Serpent full-size compound crossbow. I've checked with all the sporting-goods stores in the Greater Manchester area, but apparently they don't make them anymore. Serpent went out of business after Griffiths was convicted. Nobody wanted them. That said, you can still buy them second-hand online, but tracing any historical purchases is virtually impossible.'

'Of course it is,' said Phillips flatly.

'So what next, Guv?' asked Jones.

'I want the envelope he delivered sent over to forensics for a fingerprint and DNA check.'

'I can do that,' said Bovalino. 'I'll take it there myself.'

'The wider team can stay on the van sightings. Jonesy, find out where people go to practice using a crossbow in Manchester, and check out any clubs that our man might have joined recently. It seems he's not the shy retiring type, so there's a good chance he may have stood out.' Phillips turned to Entwistle. 'I want you to trawl through Facebook,

Instagram and any other social media sites. You're looking for societies dedicated to crossbow users, and any members or comments that stand out. Start with the local ones first, then go wider if you have to. Speak to the administrators. Our guy is cocky, and confident we'll never catch him. If the doc's correct about him, then he'll be compelled to brag or boast in some capacity.'

'But be prepared – if he is boasting, it'll likely be cryptic messaging,' Harris added.

Phillips stood. 'I'd better go and update Carter, see if he's still in one piece. I don't need to tell you, we're well behind the prize on this one, guys. Whatever it takes, we need to stop him.'

'Yes, Guv,' said each of the men in unison as she left the room.

43

'Who's my gorgeous boy, hey? Who's my gorgeous boy?' Gabe repeated as he tossed Noah into the air, caught him again in his hands, then held him above his face.

Noah smiled and gurgled, looking down at his daddy.

The TV was on low volume in the background, but Gabe wasn't watching it. Behind him, in the open-plan kitchen that annexed the family room, Jodie was busy cooking dinner. Friday was taco night, and the delicious aromas wafting from the stove were making his stomach rumble.

Placing Noah on the activity mat on the carpet, he sat back on the floor and leaned against the base of the sofa as Lola padded in and curled up next to him. The local news was starting, so he grabbed the remote and increased the volume. The lone news anchor stared out at him from a flimsy-looking news set, her expression grave as she began the bulletin.

'Greater Manchester Police are once again appealing

for witnesses who may have seen this vehicle, believed to be connected to a number of unlawful deaths in and around central Manchester.' CCTV footage of the van flashed on screen.

Gabe smiled and stroked Lola's back as the news anchor continued. *'In a live press conference given yesterday afternoon, Chief Superintendent Harry Carter refused to comment on whether the driver of the vehicle was a suspect in the deaths, but instead stressed how important it was that they track down the owner.'*

'No shit, Sherlock,' Gabe muttered under his breath.

Jodie appeared and perched on the arm of the sofa above him. 'God, it's terrifying,' she said as the news continued.

Gabe craned his neck so he could see her. 'What is?'

'Living in a city with a monster on the loose.'

'What monster? What are you talking about?'

'Him!' She pointed at the image of the van, which remained on screen. 'The man driving round the city, dragging women into that van and murdering them. Any of us could be next.'

'Don't be so silly, Jodes. They don't know for sure if the driver of the van is connected. And besides, it's not just women that have been killed.'

'And that's supposed to make me feel better, is it?' said Jodie. 'What if he breaks in here one night when you're out at work, or over at your dad's?'

'He's *not* gonna break in here.'

'How do you know?'

'Because the killer's been picking up his victims in pubs and clubs, or off the street,' Gabe said firmly.

'Says *who*?'

'Er...I...I...' Gabe stuttered. He realised he'd dropped

his guard and said more than he should have. 'I read it in the paper.'

Thankfully, Jodie wasn't really listening, as usual. 'Noah and I could be murdered in our beds and you'd know nothing about it.'

'Oh, don't start all this again,' he mumbled under his breath. 'I get enough guilt trips from my dad as it is.'

'It's *true*, Gabe. There's a killer on the loose, stalking and killing young women in Manchester, and I'm scared. You should be too. What if he killed your wife and son? What if you came home late one night and found us both dead? I know your job's important to you, and Bert's not well, but surely your own family comes first. *Me and Noah.* You must see that?'

'Will you please give it a rest? I'm sick of you going on at me all the time.'

'No, I won't give it a rest. This is important, Gabe.'

'I've had enough of this,' he said, scrambling to his feet.

'Where are you going?'

'Out!'

'But dinner's nearly ready.'

'I'm not hungry!' he shouted as he pulled on his shoes.

'You can't just leave. We're talking.'

'No. You're talking. I'm being poked like a bear.'

The sound of his parents arguing caused Noah to start crying.

'Ah God, that's all I fucking need!' Gabe growled, before heading out into the hallway.

'Don't you dare walk out!' Jodie yelled after him.

He didn't respond as he pulled on his coat and marched towards the front door.

'If you leave now, you'd better not come back.'

He reached the door and yanked it open. Noah continued to cry in the lounge, louder now.

'That's right. Run away, like you always do, you pathetic piece of shit!'

He turned to face her, anger boiling in the pit of his stomach. 'What did you say?'

'You heard me. You're *pathetic*.'

Gabe glared at her as a snarl formed on his lips.

'Look at you. A pathetic, weak little man. Just like your pitiful excuse for a father.'

Gabe closed the door slowly and locked it in place. Rage burned in his gut. 'I am nothing like my father,' he said in a low voice, before rushing headlong at Jodie, arms outstretched.

44

Floss was waiting as Phillips opened the front door, and snaked around her legs as she stepped inside the house. 'Well, *you're* a sight for sore eyes,' she said, bending down to pick her up. It was then she noticed the padded envelope sat on the doormat, covered in the same frenzied handwriting as the one delivered to Ashton House the day before. Her adrenaline spiked as she stared at the small package. This wasn't the first time an investigation had spilled into her home. Unconsciously, her eyes were drawn to the exact spot in her hallway where the very man she had been hunting in that case had tried to strangle her a couple of years ago; tried, but thankfully failed. That experience had taught her not to take any chances. Holding Floss in her arms, she retreated out of the house and hurried back to her car, where she jumped in and put Floss down on the passenger seat. Next, she called through to Uniform Control, alerted them to her rank and situation, and demanded the nearest patrol unit be sent to her address urgently.

Five minutes later, she was relieved to see the distinctive blue and yellow markings on the patrol car as it turned down her street. Leaving Floss in the vehicle, she jumped out and waved them down. She didn't recognise the two officers, but they knew her, explaining they'd seen the recent press conference and were familiar with the case. Radioing in their position, they immediately headed inside the house whilst Phillips waited on the street. She had learnt her lesson the last time, and until she knew the house was safe, she would not be going back in.

It wasn't long before the two officers returned, strolling casually down the front path to her position on the pavement.

'All clear, Ma'am,' said the first officer.

'Did you check every room?' asked Phillips.

'Yes, Ma'am.'

'Upstairs, too?'

'Yes.'

'What about the garden?'

'It looked clear from the kitchen,' said the second officer.

'Did you go outside, though? Actually into the garden?'

'No. The back door was locked.'

Phillips handed over her keys. 'It's the orange one. I need you to check it all thoroughly.'

Once again, both officers headed back inside. While she waited, her mind flashed back to the battle with her attacker on that terrifying night, a chilling memory of how close she had come to becoming a victim herself.

After a few minutes, the officers returned.

'All clear, Ma'am,' said one.

'We've even checked the shed,' said the other.

Phillips breathed a sigh of relief. 'Thanks. I just needed to be sure.'

'Not a problem, Ma'am. We're in the area all night, so if you have any problems, let Control know and we'll come straight back.'

'I will. Thank you.' Phillips headed back to her car to fetch Floss.

Despite their assurances, once inside, she conducted her own search, which included checking under the beds and inside the wardrobes. Even her large American-style fridge was given a thorough inspection. This guy really had her spooked.

Finally satisfied, she pulled on a pair of latex gloves and retrieved the package, which she carried into the kitchen. With care, she opened the seal and peered inside. Inside was another single pen drive. Placing the envelope back on the bench, she pulled out her phone and called Jones. When he answered, she wasted no time. 'I've received another package. It looks like it's from the same guy as before. I need you to meet me at the forensics lab as soon as you can.'

'Of course, Guv. I'm on my way.'

Next, she called Senior CSI Andy Evans.

Forty minutes later, she stood in the GMP forensics lab with Jones, as Evans carefully opened the package and removed the pen drive, before inserting it into his laptop. Double-clicking the only file on the disk, it began to play automatically. She was not surprised to hear the same voice talking back to her, once again distorted with a North East accent.

'*Hello, Jane. You must be feeling real stupid by now. First you walk right past me at work, and now you've* missed me at home. It wasn't hard to find out where you live, by the way. Not great for someone in your position, I wouldn't have thought. And considering your reputation, I expected you'd be much closer to finding me than you are. If truth be told, Jane, I'm finding it all a little bit too easy at the moment. That's why I've decided to give you a clue. Are you ready? Here goes: "The Angel of Death walks amongst your own kind, DCI Phillips. Like the good shepherd you are, follow the guiding star to find your salvation." Good luck, Jane. It looks like you're going to need it.' The message ended.

'So, he posted this through your letter box at home?' asked Jones.

Phillips nodded.

'How do you feel about that?' said Evans.

'Spooked, to say the least. I mean, how the hell does he know where I live?'

Jones remained silent, deep in thought, before he eventually spoke. '"The Angel of Death walks amongst your own kind...Like the good shepherd you are, follow the guiding star to find your salvation." What the hell does that mean?'

'Play it again,' said Phillips.

Evans obliged, and for the next five minutes they listened to it on repeat.

'The only thing I can think of is that, when he says, "The Angel of Death walks amongst your own kind", he's maybe telling us he's a copper?' Phillips ventured.

'Surely not, Guv?'

'It's happened before. We know that better than most. I mean, it would make sense in many ways, and would explain how he knows so much about the locations of

ANPR cameras in the city, not to mention how to avoid them. It would also explain how he got my address – from the staff records.'

'True, but if he is a copper, why would he leave DNA on Szymańska and Marsh?' said Jones. 'He'd know we'd be able to trace it.'

'And he'd also be aware that we don't keep DNA records on file unless they've been used to secure a conviction,' added Evans.

'Well, if he *is* a copper, then there's over seven thousand officers on the force,' said Jones. 'And even if we estimate that a third of those are women, then we're still looking at the possibility of over four and half thousand suspects, Guv.'

'I know that,' said Phillips, focusing on Evans. 'Andy, I was thinking. Do you know if we keep a record of coppers' heights on file?'

'I think so, yeah.'

'And what about shoe size?'

'Maybe. I assume all coppers are measured up when they start in uniform, so that information has to be stored somewhere.'

'Well, we know from your footprint analysis that our guy wears a size seven boot, and is likely to stand between five foot seven and five foot nine. If we can check the height and shoe size of all the male officers on file against those measurements, that's gotta narrow down the list of suspects, hasn't it?'

'Yeah, I think it might. I mean, I doubt there's that many male coppers with such small feet on the force,' said Evans.

'Let's start there, then. Jonesy, I want you, Bov and

Entwistle to find the records and go through them first thing on Monday. And rope in PC Lawford, too. She's good with this kind of stuff.'

'Will do, Guv,' said Jones. 'Is there anything else you need tonight? Only I left my girls on their own, as Sarah's visiting her mum for a few days. I need to get back before they decide to invite their mates over and smash through my booze cabinet.'

Phillips chuckled. 'No. We're good. You get yourself away.'

'I'd better get this lot bagged and tagged,' Evans said, and left the room.

With Evans out of sight, Jones locked eyes with Phillips. 'Are you gonna be ok at home on your own?'

'I'll be fine. I've got more locks than Hawk Green these days.'

'Are you sure, Guv? You're more than welcome to stay at ours for a few days. We've got the space.'

'Let me think. Stay at home on my own, or shack up with a couple of hormonal teenagers for the weekend? I know which one sounds the most dangerous.' She forced a smile.

Jones nodded. 'Well, call me any time if you feel uneasy.'

Phillips patted him on the arm. 'Go. I'm fine.'

'If you're sure?'

'I'm sure. Go.'

'Ok. See you Monday.'

Phillips watched Jones as he walked out. The room fell silent in his absence. Images of the killer standing at her front door flashed into her mind, and an icy chill ran the length of her spine. Who was the man behind the murders, the architect of this so-called game? She pulled out her phone and called Control for a second time that evening, ordering a patrol to check her house at regular intervals throughout the night and across the weekend. Whoever the Copycat Killer was, and whatever he was planning next, she wasn't taking any chances this time.

45

MONDAY, MARCH 16TH

Phillips and Carter sat waiting in Chief Constable Fox's outer office, watched over by her assistant, Ms Blair. In stark contrast to Carter's assistant, Cook, Blair made no effort to either make conversation or offer a hot drink – or any drink, for that matter. Phillips wasn't sure if Blair was an inherently cold person, or whether she was under instructions from Fox to act the way she did. Either way, any time spent in this environment made her feel like a naughty child awaiting punishment from the headmaster. Based on her conversation with Carter on her drive into work this morning, a reprimand was no doubt on its way. Not content with spending an hour dressing down Carter on Friday, Fox had clearly decided she needed to vent her spleen further, so had instructed the chief superintendent to bring Phillips to an emergency review meeting as soon as she arrived at HQ that morning. They therefore found themselves huddled together, awaiting their fate.

The phone on Blair's desk rang just once before she

picked it up, listened for a moment, then replaced the handset. 'You can go in now,' she said, her voice dispassionate.

Carter cleared his throat as he stood. Phillips followed his lead.

Fox's office, as chief constable, was the largest in the building, and the cold-coloured walls and lack of any personal touches – aside from the raft of photos of her alongside the great and the good of Manchester – perfectly matched her own austere exterior. 'Sit, the pair of you,' she said from behind her large desk, as if talking to children.

Carter and Phillips acquiesced and took seats opposite her.

As ever, Fox was dressed in her black and white uniform, her spectacles perched on the end of her overly tanned nose. Her shoulder-length hair was dyed blonde and, despite the obvious trappings of a six-figure salary, looked cheaply maintained. 'I understand you had a visitor to your house on Friday night, DCI Phillips?'

'Yes, Ma'am. A hand-delivered package from the main suspect in the five murders. Another voice message.'

'I see from the reports that you called in uniform immediately to check the house?'

'Yes, Ma'am. I didn't feel safe going inside by myself. I didn't know if he was there or not.'

Fox's eyes widened. 'Well, you have changed, haven't you? Not so long ago, you'd have gone charging in after him, hell bent on getting yourself killed.'

Phillips didn't react to the obvious dig.

'So, tell me exactly what the message said.'

Phillips pulled the pen-drive from her pocket and handed it over the desk. 'You can hear it for yourself.'

Fox inserted the drive and they listened as the message played. When the recording ended, Fox sat back in her chair. 'Cocky little bastard, isn't he?' she said. 'Any ideas what he means?'

'When he says "The Angel of Death walks amongst your own kind", our initial thoughts are that he might be trying to tell us he works for the police, Ma'am.'

Fox rolled her eyes. 'Oh God, not again. We just about got away with it the last time that happened.'

'Obviously we don't know for sure that's what he's saying, but it's a starting point – and would make sense, given his potential knowledge of police procedures and his ability to evade capture on CCTV and ANPR cameras.'

'So, what are we doing about it?'

'Well, Ma'am. As you know, better than most, we have almost seven thousand officers in the force currently. If we take away the females, we're left with just over four and half thousand. Based on the shoe size and height range identified by forensics – which are both quite small for male police officers – we're hoping we can narrow it down to just a few hundred.'

'Which is *still* a very large number of suspects,' said Fox.

'But a lot better than four and half thousand, Ma'am,' Carter cut in.

Fox pursed her lips as she stared at them both in silence for a long moment. 'Chief Superintendent Carter tells me you have a picture of the killer's face, taken from the CCTV in reception.'

Phillips nodded, and fished her phone from her pocket. It took her a few moments to find the image in question. She presented it to Fox. 'It's a clear shot of him face on, but we believe he's wearing a disguise in order to look like Peter Sutcliffe.'

Fox's eyes narrowed as she inspected the image. 'God, he really does look like him, doesn't he?'

'Yes, Ma'am. He's a dead ringer, if you'll pardon the pun,' said Carter. 'Dr Harris believes it's all part of the game for him.'

'Harris? You mean the criminal psych from your old patch?'

'That's her. She also thinks we should release the image of him to the press.'

'Not a chance!' scoffed Fox. 'If the public see him looking like Sutcliffe, then the Copycat Killer will become a living, breathing thing. Before we know it, the public will be whipped up into a frenzy and our man will go underground.'

Carter shook his head. 'Dr Harris doesn't think so. She believes this man craves attention, hence him reaching out to Jane. If the actual killing was what was driving him, then she believes he would be doing whatever it takes to stay off the radar and continue his spree. The opposite seems to be true: he's allowed himself to be caught on ANPR – likely to demonstrate that he's adapted his van so its impervious to the cameras. He risked everything by walking into *this* building in broad daylight, then sent messages directly to Jane – even turning up at her house. Harris reckons he wants us to know how smart he is. She believes that if we release the image to the press, it could draw him out into the open to see what people are saying about him, maybe even bask in the reflected glory. If that happens, he's more likely to drop his guard and leave a trace. Hopefully, he'll make a mistake, and that's when we'll have the best chance of catching him. Plus, even with the beard, someone who knows his face well enough may recognise him. Considering where we are, it has to be worth a shot, Ma'am?'

Fox reclined in her seat and linked her fingers together across her abdomen. 'It feels risky to me. I saw the press conference the other day, and whilst you did well to deflect the question regarding the Copycat Killer, releasing an image that is such an obvious likeness to Sutcliffe will push that theory to the top of agenda.'

Phillips cut in now. 'As you know, Ma'am, I have a good relationship with Don Townsend at the MEN —'

'God knows how. The man's a bloody snake,' spat Fox.

Phillips continued. 'The journalist who asked about the copycat theory at the press conference is called Lachlan Sims, and he works for Don. When I spoke to Don the other day, he made it very clear to me that Sims has a raft of research and information on the historical killings of Nilsen, Sutcliffe and Hardy, etc., and that he's desperate to connect to our cases. The editor over there is chomping at the bit to splash the copycat theory all over the paper, and keep doing it for as long as it takes us to catch this guy. Because of my leverage with Don, I managed to persuade him to sit on Sims for a while, but he warned me that we only had a few days grace, at best. That was Thursday, and today's Monday. It's our view that it's in our interests to get out in front of it, reduce the noise, and hopefully minimise the impact of Sims and the MEN.'

Fox sat, deep in thought, for a long moment, before eventually sitting forward and resting her elbows on the desk. 'Ok. Well, it seems like we don't have much of a choice, does it? Release the photo, but make sure it's cropped so there's no chance anyone can recognise the background as Ashton House, ok? We need to at least *try* and look like we know what we're doing.'

'Of course, Ma'am,' said Carter.

'I'll speak to the PR team straight away,' added Phillips.

Fox removed her glasses and allowed them to hang on the cord around her neck. 'I don't need to remind you both just how important the right result on this case is to your department. With budget cuts and pressure on resourcing, merging units going forward is not out of the question. We've got five bodies and very little else right now. For MCU to remain an elite team, I'm expecting that to change very quickly. Are we clear?'

'Yes, Ma'am,' said Phillips and Carter in unison.

'Good. Phillips, you can go. Chief Superintendent, you can stay. I'm not finished with you yet.'

Phillips wasted no time in getting away from Fox's lair, keen to put as much distance as possible between her and the chief constable. She felt for Carter, who she'd left behind in the line of fire, but at the same time was grateful it wasn't her sat in that hotseat anymore.

When she felt she was far enough away and sure there was no one around, she slipped into an empty meeting room and pulled out her phone to make a call. A deal was a deal, and she had a promise to keep.

He answered promptly. *'Jane. Have you got something for me?'*

'Off the record?'

'Off the record.'

'Ok. We're about to go public with an image of our main suspect.'

'Really?'

'I told you I'd make sure you got the exclusive, so I'm sending it over to you first.'

'You said you're going public. So who else is getting it?' asked Townsend.

'It'll be sent out to all media in the next hour.'

'That's hardly an exclusive, Jane.'

'Well, it's the best I can offer. At least you've got a head start on everyone else.'

'I suppose that's something.'

'And there's one more thing, Don.'

'Of course there is.' Townsend's tone was sardonic.

'In the picture, the suspect appears to be the double of Peter Sutcliffe. We're convinced it's a disguise and not what he really looks like, but I need Sims to be responsible with the information. I know he's hell-bent on making as much noise as possible, but that could cost lives. Please, Don. Think of the victims' families.'

Townsend said nothing for a moment before exhaling loudly. *'I'll do what I can, Jane – which, based on the editor's hard-on for this story, probably isn't much. I'm afraid I can't offer any more than that.'*

'Thanks, Don. I know you'll do what you can.' Phillips rang off and stepped back out into the corridor. Checking her watch, she could see it was 10.20 a.m. Despite Townsend's best efforts, she knew in her gut he would be fighting a losing battle. The story was just too explosive for Sims and the editor to resist. By midday, the only thing anyone in Manchester would be talking about would be the Copycat Killer.

46

'I've pulled that report together that you asked for, Ma'am.' PC Lawford stood in the doorway to Phillips's office, a bulging Manila folder in her hands.

Phillips beckoned her in.

Lawford took a seat, placed the folder on the desk and opened it, then began passing across separated bundles of printouts. 'Pretty much every media outlet has run the picture of the suspect, with at least five hundred words on the story,' she said.

'That's got to be some kind of record, especially considering we only released the photo three hours ago. How many of them reference the Copycat Killer?'

'A handful of the online blogs and sites, but the majority of the traditional media have just focused on the Peter Sutcliffe likeness. The MEN, on the other hand...' Lawford paused as she pulled out a thick wad of paper, which she proffered to Phillips. '...they've gone for it big time.'

Phillips's heart jumped as she gazed down at a colour copy of the front page of the paper. A huge picture of the suspect took up almost the entire page, positioned underneath the massive headline: COPYCAT KILLER PROWLING OUR STREETS. The next few pages of the file contained further copies of stories that had been lifted from the paper. Historical mugshots of Steve Wright, Denis Nilsen and Trevor Hardy stared back at her. Their individual crimes, number of victims and prison sentences were listed below each image.

'That stupid little fucker!' Phillips raged.

Lawford shifted in her seat and glanced down at the floor.

Phillips continued. 'To them, it's just a sensational story to drive hits – bloody click-bait – but to us it could mean the difference between catching him or finding his next victim slaughtered and mutilated.'

Entwistle knocked on the open door.

'What is it?' snapped Phillips.

Entwistle raised his eyebrows. 'I'm sorry to interrupt, Guv, but I've got something on the van I think you need to see.'

'Show me.'

Entwistle quickly took the seat next to Lawford. 'I've been going through the reported sightings, most of which have absolutely no value, and then I found this.' He handed across a report that had been processed the previous evening. 'I recognised the road mentioned – Harper Way – but I couldn't think why. So I googled it, and realised it runs adjacent to Hollingworth Road.'

Phillips frowned. 'What's the relevance?'

'Hollingworth Road is where the Cedar Pines Care

Home is located. It looks like the van was spotted in that vicinity the night Yates was killed.'

'Did the witness see the driver?'

'No, he said it was too dark. But there's more...'

Phillips moved to the edge of her chair. 'Go on.'

'Well. I called the care home again this morning and spoke to the manager, Diana Kirby. I asked to see their staff and treatment logs for that evening. She sent them over a couple of hours ago, and I've been working my way through them. To be honest, I wasn't entirely sure what I was looking for, but then I noticed that another resident had been taken to hospital in an ambulance the night Yates died. I called Kirby back and asked who had made the call to the emergency services that night, as it wasn't in the log. Kirby didn't know, but said she'd find out. Anyway, she called me back about ten minutes ago and said it wasn't any of her staff – it was an on-call doctor. His visit should have been written up in the log, but because the patient was taken away in an ambulance, he got mixed up in all that paperwork.'

'So, do we know the doctor's name?' asked Phillips.

Entwistle locked eyes with Phillips. 'Dr Anderson. The same guy who prescribed Sean Hamilton's medication.'

A spike of adrenaline shot through Phillips's body. 'Bloody hell!' she said, jumping up from her chair and rushing into the incident room. 'Jonesy. Come with me.'

Jones looked taken aback. 'Where are we going?'

'Back to Manchester Central Surgery. I think we've finally got a breakthrough.'

47

The receptionist at the surgery frowned. 'Dr Anderson? I'm afraid we don't have a Doctor Anderson.'

Phillips was in no mood for games. 'He's a locum. I spoke to him here myself just a couple of weeks ago.'

The receptionist's face softened. 'Ah right, I see. I only started last week. That's why it didn't register. He mustn't have been in recently.'

Phillips's frustration was building. 'Well, in that case, we need to speak to Dr Goodwin urgently.'

'I'm afraid she's with patients at the moment.'

'I don't give a shit who she's with. Bloody well interrupt her!' growled Phillips.

At that moment, Phillips spotted Dr Goodwin out of the corner of her eye as she walked to the edge of the waiting area. It appeared she was about to announce her next patient, then spotted them. Her agitated expression suggested she was less than happy to see Phillips and Jones.

She marched over. 'Can I help?'

'We need to speak to Dr Anderson urgently,' said Phillips, louder than necessary, drawing attention from the waiting patients.

Goodwin pulled them to one side, away from prying eyes and ears. 'He's not in today. In fact, he's not been in for over a week. The agency we book him through said he was taking some time off.'

'Did they say why?'

Goodwin shrugged. 'Personal reasons, or something to that effect. Can I ask what this is about?'

'We think he might have information that could help us identify a suspect in a serious crime,' said Phillips, playing down his importance.

'When did you last see him?' asked Jones.

Goodwin took a moment to think before answering. 'His last shift was probably the day you guys spoke to him here. I tried to book him in for a few days the following week, but that's when the agency told me he was out of action for a while.'

'Were you aware that Dr Anderson treated a patient at Cedar Pines the night Michael Yates was poisoned?'

Goodwin did a double take. 'Really? Says who?'

'The manager, Diane Kirby. Apparently he was called out to visit Arthur Mayhew around 10 p.m. He called an ambulance and had Mayhew admitted to the MRI soon after.'

'He never said anything to me about that, but it may have slipped his mind. Let me check the logs.' Goodwin moved into the reception area and sat down at the spare computer. She took a moment to log on, then a minute or so to find what she was looking for. 'I'm afraid there's nothing in here about a Cedar Pines visit on that night. Are you sure it was him?'

'According to Diane Kirby, yes.'

'Do you know if Dr Anderson visited Cedar Pines on any other occasions?' asked Jones.

'Off the top of my head, no. But I'm pretty sure he will have done at some point. There's thirty residents living in the home, and they are all registered with this practice. If either Dr Singh or I wasn't around and he was on duty, then he would have been the first port of call.'

Jones continued. 'And what about Michael Yates? Did Anderson ever treat him?'

'Well, the same applies. If we weren't available and Mr Yates needed attention, then he would have seen him, yes.'

Phillips and Jones glanced at each other. The pieces were starting to fall into place.

'Have you noticed anything different about his behaviour lately?' asked Phillips.

'In what way?'

'Well, was he moody, agitated, aggressive, hyper, even?'

'Dr Anderson, aggressive?' Goodwin scoffed. 'That man wouldn't say boo to a goose. I'm lucky to get a hello out of him most days. Not that I mind, though. He's a very good doctor, and the patients seem to like him. Plus, I've rarely seen any doctor who can manage their appointments schedule as efficiently as he can.'

'I know you say he was quiet, but did he ever talk about his home life?' Phillips asked.

'Not really. I mean, I know he's married and they recently had a baby, but other than that, not much else.'

Phillips nodded. 'We're going to need his address and mobile number.'

'Of course. I can get them for you now,' said Goodwin as she tapped into the computer. 'Here it is.' A moment later, Goodwin scribbled the details on a Post-it Note, then passed it across the reception desk.

'And because of the sensitive nature of the case, we'd appreciate it if you'd keep this conversation confidential for now,'

'I understand, Chief Inspector.'

'Thank you, Dr Goodwin.' Phillips turned and headed for the door.

48

Phillips led the way with Jones tucked in behind as they walked up the short garden path to Anderson's home, a well-appointed semi-detached property in the leafy suburb of Finney Green, just a stone's throw from the highly desirable South Manchester village of Wilmslow. She pressed the ornate metal doorbell fixed to the side of what looked like a recently fitted modern door, praying Anderson was inside. When there was no answer, she tried again with the same result.

'Check the back,' she told Jones, as she stepped into the front garden to look through the large bay window.

Inside, she could see from the lounge right through to the kitchen at the opposite side of the house. Everything appeared in order, so she made her way back to the front door.

Jones reappeared from the path at the side of the house. 'No sign of anyone at the back, Guv.'

Phillips bit her lip as she considered her next move.

'Shall we get uniform to sit on the house?'

A muffled noise from within the house caught Phillips's attention. 'Did you hear that?'

'Hear what?'

'There it is again,' said Phillips.

'I can't hear anything, Guv.'

Phillips moved to the front door and crouched as she peered through the letterbox. Annoyingly, there was a wind-break flap on the other side that obscured her view. 'Pass me your pen, will you?'

Jones obliged.

Gripping the pen between the thumb and forefinger of her right hand, she lifted the flap, just a little at first, but with a slight adjustment she managed to open it fully. 'Oh my God!' she said as she stared at the prostrate body of a woman lying motionless in the hallway. 'We need to get inside, now. There's a body in there!'

'Follow me,' said Jones as he headed for the side of the house once again. 'There's a glass-panelled door at the back.'

A moment later, Jones grabbed a heavy terracotta plant pot from the patio, spun, and hurled it through the glass, which shattered noisily. Next, he reached through and released the latch.

Phillips rushed inside and along to the hallway, Jones in tow. A second later, she knelt next to the woman and checked her neck for a pulse. 'She's dead.'

Jones exhaled loudly. 'Jesus, Guv.'

The sound of a dog barking incessantly, along with high-pitched muffled cries, filled the air. They were coming from upstairs. 'That's what I heard outside.'

'What if he's still in the house?' Jones whispered.

The same thought had occurred to her, and she swallowed hard as her adrenaline spiked. 'Stay close. Any sudden movement, get the hell out of the way.'

Jones nodded, and tucked in behind as Phillips padded slowly up the stairs.

A moment later, they reached the landing. The dog's deafening barking, mixed in with the faint cries, came from behind the closed door to the front bedroom. Resisting the urge to rush along the landing and charge in, she gave Jones silent instructions to check the bathroom behind him at the top of the stairs while she opened the door to the second bedroom on her left. Both were empty, so they continued down the hall to stop outside the front bedroom. The dog was going ballistic on the other side, barking and scratching at the door.

'I bloody hate dogs,' Jones whispered.

'Me too,' said Phillips, before taking a long breath. Gripping the door handle, she silently mouthed, 'One, two, three', then swung the door open. A black dog rushed towards them, causing Phillips to jump with fright. It growled and clamped down onto her trouser leg.

Jones was on it in a flash and yanked the dog away. 'It's all right, mate, it's all right,' he repeated as he tried to calm the animal.

The sight that greeted Phillips broke her heart: a little baby boy, dressed in a powder-blue sleepsuit, lay in his cot screaming his lungs out, his face red and swollen. She rushed towards him and scooped him up as Jones carried the dog out of the room.

'There, there. Ssh, you're ok. Ssh, everything's ok,' she whispered, gently rocking from side to side even as she knew the exact opposite was true, what with the little lad's mother dead, and his father their prime suspect in several murder cases. Reaching into her pocket, she pulled out her phone and called Entwistle.

'We're at Anderson's house. We've discovered a deceased female and an abandoned baby. I need an ambulance and forensics down here immediately.'

'*I'll get straight onto them,*' said Entwistle.

'Oh, and I also need a dog handler. Jones is currently downstairs trying to restrain what looks like a manic cockapoo.'

'*On it, Guv.*'

WHILST THE VARIOUS teams and services descended on the house and took care of the baby and dog, Phillips and Jones gloved up and joined Andy Evans and his team as they searched for clues as to what had killed the woman. Based on a joint bank account statement pinned to the corkboard in the kitchen, along with framed photos scattered around the house, there was no doubting the woman was Jodie Anderson. And, according to a healthcare worker's report – also attached to the corkboard – the baby's name was Noah, and he was three months old.

After working in separate rooms for a time, Phillips and Jones reconvened in the kitchen.

'Do you think he did it?' asked Jones.

'I couldn't say for sure, but it looks likely.'

'If he *is* the Copycat Killer, then who's this one supposed to be emulating?'

Phillips shook her head. 'I have no idea, and to be honest, right now I don't care. I just want find Anderson before he kills again.'

Jones let out a frustrated breath. 'So where the bloody hell is he?'

Phillips didn't reply, her attention drawn to a grainy old photo stuck to the fridge door. She stepped forwards and removed it. 'Who's this guy with Anderson?'

Jones took a closer look. 'No idea.'

Phillips turned it over to find writing on the back, written by the same hand as on the envelopes containing the audio messages. '"Dad's first farmer's market, 1999".' She flipped it back again and scrutinised the photo further, before tapping the far edge of the image. 'Can you see that?'

Jones took it from her.

'Does that look like the rear bumper of an old green van to you?'

Jones's eyes narrowed. 'There's not much there to see, but now you mention it, I think it does.'

Phillips called Entwistle once more.

'I need you to find me the name and address of Anderson's father, quick as you can.'

'Give me ten minutes,' said Entwistle and rang off.

49

Phillips keyed Anderson's father's address into the car's Sat Nav, which suggested the journey time from Finney Green to Styal would be less than ten minutes. Thanks to the wonder that was Google Maps, she was able to source an aerial shot of the old farmhouse and surrounding land, which she shared with Jones. After a brief discussion regarding the available options – recalling a similarly remote location just six months earlier, when Jones had almost lost his right arm chasing down a murder suspect – they decided they should call in the Tactical Firearms Unit for support. There was no guarantee Anderson was there, of course, but it was better to be safe than sorry. Luckily, there was a mobile TFU stationed at Manchester Airport, which meant they would be on scene within quarter of an hour.

As they made their way to Styal, Phillips called Entwistle.

'*Any luck with Anderson, Guv?*' he said, his voice booming through the car's speakers.

'He wasn't at home, but we got a lead on the van. We're about to check out his father's address in Styal.'

'Do you want me to call in TFU?'

'Already done.'

'What about a warrant to search the house?'

'Thanks, but because we suspect Anderson is involved in the deaths of at least five people we don't need one based on the imminent threat to life.'

'Fair enough.'

Phillips continued. 'But I do need a full background on Dr Anderson and his father, Albert Anderson. Apparently he was a CID detective, went by the name of Detective Sonny. And see if either of them holds a firearms license as a matter of urgency.'

'I'll do that right now,' he said, and hung up.

A couple of minutes later, Jones guided the squad car down the bumpy dirt track leading from the main road towards the farmhouse. He stopped just outside the gate to the property. About five hundred yards farther up the track stood the farmhouse, which, to all intents and purposes, looked empty, derelict even. There was no sign of a van, but with a host of outbuildings surrounding the main house, Phillips reasoned it could easily be hidden in any one of them.

As they waited for the TFU to arrive, Entwistle called back.

'Any joy?' asked Phillips.

'You'll be pleased to know that neither of them has any record of owning firearms—'

'Doesn't mean they don't have them, though,' Jones cut in.

Entwistle continued. 'I've only been able to do a top-line check at the moment, but I can tell you Dr Anderson's *full name is Gabriel George Anderson. Date of birth is 29th of September, 1977. He studied medicine at Leeds University, and qualified as a doctor from Manchester Royal Infirmary in 2000. He's been a GP ever since.'*

'Any history of violence or mental health issues?' asked Phillips.

'No record of violence, but all medical records are confidential, so without a Section 23, I can't get access to any information on that one.'

'What about the father?'

'You were right, Guv. Albert Anderson was a decorated detective sergeant in GMP CID for over thirty-five years. He retired in 1999, aged fifty, with a full pension.'

'That was just before I joined. That explains why I've never heard of him,' said Phillips.

'Bert's registered on the electoral role as living at 35 Old Styal Lane, Wilmslow. He's been there for over forty years.'

'Anything else?'

'That's all I've got at the moment, Guv.'

'Ok. Well, keep looking.'

'Will do.'

Just then, the whoop of police sirens filled the air. 'We'd better go, sounds like the cavalry have arrived,' said Phillips, and ended the call. Glancing in the wing mirror, she could see the flashing lights of the TFU's BMW X5. 'Jesus, they don't do things discreetly, do they?'

'Well, if the Andersons didn't know we were coming, they do now,' said Jones, curtly.

Sergeant Roy Matthews, leader of the TFU, knocked loudly and repeatedly on both the front and back doors of the property. When there was, at length, no response, Phillips gave Matthews the green light to break the door down. Using a hand-held metal battering ram, the TFU boys made light work of the front door, then rushed inside shouting "Armed police!", their MP5 semi-automatic machine guns ready, the extended stocks pulled hard into their shoulders in case of attack. Butterflies churned in Phillips's stomach as she waited to find out what was going on.

A few minutes later, Matthews returned to the front door. 'It's all clear, Ma'am. No sign of anyone here, but there's an ungodly smell in one of the rooms.' He beckoned her in. 'Come on, I'll show you.'

Phillips stepped inside, Jones just behind, and followed Matthews through the dilapidated kitchen. Every surface was covered in empty food cans, takeaway cartons, and filthy plates and cups. As they reached the door on the far side of the room, the stench hit them.

'Jesus!' said Jones, clamping a hand over his nose and mouth.

Phillips was forced to turn away as she retched, fighting off the urge to vomit.

'I told you it was bad,' said Matthews.

'God. You weren't kidding,' replied Phillips, coughing hard. 'Where's it coming from?'

Matthews pointed into the room ahead. 'It's strongest just over by the window.'

Phillips breathed through her mouth as she pulled on a pair of blue latex gloves. Then, covering her nose and mouth, she moved carefully across the room, stopping just in front a large rug that has been placed on the floor below the window. The room fell silent for a moment as she tried to pinpoint the exact source of the vile stench. 'Can you hear that?' she whispered.

'Hear what?' asked Jones.

Matthews appeared puzzled.

'That low, humming noise,' said Phillips.

Jones's eyes narrowed. 'I can't hear anything, Guv.'

Phillips remained silent as she beckoned him over.

Jones moved next to her, and his eyes widened. 'Oh, yeah. I can hear it now.'

'It's coming from under the floor.' Phillips took a knee and pulled back the rug, revealing a large hatch cut into the floorboards, with a recessed handle.

She glanced up at Jones, then at Matthews, whose eyes were fixed on the hatch. 'Have you got a torch?'

Matthews nodded, and pulled it from his belt before switching it on and handing it over.

Jones swallowed hard. 'What the hell's down there?'

'Well, there's only one way to find out.'

Phillips exhaled loudly, then turned the hatch with a heavy click. It felt surprisingly light in her hand. 'Are we ready?' she whispered.

Jones nodded.

Matthews readied his MP5.

Yanking it open, she immediately jumped back in horror as thousands of flies rushed from the darkness below, the buzzing almost deafening as they swarmed around the room. Each of them attempted in vain to swat away the flies, but there were just too many. Beating a retreat, they ran from the house back out into the yard.

Phillips and Jones gulped in fresh air once outside, whilst Matthews regrouped with his men before retrieving gas masks from the X5 and heading back into the house. A minute or so later, every window in the place had been opened. The flies poured out like plumes of black smoke escaping a burning building.

When the flow of flies had slowed to a trickle, Phillips and Jones returned to the open hatch. In the torch light, a set of steep wooden steps was now visible. She could hear voices coming from below.

Jones gazed down into the hole. 'Should we send Matthews in first?'

'No chance. I wanna see what's down there for myself,' said Phillips, and placed her foot on the top step.

'Seriously, Guv. I think we should leave it to Matthews and his team. I'm not getting hurt again,' he said, unconsciously rubbing his right arm where he'd been hit with a machete just six months ago.

Phillips paused. She could see genuine fear in his eyes. She relented. 'Ok. Call him in.'

A few minutes later, Matthews and his men had descended into the darkness, with Phillips and Jones falling in behind. As they reached the bottom, the stench became unbearable. Phillips could hear the buzz of more flies, along with voices and music. Arcing the torchlight across the wall closest to him, Matthews found a light switch and flicked it on, illuminating the space. They were in a small room. A battered old door was ahead of them, paint peeling from its surface. Phillips's heart pounded in her chest as Matthews stepped closer. The low hum of flies came from the far side, and the voices were louder than ever, yet somehow distant. The TFU boys made ready with their MP5s once more as Matthews took a deep breath, braced, then grabbed the door handle and pushed it open. Another swarm of flies rushed out. Phillips covered her face and ducked as she attempted to get out of their path. She held her breath for as long as she could before exhaling loudly and uncovering her face.

The sight that greeted her made her blood run cold; a ravaged corpse lay on a bed in the centre of the room, maggots and flies feasting on what little flesh remained. A raft of cannulas was attached to the skeletal wrists, and a hissing oxygen tube was inserted into what had been the person's nose. A TV blared from atop a chest of drawers facing the bed, packets of unopened cigarettes piled high next to it.

'My God,' whispered Matthews, lowering his gun.

Jones stepped out from behind Phillips to get a better look, his hand covering his mouth. Without warning, he turned away and vomited.

Phillips gave him a minute to compose himself.

'Jesus, Guv!' he said finally, wiping his mouth.

'I think we might have found Bert Anderson,' she said, stepping as close to the body as her senses would allow.

'How long's he been dead?' asked Matthews.

'I dunno, but long enough to become maggot food.'

'I need some air,' said Jones, and rushed from the room.

Phillips followed him out, along with Matthews and his men.

Once outside, she called Andy Evans and ordered a full forensic sweep of the house.

When she was confident Jones was ready to get to work again, she sent him off in search of the van whilst she headed back into the house to search for clues as to Gabe Anderson's whereabouts.

For the next thirty minutes – whilst trying to ignore the foul smell and breathing through her mouth – she searched every cupboard and drawer she could find.

Jones reappeared. 'There's tyre tracks heading away

from one of the outhouses, Guv. They look fresh, and I'm pretty sure they're a match for those we found at the crime scenes. I followed them for about half a mile down an old track that loops back round to the main road. Looking back down the hill, there's no way we could have seen him from the gate. I think we just missed him.'

'Shit!' said Phillips, her frustration boiling over.

'What have you got there?' asked Jones.

Phillips handed over a pile of old photographs she'd found in one of the drawers.

'It looks like the van,' said Jones, as he inspected the top photo at the top of the stack. 'A bit newer there, though.'

'Yeah, the timestamp says it was taken in 2001. Look at the logo on the side.'

'*Anderson's Produce.*'

'Which explains the writing we *thought* we saw on the side of the van. It wasn't "And Son", it was *Anderson*.'

Jones stared at the photo as Phillips opened another drawer.

'What's this?' she said, lifting out a large sports rucksack. 'It's heavy,' she added, and carried it to the kitchen table. Carefully, she unzipped the bag, pulled out a laptop and placed it on the table before switching it on. Frustratingly, it was password-protected. 'Call Entwistle. I want to see what's on this ASAP.'

Jones nodded and fished out his phone.

Phillips emptied the remaining contents onto the table. 'Look at this,' she said, holding a small digital recording device in her hand. She pressed play, and the familiar, distorted tones of the killer filled the air. *'Hello, Jane. You must be feeling real stupid by now. First you walk right past me at work, and now you've missed me at home—'*

She'd heard enough. 'Well, there's no doubt about it. Anderson's our killer,' she muttered under her breath.

Jones looked up from the laptop. 'I can't get into this remotely, Guv. Entwistle says I'll need to take it back to base so he can have a go at it.'

Phillips nodded absentmindedly, then pulled out her phone.

'You ok, boss?'

'I need to call Carter. If Anderson knows we're onto him, he's got about an hour's head start.' Phillips marched outside. A moment later, the call connected.

'Jane. Tell me you've got good news,' said Carter, sounding defeated.

'I wish I did, sir.'

50

It was going to be a long night. Whilst Jones and Bovalino grabbed some sandwiches for the team from the canteen, Phillips pulled up a chair next to Entwistle, who made light work of cracking the password on the laptop. Once inside, he began scouring the drives for anything that might help them locate Anderson. After about ten minutes of digging around, something caught his attention.

'Look at this,' he said.

Phillips leaned forward and inspected the Excel spreadsheet on the screen. 'What is it?'

'It's the patient database for Manchester Central Surgery, including their home addresses and phone numbers.'

'Is that something a locum doctor would normally have access to?' said Phillips.

'I'm not sure. Let me check something…' Entwistle tapped the keyboard, and a second later, the screen changed. 'Well, look at that.'

Phillips hated Excel – *almost* as much as she hated people not getting straight to the point. 'What?' she said, barely able to hide her mounting impatience.

'Yates, Hamilton and Marsh are all on the patient database.'

'Which would likely explain his connection to them, and probably why Marsh was happy to get into the van that night.'

'It would make sense, wouldn't it?'

Phillips tapped her pen against her teeth. 'Because who is the one person people trust above all others?'

'Their doctor,' said Entwistle.

Phillips continued. 'We know Szymańska worked at the care home, but how does Gillian Galloway fit into it?'

'I'll keep looking,' said Entwistle.

Phillips patted him on the shoulder as she stood and made her way over to her office. Unlocking the door, she moved across the darkened room, dropped into her chair, and closed her eyes for a moment. She felt overwhelmingly frustrated; they had come so close to catching Anderson and now he could be anywhere. Her eyes remained closed for a few minutes as she replayed the events of the day in her mind's eye.

'I've found something,' said Entwistle, rousing her from her thoughts.

Phillips opened her eyes and switched on the desk lamp as Entwistle placed the laptop in front of her. 'Remember Gillian Galloway went on a date the night she died? The guy who the landlord said looked like a Thunderbird and carried her out of the pub?'

'Yeah, his name was Conrad Eve, wasn't it?'

Entwistle tapped the laptop keyboard, and the familiar Tinder photo of the man on the beach appeared on the screen. 'Meet Conrad,' he said. 'Based on their messages to each other, Anderson was posing as Conrad, and *he* was definitely the guy she met in the pub that night.'

Phillips stared at the image of the gorgeous, tanned young man. 'God. She must have been disappointed when Anderson showed up. I mean, he looks absolutely nothing like that fella. I'd have run out the door if it was me.'

'Galloway's flatmate said she was a kind soul. Maybe she took pity on him,' said Entwistle.

'And in return he spiked her drink and strangled her,' replied Phillips. 'The poor thing.'

'Looks like you've got a voicemail, Guv,' said Entwistle pointing at the flashing light on the desk phone console.

'Oh, God. The only person that uses that is Fox, which usually means I'm in for a bollocking.' Phillips huffed as she pressed the message button.

'Hello, Jane.' It was Anderson's voice, this time without any effects, the accent all his own. *'You were so close, Jane. So, so close. In fact, if it wasn't for your boys in blue and their sirens blaring across the Cheshire countryside, I'd probably be sitting in one of your cells right now. I must remember to thank the firearms boys when I see them next.'* He chuckled. *'I'm not sure how you found my hide-out, but Bert was right: you are a smart girl, Jane. And a much better detective than he ever was, the drunken old fool. Anyway, I expect he's told you everything he knows by now, but I can assure you, it won't help; I'm still one step ahead of you. You see, dear old Bert only knows the basics of my plan, and he has absolutely no idea what's coming next. But don't worry. You will, soon enough. If you want to find me, all you need to do is solve the clue that I gave you. Think hard, Jane, because the answers you seek are right in front of you, liter-*

ally staring you in the face.' He paused for a moment. *'When this is all over, I'm looking forward to meeting you, Detective Chief Inspector. I really am.'* The message ended.

Phillips's brow furrowed as she considered his words. 'What did he mean when he said his dad would have told us everything by now? Evans reckons if that body belongs to Bert Anderson, he's been dead for over a month.'

At that moment, Jones and Bov walked back into the incident room carrying food.

'In here, guys,' Phillips shouted.

As both men stepped inside her office, Phillips replayed the message.

When it finished, Jones's immediate reaction was the same hers. 'His *dad*'s told us everything? His dad's bloody maggot food!'

Phillips turned to Entwistle. 'Can you trace the call?'

'Depends if it came through the switchboard or direct to your extension,' Entwistle picked up the handset and dialled 1471. They were in luck. 'He dialled you directly,' he said as he wrote down the mobile number used to make the call. 'I'll get a trace on it right away.' He left the room.

Picking up her own mobile, Phillips called Dr Harris.

'Hi Jane. I hear you've identified the killer. Congratulations.'

Phillips was in no mood for faint praise. Until Anderson was in custody, they'd achieved nothing. 'Have you got a minute?'

'Of course.'

'I don't suppose you're still in the building, are you?'

'I am. I was just finishing up with the chief super.'

'Would you mind popping down to my office. I have something I'd like your take on.'

'*Sure. I'll come down now.*'

'Thanks,' Phillips hung up.

Bovalino must have overheard what the doctor had said. 'Been shagging Dirty Harry, has she?' he joked.

'Who told you that?' said Phillips curtly.

The big Italian raised his hands in defence. 'It was just a joke, Guv.'

'Well, we can do without shitty rumours like that going round the station, and this is no time for fucking about, Bov.'

'Sorry, Guv.' He looked like a chastised schoolboy.

Phillips shook her head and blew her lips. 'No, mate. It's me that should be sorry. I'm just so bloody frustrated at how close we came to catching this bastard, and I'm taking it out on you.'

Bovalino offered a coy smile and handed her a cheese sandwich. 'Peace offering?'

Phillips grabbed the packet. 'You spoil me sometimes,' she said with a chuckle.

'It's the Latin blood in me, Guv,' he replied, before demolishing half of his own baguette in one bite.

HARRIS EXAMINED the photos of the body at the farmhouse. 'It looks reminiscent of an old field hospital.'

'The SOCO team found vials of morphine, as well as a bunch of empty oxygen tanks,' confirmed Jones.

'As he's a practising doctor, he could well have been treating his father at home,' Harris said.

'I get that might have been happening at some point, but why did he say his father was likely to tell us everything when his body has been rotting in the cellar for weeks?'

Harris shrugged. 'Two options, as I see it. The first, he's continuing the game, speaking metaphorically and suggesting his father's body would somehow explain his crimes—'

'And the second?' pressed Phillips.

'He's suffering from schizophrenia or similar mental health issues and he believes his father is somehow still alive. As was the case with Graham Young and Peter Sutcliffe, schizophrenia is a common trait amongst vicious killers, and it's often the voices they hear that urge them to murder.'

Jones folded his arms across his chest. 'I understand that some people hear voices, Doc, but nobody on earth could believe that the body in that bed was still a living, breathing thing. I mean, the stench was ungodly, and there were literally *millions* of flies down there, not to mention maggots had eaten the eyeballs and tongue down to virtually nothing.'

'Sergeant, the brain is the most powerful organ in the human body,' said Harris, firmly. 'People suffering from a condition such as schizophrenia live in an alternate reality. If Anderson believes his father is still alive, then where you and I would see a skeletal corpse, he sees his father exactly as he was when alive. They'll have conversations that appear real, but are likely just echoes of memories, replaying within his own mind. In fact, if he was treating his father, then his death could have been the event that triggered the delusions. Trauma is a common root cause for schizophrenic behaviour.'

'Ok, so what next?' said Phillips. 'What does he mean about "we'll know soon enough?"'

'As we've seen, Anderson loves to play games,' said Harris. 'He's enjoying the challenge of staying one step ahead of you, Jane, and he's made the game personal now. It's about you and him and who comes out on top. I know you're worried he'll go to ground, but I suspect the opposite is actually true and that he plans to kill again – and very soon. Considering he knows you're onto him, I'd say he'll take his next victim within the next twenty-four hours.'

Phillips rubbed her temples hard with her fingers as she tried in vain to fend off a crippling headache. 'Where are we at with the Crossbow Cannibal theory? Any luck with crossbow societies?'

'I've spoken to all of them in the North West, and there's been no new members join in the last twelve months.' said Bovalino. 'It's quite a niche sport, I'm afraid, and no one stood out as being different or potentially unhinged.'

Phillips tapped her clenched fist against her mouth. 'Check them again, and this time you're looking for anyone that resembles Anderson.'

'On it, Guv.'

'The trace has come back on the phone used by Anderson,' Entwistle cut in.

'And?'

'It's an unregistered number, and the phone last connected to the mast at the airport at around 4 p.m.'

'When we were at the farmhouse,' said Jones.

Entwistle continued. 'The call could've come from anywhere within a five-mile radius of the mast. It was switched off after the call was made, and it's not been switched back on since.'

Frustration gnawed at every cell in Phillips's body.

How could they have come so close to catching Anderson and still have no idea where he was or what he was planning next? She checked her watch: 8.03 p.m. 'I want all of us to go back through the five cases with a fine-toothed comb. Now we know it's Anderson, there must be something in one of them that is the key to catching him.'

Each of the men nodded.

'Would you like me to stay and help?' asked Harris.

Phillips smiled. 'We could be here all night, Doc.'

'Fine by me. Beats going back to that hotel on my own.'

'In that case…' said Phillips, handing her the Michael Yates file, '…see what you can find in that lot.'

51

'You're loving this, aren't you?' said Don Townsend across the open-plan office.

Lachlan Sims, the only other person in the room, looked up from his laptop a few desks away. 'Loving what?'

'The thrill of the hunt for the Copycat Killer. Great name, by the way.'

Sims smiled. 'Thank you. It was an open goal, to be fair.'

Townsend reclined in his chair. 'So, what's the plan now? Where are you taking your readers next?'

Sims sat forwards, bristling with excitement. 'I've just scheduled a poll asking the readers how safe they feel in Manchester right now, and how effective they think the police are. It's a little bit of karma for Chief Superintendent Carter for embarrassing me at the press conference the other day, suggesting I was too inexperienced to write proper stories.'

'Don't mess with Lachlan Sims,' chuckled Townsend.

Sims grinned. 'Honestly, with the historical link to the previous serial killers, this story is a *goldmine*. There's so much backstory on those guys. My plan is to run a piece each day this week, comparing each recent murder with its infamous counterpart. A contact of mine at the MRI said the Polish girl's breast was bitten clean off, which is a carbon copy of Terry Hardy, aka the Beast of Manchester. I mean, seriously, this stuff writes itself.'

Townsend smiled. 'Oh, to be young and enthusiastic,' he quipped.

Just then, Sims's mobile began to ring; the number withheld. 'Hello?'

'*Lachlan Sims,*' said the voice at the other end.

'Yes. Who's this?'

'*You don't recognise me? I'm disappointed, Lachlan.*'

'Er, well, I speak to a lot of people every day.'

Townsend watched Sims, an eyebrow raised.

'*Maybe, but I'm the* only one *who knows the identity of the Copycat Killer.*'

Sims's pulse quickened. 'The Copycat Killer, you say?' He said it loud deliberately, for Townsend's benefit.

Townsend sat forwards, his full attention now on Sims.

'I'd love to hear more about the Copycat Killer,' said Sims.

'*I know you would. I want to meet.*'

'Meet? What for?'

'*You want to know who he is, don't you?*'

Sims swallowed hard. 'Yes, of course.' His imagination was running wild. He could see the intoxicating headlines in his mind's eye, along with record sales for the paper, millions of hits online, notoriety within the industry; a book deal even, and all before his twenty-fifth birthday. He tried his best to play it cool, but his voice betrayed his excitement. 'But tell me, if you really do know who he is, why not just go to the police and help them catch him?'

'*Where's the fun in that? They'll try to bury what I know, whereas you'll do the exact opposite.*'

'Ok, so why meet? Why can't you tell me over the phone?'

The man chortled. '*Two reasons, Lachlan. The first being, I want to see your face when you realise who the Copycat Killer actually is. And the second being, this information is worth a lot of money, and I want what I'm owed. In cash.*'

'How much do you want?' Sims asked.

'*Five grand should cover it.*'

'Five grand?'

Sims locked eyes with Townsend, who shook his head and inverted his thumb, indicating Sims should go back with a lower offer.

'I don't think I can access that kind of money.'

'*Well, then I'll take my information to a paper that can. Goodbye, Lachlan—*'

'No! Wait. Wait. I'm just a junior reporter. Let me speak to my boss.'

'*Is he there now?*'

'Yes, he is.'

'*Well, talk to him. I'll call you back in five minutes. No money, no story.*' The phone went dead.

Sims stared at his phone for a long moment before turning his attention to Townsend. 'He says if we don't give him the money, he'll take it to another paper.'

'Do you believe him?'

'I don't know.'

Townsend sat forwards. 'Has he said *how* he knows who the killer is?'

'No. Just that he does and, to be fair, he was the one who made the connection between the current murders and the historical cases. I would never have put it together without him, so I think we should take what he says seriously.'

'And what if *he's* the killer?'

Sims scoffed. 'Well, if that was the case, why admit it to me? He must know we'd have to inform the police.'

Townsend sat in silence for a moment. 'I'm wondering if we shouldn't inform the police already. If we have a source that has information regarding an open case, we're duty-bound to report it.'

'Oh come on, Don. If we do that, this story's finished. And besides, we have absolutely no idea if he's telling the truth or not. Why don't you let me check him out and if I hear anything that I think the police should know, I'll tell them.'

Townsend considered his suggestion before nodding. 'Ok. I can live with that.'

Sims grinned. 'All we need now is the cash.'

'Well, there is source money in the safe for this sort of thing,' said Townsend.

'How do we get access to that?'

'As a senior reporter, I have access, but the brass won't like it if you spunk five grand on some loony who's full of shit.'

'So, what do we do? Maybe he is talking bollocks, but if he's not and he *does* know the identity of the killer, this is the story of a lifetime, Don.'

Townsend appeared deep in thought. 'Ok. Here's what you should do. Tell him he can have the five grand, but only if he has concrete evidence to back up his claim. Theories are out. We want hard facts.'

Sims nodded eagerly.

'And it'll come in two payments. Half now if it looks like good intel, and half once our editor approves the story. See what he says to that.'

'Ok.' Sims's phone began to vibrate again. 'Hello?'

'*Did you get it?*'

'Yes. But there are a couple of conditions.'

'*I'm listening.*'

'I can give you two and half grand up front if the info is kosher and factual...'

'*Go on.*'

'And the other half once the editor approves my story and we run it.'

Silence.

Sims's heart beat so loudly, he was sure the man could hear it on the other end.

'*Ok, Lachlan. You've got yourself a deal. Meet me at ten p.m. tonight—*'

'Tonight?'

'*No sense in wasting time, Lachlan. We're both on a deadline.*'

'Where?'

'*The White Horse pub in Woodford. Do you know it?*'

'I'll find it.'

'*Good.*'

'How will I know what you look like?'

'*You won't. But I'll know you. And come alone. I see anyone else, I'm gone.*' The man hung up.

Sims stared at the phone before replacing the receiver.

'He went for it, then?' asked Townsend.

Sims let out a nervous laugh. 'Yeah, he did. I'm meeting him at The White Horse pub in Woodford, in an hour.'

'It's not a bad boozer, that.' Townsend stood. 'I'll be back in a minute.'

'Where are you going?'

'To get your money.'

Ten minutes later, he returned with five bundles of notes, which he deposited on Sims's desk. '*Et voilà*, two and a half grand,' he said.

A surge of excitement shot through Sims's body. He'd never seen so much cash in one place. 'Bloody hell, Don. That's amazing.'

Townsend handed him a docket. 'Well, don't get too excited. With large amounts of source-money comes great responsibility. You need to fill this out. This is *your* story, and *your* balls on the line. Make sure you get what you're paying for, or your glittering career will be over before it's even begun.'

Sims nodded, and proceeded to fill out the requisition order.

'That's a lot of money to be carrying round on your own. Do you want me to come with you?' asked Townsend.

'No. He expressly told me to come alone. Said if he saw anyone else but me, he'd disappear.'

'Ok. But be careful,' said Townsend. 'A lot of nutters call us every day claiming they know who killed Diana, or that John Lennon is still alive and living in Gorton above the Domino's Pizza. Dealing with crazies is an occupational hazard in our line of work. My advice is, get there before he does and choose a seat that's visible to other customers or the bar staff – better still, both. If you suspect anything is off, that he's a crazy or a weirdo, or you feel threatened, just make your excuses and leave. Believe me, no story is worth getting hurt over.'

'Thanks, Don. I'll be careful.'

Townsend checked his watch. 'Well, in that case, you'd better get going.'

Sims nodded, and began packing the money into his backpack.

'I'll be here for another hour or so, but my mobile will be on all night. Call me if you need me, ok?'

'I will,' said Sims, standing. 'Wish me luck.'

'Your Pulitzer Prize awaits!' said Townsend, affecting a fake American accent.

'Piss off,' chuckled Sims, then grabbed his bag and car keys, and headed for the lift.

52

'Take a look at this, Guv,' said Entwistle, angling his laptop so Phillips could see his screen.

Phillips placed the file she'd been reading on the desk and moved to his shoulder.

'I found this in one of the folders on here,' Entwistle tapped the screen with an index finger. 'A bunch of old newspaper articles on each of the killers, plus a load of others we've not encountered yet. There must be thirty or forty different names listed here.'

'Jesus. His next kill could be a copycat of any one of them. Is there anything in there on the Crossbow Cannibal?'

Entwistle scanned down the long list of files on screen. 'Doesn't look like it, Guv.'

Phillips removed her glasses and rubbed her hand down her face. 'Well, if that's the case, then we've been chasing our tails on the crossbow angle.'

'I think you're right, Guv,' said Bovalino, dropping his pen on his notepad with a sigh. 'I've found nothing online to link Anderson to any of the crossbow associations, and I've checked them all.'

'Well, we can't afford to waste any more time on it if that's the case. Park it and let's move on.' Phillips turned her attention back to Entwistle. 'Can you print off each of the old articles?'

'Sure. It'll take some time, though.'

'Do it. Run them off in alphabetical order, and we can start working through them.'

Entwistle nodded, and got to work.

At that moment the door to MCU opened behind them, causing Phillips to turn.

'I thought I'd check in on the troops,' said Carter as he strode across the office. 'How are you getting on?'

'Slowly, sir,' said Phillips. 'Entwistle's just found a stack of old articles on Anderson's laptop related to historical serial killers. There's between thirty and forty names, including the killers he's copycatted so far.'

'Bloody hell,' said Carter, frowning.

'*But*…nothing related to the Crossbow Killer. So, with time running out, we're ditching that theory. Entwistle's printing each of the articles off now, and then we'll start working our way through them.'

'Need some help?'

Phillips smiled. 'That would be great, if you have time.'

'Well, as there's no-one at home at the moment, I've got all the time in the world. Plus, I can't let Dr Harris take all the credit, can I?'

Harris looked up from the file she was working on and smiled.

'Where do you want me?' asked Carter.

'Take that desk.' Phillips pointed to one on her right.

Entwistle returned from the printer with the first few printouts, which he handed to Phillips.

'You can get stuck into these, sir,' she said, passing them over to Carter. 'You're looking for any similarities to his previous murders with regards to scale and profile. And, based on the pattern that's emerged, a different method of murder to any of his kills so far.'

Carter took a seat and began working his way through the sheets.

Phillips walked across to one of the large whiteboards fixed to the wall and began writing. 'Also, look for anything that makes sense of the clue: "The Angel of Death walks amongst your own kind, DCI Phillips. Like the good shepherd you are, follow the guiding star to find your salvation".'

Entwistle produced another set of printouts.

'I'll have those,' said Phillips, and took her seat at the desk next to Carter's.

Over the next thirty minutes, Entwistle continued rolling off the articles and, in turn, Jones, Harris and Bovalino began trawling through them; the only sound in the room came from the heavy-duty printer working overtime in the corner.

Having exhausted her stack, Phillips sat back and closed her eyes for a moment. She'd found nothing relevant. Opening her eyes again, her gaze fell on the whiteboard and the clue. '"The Angel of Death walks amongst your own kind, DCI Phillips. Like the good shepherd you are, follow the guiding star to find your salvation".' She whispered it over and over until the words no longer seemed to make sense. It was time for a break. 'I need some air,' she announced, and left the room.

She made her way out into the rear yard, located next to

the custody suite. The cold night air was crisp, her breath visible in front of her. The skin on her cheeks tightened as she folded her arms across her chest to keep warm. Uniformed officers milled around the yard, chatting, smoking and laughing. For a moment, she longed for the simplicity of street policing. No riddles, no games, just the chance to lock up villains with every single shift. Right now, with the clock ticking and no idea what Anderson was planning next, that life seemed like heaven. She ran the clue over in her mind once again. If he wasn't referring to a copper when he said "your own kind", then what *did* he mean?

The automatic gates to the yard began to roll open and, a minute later, a patrol car moved through, coming to a stop in a parking space just a few feet from where Phillips stood. Two officers jumped out. The fact that they were both women caught her attention. Chatting away, the pair made their way inside, nodding and offering respectful 'Ma'am's as they passed her. She watched them until they disappeared inside the building, the double doors closing behind them with a heavy thud before the automatic lock clicked into place. Then it suddenly dawned on her. 'Your own kind...your own kind...that's it!' she muttered under her breath, then rushed inside and upstairs.

A few minutes later, Phillips burst through the door of MCU. 'I think I've figured out what he means by the Angel of Death walking amongst my own kind!'

Everyone stopped what they were doing and stared at her.

She continued. 'We initially thought *my kind* was referring to me being a copper, but now we know the killer is Anderson, we can rule that out. So, the next most obvious thing I am is a woman.'

Puzzled looks filled the room.

'But Anderson's a man, Guv,' said Jones.

'Yes. I know he is. But for every murder he's committed, he's pretended to be someone else: a poisoner, a strangler, a gay guy, a vicious maniac, a stalker... Why couldn't he pretend to be a woman for his next kill?'

'It would certainly fulfil his desire to go one step further with each murder,' said Harris.

Phillips felt reenergised. 'Right. Entwistle, set your laptop up in the conference room and pull up the names of every female serial killer from the last fifty years. We'll go through them together, one by one.'

Soon after, the team was huddled around the large conference table, their eyes locked on the screen on the wall. One by one, as female mugshots appeared, Entwistle narrated their crimes: 'Myra Hindley – murdered children with her boyfriend Ian Brady; Rose West – killed her own children, as well as lodgers, with her husband Fred, then buried the bodies in the house and garden; Beverley Alit – the paediatric nurse who murdered sick children in her care. And according to this, Guv, she was nicknamed The Angel of Death.'

Was Alit to be the next copycat? Phillips wasn't so sure. 'The nickname makes her the obvious choice, but she only killed kids. Our guy has stuck to adults through the five murders so far – six if he was responsible his wife's death. I'm not an expert, but is it likely that he would he suddenly stray from that pattern, Doc?'

'I don't think so,' said Harris. 'As much as he's a psychopath, as you rightly say, his victims up to now have all been adults. After five kills, I can't see that changing. I agree. I think his next target will be an adult as well.'

'Just in case, let's keep Alit in mind, but I'm keen to see

if we can find anyone else who fits his MO more closely,' Phillips said.

'So, going back to the wife. Does her death look like it could be a copycat?' asked Jones.

'The honest answer is, we don't know at this stage,' said Phillips. 'There's nothing obvious to suggest it was, but we'll know more once we get the post-mortem results in a few days.'

'Having seen the preliminary SOCO report on the crime scene, I'd say that, unlike the rest of the murders, his wife's death looks unplanned,' said Harris, 'and certainly not the crime he's imaging in his messages. In his mind, whatever he's referring to in those will need to be a lot grander than strangling his wife at the bottom of the stairs.'

'I agree,' said Phillips. 'And even if it does turn out to be a copycat, it's not going to help us catch him now. So, let's get back to the search.'

Entwistle obliged. Maxine Carr, the co-conspirator in the Soham murders in 2002, where two young girls were lured into her boyfriend's home and murdered, appeared next.

'Kids again,' said Phillips. 'Move on.'

The next mugshot to appear on the large screen sent a chill down Phillips's spine. The face staring back at them epitomised evil. Black eyes, framed by lank brown hair, with a large star tattoo filling her right cheek.

'Joanna Dennehy, aka the Peterborough Ditch Murderer. Stabbed four men in March 2013, killing two of them, before dumping the bodies in drainage ditches outside Peterborough,' said Entwistle.

'God. I remember her,' said Bovalino.

'Me too,' added Carter.

'It was a huge case in the profiling world,' said Harris.

'Mainly because it was the first time a woman had committed multiple premeditated murders on men as the aggressor – as opposed to acting in self-defence.'

Phillips stared at the face for a long moment, then walked up to the screen. She tapped her fingers on the large tattoo. 'Follow the guiding star,' she said, then turned back to face the team. 'Joanna Dennehy. A masculine woman who committed a series of high-profile murders in the glare of the media, famous for the star tattoo on her cheek. My gut's telling me she's our next copycat.'

53

Sims arrived at The White Horse pub twenty minutes early. It was relatively busy, and the hum of chatter hung in the air. After ordering a diet coke, he sat down at a booth in full view of the bar, close enough to neighbouring tables to be seen, but far enough away so as not to be heard. He placed his bag containing the cash out of view on the bench next to him, pulled out his notepad and pen, and waited.

Ten minutes later, a long-haired man wearing a beanie hat, with a facial tattoo and dark painted fingernails, sat down opposite him, cradling a bottle of cider.

'That seat's taken,' said Sims, unimpressed.

'I know it is. I'm sitting in it.' His voice sounded masculine, but high-pitched and affected.

'Look, I don't mean to be rude, but I'm waiting for someone. They're due any minute.'

'They're already here, Lachlan,' said the man.

Sims's brow furrowed.

The man offered his hand. 'I'm Gabby.'

Sims was confused. A man with a woman's name?

'*I'm* your source.'

'I'm sorry?'

'Do you have my money, Lachlan?'

Sims frowned. '*You're* the person I've been talking to about the Copycat Killer?' His voice was almost a whisper.

Gabby grinned, then took a swig from the bottle. 'You were expecting somebody, or maybe *something*, else?'

'Well, yeah. I guess so. You sounded different on the phone.'

'Everyone says that. So, back to my question. Do you have my money?'

Sims shot a glance down at the bag, then back at Gabby. 'Yeah, but as we agreed, I need printable facts before I can hand it over.'

'Oh, I've got plenty of facts, Lachlan. I know everything there is to know about the Copycat Killer.'

Sims grabbed his notepad and pen. 'So, what can you tell me about him?'

Gabby's gaze moved to the bar for a moment, where the barman was busy making a cocktail of some kind. 'What do you think of DCI Phillips?'

Sims narrowed his eyes. 'I don't know her.'

'Yeah, but how do you think she's handling the copycat murders?'

'Well. I'm no expert, but she seems a bit lost, if I'm being honest. I mean, he's killed five people so far and the police appear no closer to catching him.'

Gabby's grin reappeared. 'No, they don't, do they. What about the killer?'

'What about him?'

'What do you think of him?'

'Er, well, again, I have no idea who he is, but based on

what I know about the murders so far, I'd say he's clearly smart, calculated, and seems one step ahead of the people trying to catch him.'

'I like that description,' said Gabby, taking another drink.

An uncomfortable silence descended as they eyed each other.

Everything about Gabby unnerved Sims. 'You said on the phone that you knew his name.'

Gabby nodded. 'I do. But that's not important right now.'

'It is to me. It's the whole reason I'm here.' Sims was struggling to hide his frustration.

'All in good time, Lachlan, all in good time,' said Gabby. 'So, tell me, what you think of *me*.'

Sims coughed nervously. 'I'm not sure what you mean?'

'Do you like how I look?'

'Sure,' he said without conviction.

'What about my tattoo?'

Sims glanced at it for a moment. 'It's very impressive.'

'It's new,' said Gabby proudly.

'Must have hurt.'

'Yeah. I did it myself.'

Sims nodded, unsure of where the conversation was going.'

Gabby leaned forward across the table and locked eyes with Sims. 'You can't tell if I'm a man or a woman, can you Lachlan?'

Sims blushed before choosing his words carefully. 'If I'm being honest, no, I can't.'

Gabby nodded, then drained the contents of the bottle

before setting it down carefully on the table and stepping out of the booth. 'I need a piss.'

Sims watched Gabby head inside the ladies' toilet. Confusion fogged his brain. This was without doubt the weirdest meeting with a source he'd ever had, and he was getting nowhere fast. Just then, his phone vibrated in his jeans pocket. Pulling it out, he saw Don Townsend was calling. 'God, Don. Your timing couldn't be better.'

'*Why? What's up?*' asked Townsend.

'My source, that's what's up.'

'*What? Is he a no-show?*'

'No, they're here, but it looks like *he*'s actually a *she*.'

'*What?*'

'I'm seriously confused, Don. I definitely spoke to a guy on the phone earlier tonight, as well as the first time he called, before the press conference, but the person who's turned up now sounds kinda like a woman – albeit with a masculine tone – has long hair, painted nails, and calls herself Gabby. Plus, they've just walked into the ladies' loo.'

'*Are you sure it's the same person you spoke to before?*'

'I think so. I mean, she identified herself as my source, knew my name, and asked about the money as soon as she sat down.'

'*So what's the issue? Maybe she's transgender. This is Manchester after all, Lachlan, the LGBTQ capital of the UK,*' said Townsend.

'Maybe so, but she's seriously freaking me out!'

'*What? Because she's trans?*'

'No. I couldn't care less if she's trans, Don. That doesn't bother me at all. No, it's *her*. The way she talks, the way she looks at me, *and* she has this massive homemade star tattoo on her cheek. It's creepy as all fuck.'

'Well, has she given you any information on the killer yet?'

'No. She just keeps talking about DCI Phillips.'

'Really? What's she said about her?'

'Asked me what I thought of her and how I thought she was handling the case. Then after that, she wanted to know what *I* thought of the killer.'

'And what did you say?'

'I said I thought he was one step ahead of the police, which seemed to please her.'

'Sounds like you might have a crazy on your hands,' said Townsend.

Sims blew his lips. 'That's exactly what I was thinking."

'It happens, mate. The high-profile cases do tend to bring out the nut-jobs, I'm afraid. Look. If it doesn't feel right, then just get out of there. You've still got plenty of copycat content for the next few weeks, and I'm sure more will come up before long.'

'Yeah. Sounds like a plan,' said Sims.

'Ok. But before you go anywhere, I've had the boss on the phone wanting to know when your poll on public safety and the effectiveness of the police is going live. I told him I thought you'd already done it earlier, but I've looked and there's nothing on the website or social media.'

'That's odd,' said Sims. 'I set it to go live from 8.30 this evening. I'll double-check it.'

'Ok, well, I've been in the office for long enough, so I'm going home now. If you need me for anything, call me on the mobile,' said Townsend.

'Will do. Thanks, Don.'

Sims hung up and attempted to login to his work profile remotely, but the 3G signal was pretty much non-existent inside the thick stone walls of the ancient pub. He glanced up at the ladies' toilet, wondering where Gabby had got to. If she *had* just gone for a piss, as she had claimed, then it was probably the longest wee ever. Checking his watch, he realised it was approaching 10 p.m. It had been a long day and, having worked all weekend, he'd run out of steam. With no sign of Gabby returning, he decided it was time to go. He had zero confidence his so-called source had anything of real value to tell him, so, grabbing his bag and coat, he slid out of the booth and headed for the door.

Once out in the car park, he checked his phone in the hope of finding a 3G signal. Finally, one bar appeared on the screen, and as he moved farther away from the building, it changed to two and eventually three. He quickly reopened the remote login window on his phone and double-clicked on the poll he had set up. Scrutinising the details for a moment, he soon realised his mistake: he'd keyed in a broadcast date of 8 p.m. tomorrow, instead of tonight. Cursing himself, he revised the date and set it live.

'Going somewhere?' asked the now-familiar voice from behind him.

Sims spun around to find Gabby staring at him. The leering look that filled her face sent a shiver down his spine. Without thinking, he stepped backwards. 'Erm, it's getting late. I think I'm gonna go.'

Gabby's eyes bored into him. 'But I haven't told you who the killer is yet, Lachlan.'

'Look, no offence, Gabby, but in the half hour that we've been here, you've talked a lot but actually told me very little. And, to be honest, it seems like this is all just a game for you.'

A snarl formed on Gabby's lip. 'You don't think I'm serious, Lachlan?'

Sims sensed Gabby's anger, and took another step backwards. 'Look, I'm just gonna go, ok? No hard feelings.'

Gabby stared at him in silence and nodded her head. 'I see,' she said, then lifted up her baggy jumper.

Sims's eyes were drawn to a huge combat knife wedged inside the top of her jeans.

'How serious is this?' asked Gabby, and yanked the knife out in one fluid movement and thrust it at Sims.

Before he could do anything, an ungodly pain exploded in his right leg. He screamed in agony as Gabby stepped closer and clamped a hand over his mouth to silence him, using her shoulder to hold him upright. The overwhelming pain made him want to vomit.

Gabby pulled the knife free before pushing him backwards. 'We're going for a little ride in my van, Lachlan.'

Unable to speak or cry out, he staggered backwards under Gabby's control. Everything was happening in a blur. He heard doors opening, then was forced backwards onto the hard metal floor of a foul-smelling van. A moment later, the doors slammed shut and he found himself entombed in darkness.

54

Phillips and the team stared at the large screen on the wall of the conference room as Entwistle continued to pull up information on Joanna Dennehy's crimes.

'So,' Carter ventured, 'if Anderson does copycat Dennehy, then by the looks of it, the next victim is likely to be male.'

'I'd say so, sir,' Phillips replied.

At that moment, Entwistle's phone beeped loudly, followed by Jones's and Bovalino's in close succession.

Phillips frowned as each of them checked their screens. 'Seriously, guys, can we stay focused here, please?'

'Sorry, Guv,' said Entwistle. 'It's a notification from Twitter. I set up an alert for any stories relating to the Copycat Killer.'

'He did the same for me,' said Jones.

'And me,' added Bov, holding his phone up so his screen was visible to the room.

Entwistle explained what he was looking at. 'It's a

Twitter poll that's just been posted by the MEN. It's asking how safe readers feel in Manchester with the Copycat Killer on the loose, and how well they think the police are handling the investigation.' He passed his phone over. 'There's already hundreds of comments. It doesn't make for good reading, Guv.'

Phillips began scrolling down through the live comments. 'Shit! This is a feeding frenzy!'

Carter's phone began to ring. He stepped up from his chair to answer it. 'Ma'am,' he said as he made his way out of the conference room.

'Looks like he's getting another bollocking from Fox,' said Jones.

'Believe me, he won't be the only one,' Phillips shot back.

Entwistle brought up the *Manchester Evening News*'s website on screen. 'The poll's running on their site too. Looks like Lachlan Sims is the journo behind it.'

'That little prick,' growled Phillips.

Carter opened the door, a grave look on his face. 'Jane, have you got a minute?'

She followed him out into the now-empty main office. 'I take it that was Fox, sir?'

'Correct, and she's *seriously* pissed off.' Carter let out a loud sigh. 'It seems she's just read the online article by Sims, and taken exception to the fact he's suggesting the force has gone backwards since she took over as chief constable and I became chief super of Major Crimes. Seems she's blaming me and you for the fact Sims has singled her out.'

'Oh, God. That's all we need.'

'I thought Townsend had put a leash on Sims?' said Carter.

'Knowing Don, he will have tried, but he also said the editor was actively encouraging Sims to make as much noise as possible about the Copycat Killer to drive more click-bait.'

'Seriously, Jane, we need to get a hold of this, and quickly. Fox is looking for a neck for the noose, and I can feel it tightening around *mine* with every hour that passes.'

'Probably mine, too. I'll call Don now and find out what the hell's going on. See if there's any way we can mitigate some of this shit.'

Phillips pulled up Townsend's number and headed for her office. His phone rang for about thirty seconds until the voicemail greeting kicked in. Phillips tried again with the same result. 'Jesus, Don. Answer the bloody phone!'

She tried a third time.

Finally, he answered. *'Sorry I missed you, Jane. I was getting petrol and left my phone in the car. Everything ok?'*

'No it's bloody not, Don,' spat Phillips, as she paced around her office. 'That little shit who works for you has just made my job a hundred times harder.'

'I work with a lot of little shits,' joked Townsend. *'You'll have to be more specific.'*

Phillips wasn't in the mood. 'Sims, and that bloody poll he's just put out online. Fox has seen it and is going mental. The comments alone are bad enough, but it seems Sims has suggested Fox's leadership isn't as good as that of Chief Constable Morris.'

'Oh, dear. I didn't know he'd done that.'

'I thought y*ou* were his boss, Don? Don't you check his articles?'

'Ordinarily, yes, but the editor has taken a shine to him at the moment and he's proofing everything to do with the

Copycat Killer. I'm just watching from the sidelines like a spare dick at a wedding.'

'It's not funny, Don. We need to get this stuff under control. My team is spending every waking minute trying to catch this guy, and shit like this not only batters the morale of an already exhausted team, but it riles up the public and makes us look incompetent.'

'I know. I know. I'm sorry, Jane.'

'Can you send me Sims's mobile number? I want to talk to him myself.'

'I'll be home in fifteen minutes. I'll ping it over to you then,' said Townsend.

'As quick as you can, Don. I'm gonna make sure the little bastard won't be printing anything else about us in hurry.'

'Ok, Jane. And look, I know you're angry, but try not to be too hard on Sims. He's young and just trying to make a name for himself. We've all been there. Plus, he's had his fingers burned tonight with a source who claimed to have information on the Copycat Killer, but turned out to be nut-job, so he'll be feeling a bit wounded right now.'

'What source?' asked Phillips.

'He took a call from a guy this evening who said he knew who the Copycat Killer was. It turns out it was the same person he spoke to before your press conference, the one that put him onto the copycat theory in the first place.'

'Go on.'

'So, this guy calls into the office tonight about 8, saying he would give Sims the name of the killer in exchange for a few grand cash.'

'And your junior reporter didn't think to call and share this information with us, with a serial killer on the loose?' Phillips was struggling to keep her cool.

'To be fair, Sims did ask why he wasn't passing that information over to the police, but the guy said you'd bury it. He wanted to make as much noise as possible, as well as a few quid. We're journalists, Jane. It's in our DNA to get as much of the story as we can before handing it over to you lot.'

'So, what happened?'

'Turns out the source was just a wannabe and a bit strange, by all accounts.'

'In what way strange?'

Townsend chuckled. 'Well, it seems he came dressed as a woman, sporting a huge facial tattoo and calling himself Gabby.'

Phillips stopped pacing.

Townsend continued. 'It seems the guy said nothing about the killer the whole time they were together, and instead spent all his time talking about you and how you were handling the investigation.'

'Did you say the source had a facial tattoo?'

'Yeah. Homemade, apparently.'

Phillips marched back towards the conference room. 'Did Sims tell you what kind of tattoo?' She opened the door and stepped inside.

'A star, I think.'

Phillips stared at the historical mugshot of Dennehy on the big screen in front of her. The face of evil stared back, complete with a star tattoo on her cheek. 'Don. Sims is in danger!'

Everyone in the room turned and stared at her.

'What do you mean he's in danger?' asked Townsend.

Phillips pressed on. 'Where is Sims now?'

'He was at The White Horse pub in Woodford when I

spoke to him about ten minutes ago, but he said he was gonna head home.'

'I need you to hang up and call him immediately. The person you've described as his source could well be the killer, and Sims his next victim.'

'You what?'

'I don't have time to explain, Don. Just call him and tell him to get the fuck out of there.'

'I'll do it now.' Townsend's voice was laced with panic.

A sea of expectant faces greeted Phillips as she ended the call. 'That was Don Townsend. He's just told me Lachlan Sims met a man tonight who was dressed as a woman, with a large facial tattoo of a star on their face – just like Dennehy's.' Phillips pointed to the face on the screen. 'The person claimed to know who the Copycat Killer was, and lured Sims to The White Horse pub in Woodford. Called herself *Gabby*. We have to assume this person is actually Gabriel Anderson dressed up as Dennehy, and that Sims could be our next victim. I want the nearest uniformed patrol unit over to that pub immediately.'

'I'm on it!' said Jones, picking up the internal phone.

'Tell them to look out for the transit van, or anyone leaving the pub that looks like Joanna Dennehy. Share her mugshot with control. They need to be discreet and watch from a distance until we get there. We want to catch Anderson, not spook him.'

Jones nodded and made the call to Control.

Phillips threw her car keys at Bovalino. 'We need to get Woodford yesterday, Bov, so you're driving.'

55

Gabe could hear the groans coming from Sims in the back of the van. He hadn't planned to stab him at the pub; he'd lost his cool and it had just happened. He was annoyed at his momentary lapse in concentration, but at the same time, his plan was still in play and he was even closer to the end game now. The incident with Sims had merely accelerated the timeline.

The dark country road that led away from Woodford was mercifully quiet. As impatient as he was to reach his final destination as quickly as possible, he forced himself to stick to the speed limit. He was too close to the end now to mess it all up by drawing unnecessary attention to himself.

In an attempt to settle his racing mind, he switched on the radio and quickly flicked through the glut of so-called hit music channels until he found Classic FM. A live orchestral version of Vivaldi's 'Four Seasons' was playing, and he recognised the dark, foreboding sounds of Winter. How apt, he thought, and smiled to himself. A few moments later, as he rounded the next bend, he spotted a car heading towards him and switched his headlights from full beam to normal so as not to dazzle the oncoming driver. As the car drew closer, he realised it was a police patrol car. His pulse quickened. Holding his breath, he stared ahead and tried his best to appear non-plussed and natural. As soon as it had passed by, he fixed his gaze on his wing mirrors, watching as it continued on away from him. He exhaled loudly and celebrated his good fortune, but his relief was short-lived when his attention was drawn to a flash of brake lights in his mirrors. To his horror, the car stopped, then turned around.

'Shit!' he said to himself, trying remain calm as the car began to follow him.

On the radio, the classical music rose, building towards its crescendo. It only added to his anxiety and sense of foreboding. 'I can't hear myself think!' he growled, and switched it off.

Checking his mirrors, he saw the patrol car drawing closer. His mind raced. Had they recognised the van? Were they following him? Had someone seen him stab Sims in the car park and called it in? *Or* was it as simple as the patrol car was needed back in the direction it had just come from? He checked the speedometer; he was doing 55mph on a stretch where the limit was 60. Not too fast, and not too slow.

'Come on. Pass me, pass me,' he muttered under his breath as the patrol car sat behind him, matching his speed.

He began to consider what he would do if they did try to stop him. There was absolutely no doubt in his mind he would finish what he started – *no matter what it took*. He considered trying to outrun them, but he knew full well there was little chance he could lose a virtually brand-new police car in this old banger. There was the possibility he could charm his way out of it. Had he been dressed as Dr Anderson, he'd have stood a chance, but tonight, dressed and looking as he did, would make it all the more difficult.

The blue lights of the patrol car began flashing in his mirror, followed by a single whoop of the siren, indicating they wanted him to pull over.

'Fuck!' he yelled as he contemplated making a run for it once again. But he knew that would only attract more cops, which was the last thing he wanted.

A sudden sense of clarity, followed by calm, washed over him. He knew exactly what he had to do. He began to slow the van down before pulling it off onto the side of the road, where he stopped.

He watched in the left wing mirror as one of the officers approached his passenger door, then tapped on the window.

Gabe leaned across and wound it down. 'I wasn't speeding was I, officer? I'm sure this is a sixty on here?'

The officer stared at him, his expression deadpan. 'Is this your vehicle?'

'No. It's my dad's, actually. You might know him. He used to be one of your lot,' Gabe said, with forced levity.

'Can I see your license?'

'Er, I don't have it with me, I'm afraid. It's at home.'

'I see, sir. Would you mind showing me what you've got in the back, please?'

'Can I ask why?'

'It's just procedure.'

Reluctantly, Gabe got out of the van and, a moment later, arrived at the rear doors, where the first policeman had been joined by his female partner. Both officers carried torches in their right hands, and each did a double take when Gabe's full appearance became clear under the car's headlights.

'Open up, please,' said the male officer.

'There's nothing in here,' said Gabe.

'Well, you won't mind us having a look then, will you?' said the female officer.

Gabe shrugged and turned his back to them as he grabbed the door handle with his left hand and began opening the door slowly. His right hand was positioned close to the knife he'd secreted in his jeans.

At that moment, a call came over the radios attached to the officers' chests. *'Control to all units. Is anyone available to attend The White Horse pub in Woodford urgently?'*

The two officers glanced at each other before the female responded. 'Control, this is Alpha Bravo Five. Go ahead.'

'Alpha Bravo Five, Major Crimes urgently request a patrol team to monitor a suspect thought to be travelling in a dark Mark II Ford transit van. The driver is believed to be armed and very dangerous—'

Before the operator had even finished his sentence, Gabe made his move. In a flash, he unleashed the large blade at lightning speed, thrusting it sideways into the male officer's armpit, just above his stab vest. Screaming in agony, the man dropped to the ground like a stone. The female officer panicked as she fumbled for her taser, but was no match for Gabe as he rushed headlong at her, lifting her off her feet before slamming her down onto the bonnet of the car. Winded, she tried to call out, but was silenced as he rammed the back of her head onto the bonnet repeatedly until she stopped moving. Stepping back, he watched as she slipped off the car like a ragdoll and onto the road. Gabe turned back to the male officer, who was lying on the ground, moaning. The glow of the headlights cast a metallic sheen to the dark blood pooling around his torso.

Wasting no time, Gabe opened the back doors to the van. Then, grabbing the male officer by his stab vest, he dragged him along the rough road, leaving a shimmering trail of blood in the dirt. The officer was pretty much a dead weight, and it took all of Gabe's strength to pull him up and into the van. He laid him down next to Sims, who was now unconscious, but still breathing.

Throughout the melee, both radios had continued to fire off messages. The operator sounded anxious, having received no further response from the pair. *'Control to Alpha Bravo Five. Come in, Alpha Bravo Five.'*

Gabe removed the male officer's radio and pushed it into his pocket as he jumped down from the back of the van. Closing the doors, he moved quickly back to the cab and, a moment later, screeched away at speed.

His plan was on track and his final destination so close, he could taste it.

56

With Bovalino at the wheel, Phillips in the passenger seat and Jones in the back of the car, they raced towards Woodford at breakneck speed under blues and twos, the siren blaring as they snaked through the inner-city traffic. As soon as they reached the country lanes, they would go silent so as not to alert Anderson to the fact they were chasing him down.

A few minutes prior, Townsend had called with an update on Sims who, it seemed, was no longer answering his phone. She was also still awaiting confirmation on which patrol team had been dispatched to The White Horse. Phillips's impatience was mounting.

Grabbing the car radio, she connected through to Control. 'Control, this is Mike Charlie One en route to Woodford. Can I get an ID on the first responder team for The White Horse?'

She waited a moment.

'Mike Charlie One, this is Control. Alpha Bravo Five

responded a few minutes ago, but have since gone silent. I've been trying to reach them, but nothing is coming back.'

'What was their location when they responded?' asked Phillips.

'They didn't get chance to say. They were the first to answer the alert and asked for details, which I relayed. But then they didn't reply.'

'Is that normal for Alpha Bravo Five?'

'*Not at all.*'

Phillips's gut told her this was somehow connected to Anderson.

'*Hang on, Mike Charlie One,*' said the operator. '*I have something coming in from Alpha Bravo Five now.*'

'Patch them through to the open channel so I can talk to them,' ordered Phillips.

'*Doing it now, Ma'am. You have control.*'

A moment later, a faint female voice came through the car speakers. '*This is Alpha Bravo Five. Officers down, I repeat, officers down.*'

'Alpha Bravo Five, this is Detective Chief Inspector Phillips from Major Crimes. What is your location?'

'*One mile east of Woodford on Church Lane, Ma'am.*'

'And what is your situation?'

'*Officer Hastings has been stabbed in the chest and driven away in a van.*'

'What van?

'*I think it's the one everyone's been looking for. A Ford transit. We stopped it because it appeared suspicious and asked to look in the back. As we were in the process of doing that, the call came through from Control asking us to look out for the exact same vehicle. Before we could respond, the driver attacked us.*'

'Are you injured?'

'*Just a few cuts and bruises. He attacked Hastings first, so I went for my taser, but he was too fast. He beat me up and knocked me out.*'
'*Can you describe your attacker?*'
'*He had a man's voice but was dressed like a woman.*'
'Did he have a facial tattoo?'
'*Yes, a large star on his cheek.*'
Phillips closed the radio link for moment. 'Shit. It's Anderson.'
'He can't be thinking of killing a copper, surely?' said Jones.
'Can't he?' replied Phillips. 'Like Harris said, he's escalating with each kill.'
Jones's face fell. 'Jesus, Guv. We can't let that happen.'
Phillips opened the radio link once more. 'Alpha Bravo Five. Which way was the suspect heading when you stopped him?'
'*East.*'
'Ok. Stay where you are. We're on our way. We'll get a paramedic out to you as soon as we can.'
'*I'm sorry, Ma'am, I tried to stop him, but he was too strong.*'
'You've got nothing to be sorry for. In fact, you're lucky to be alive.'
Phillips turned her attention back to Control. 'Control, we need all units to be on the lookout for the suspect's vehicle. I want updates as they come in. Any units responding are to follow the suspect at a distance. They must under no circumstances engage. He is armed and highly dangerous. And, Control, I want helicopter support from X-Ray Eleven as well as the TFU, right now!'
'*Yes, Ma'am.*'
Phillips closed the radio link.

'Where to, Guv?' asked Bovalino.

'Head towards Church Lane. He can't have got too far from there in that shitty old van. I'm praying that once the helicopter is up, we can get a more accurate idea of his position.'

Bovalino nodded, and hammered the accelerator.

57

He'd been expecting it, of course, having heard Phillips give the order twenty minutes ago over the copper's radio. However, the police helicopter had arrived quicker than he'd planned for, the thunderous growl of the rotor blades pressing down on him from above, along with the white light from the enormous spotlight, which lit up the dark country roads like a football stadium. The helicopter was not his only companion, as two patrol cars followed, matching his considerable speed, tucked in behind his van. He'd seen this kind of thing on TV a hundred times before: a suspect involved in a high-speed chase with myriad police cars in pursuit, his every move being watched from the dark sky above. Tonight was different, though. He was aware of that. Thanks to Phillips's desire to catch him herself, he'd heard with glee that every officer in the Greater Manchester Police had been ordered to maintain a safe distance. To watch, observe and follow, but not engage with the armed and highly dangerous suspect.

He allowed himself a smile. He was almost done. All he had to do was stay ahead of the tenacious DCI Phillips for just another fifteen minutes or so, and he could complete his plan. Tonight, at last, he would cement his own notoriety whilst tearing down Bert Anderson's oh-so-precious legacy. Just a little farther, he thought, checking his wing mirrors for any signs of Phillips and her team.

As he raced through the winding country lanes, he could hear the two men rolling around in the back of the van, banging up against the metal sides with each turn. Despite his years as a doctor – which *had* included the occasional shift in accident and emergency – he had never had cause to deal with a stab wound, which meant that at this moment in time, he had no idea whether either Sims or the officer were still alive. Again, it didn't matter. The plan had always been to kill Sims and another male victim, just like Dennehy had done. He'd got lucky with the cop, saving him the time it would have taken to hunt down a second man on the street.

But was it really luck? Or was it his destiny?

He smiled at the thought and accelerated, taking the van up to a trembling 73mph. Any higher and he risked the old girl falling apart. His mind was drawn to the closing scenes of *The Blues Brothers*, where the faithful old black and white sedan finally gave up the ghost, crumbling into pieces as Jake and Elwood jump out and make the final leg of their journey on foot in order to complete their mission from God. By complete contrast, he was certain his divine guidance came from somewhere entirely different.

At last, he could see the signs for the old farm up ahead; only half a mile to go.

His eyes were drawn now to the flashing lights of an

unmarked car approaching from the rear at speed. He was pretty sure its siren was whooping, but if it was, it was drowned out by the noise of the helicopter overhead. Whoever was driving was determined to pass the patrol cars. *Phillips.* He turned up the police radio in the hope of an update on her position, then pressed the accelerator flat to the floor, pushing the van harder and harder.

'Come on, girl! You can do it. Come on!' he yelled as he edged closer to the gateway to the farmland.

A few minutes later, he slammed on the brakes, then dragged the van off the road and onto the bumpy old track. He checked his mirrors as, behind him, the driver of the unmarked car expertly drifted before pulling off the road and through the gate at high speed. If it was Phillips behind the wheel, she was one hell of a driver.

The helicopter's spotlight followed him as he lurched up and down at speed along the rough terrain. At last he could see the final destination up ahead, resplendent in all its glory, bathed in white light from above. He smiled to himself as he listened to Phillips's every word over the radio. She was desperate to know where he was headed, but not one of those idiot coppers had a single clue. Fighting the large, heavy steering wheel, he abruptly pulled the van off the track and into the field, then surged towards the huge drainage ditch up ahead. After the heavy rain of recent days, the ground was waterlogged and incredibly muddy. A few seconds later, the van's wheels began to spin, and it shuddered to a stop.

There was no time to waste. He leapt from the cab and dropped down into the thick mud, which enveloped his boots like glue. His steps were laboured as he made his way to the back of the van, glancing back to the road where police car after police car was turning down the track and heading straight for his position.

His heart raced as adrenaline coursed through every fibre. He yanked open the back doors and climbed inside.

58

Bovalino raced along the bumpy track after Anderson.

'Where the hell's he going?' shouted Jones from the back seat. 'And what's he planning on doing in a bloody great field?'

Whatever it was – considering Anderson's previous murders – Phillips didn't believe they'd arrived at this location by chance.

Since the pilot had spotted Anderson's transit ten minutes ago, Phillips had been in direct contact with him. She connected with him now. 'X-Ray Eleven, this is Mike Charlie One. Can you see where the suspect is headed?'

There was a momentary pause. *'This is X-Ray Eleven. The track leads to outbuildings about half a click away. They appear to be stables of some kind.'*

Phillips wracked her brain for anything in Dennehy's history of crimes that involved such a location.

'Jesus! What's he doing now?' shouted Bov. Up ahead, Anderson's van swung violently off the track and into the thick mud of the adjacent field. 'I can't take this in there, Guv. We'll get bogged in seconds!'

They skidded to a halt.

The helicopter hovered overhead, illuminating the field to their right. All three of them leapt out of the squad car and watched as the transit tried in vain to navigate the thick mud. It ground to a halt no more than a hundred yards away, the tyres spinning violently, throwing up lumps of muck but getting nowhere.

'This is X-Ray Eleven,' said the pilot a moment later. 'The suspect is out of the vehicle and on foot. I repeat, the suspect is out of the vehicle and on foot.'

'We can't lose him!' shouted Phillips as she prepared to give chase, but halted when she saw Anderson move awkwardly through the mud towards the back of the van. He opened the doors and climbed in before pulling them closed behind him.

Farther back down the track, two four-wheel-drive vehicles approached at speed, sirens whooping and lights flashing.

'TFU, Guv,' said Jones.

Phillips kept her eyes locked on the van. A minute later, the BMW X5s came to a halt nearby, casting the area in alternating blue and red light.

Sergeant Roy Matthews was once again the senior officer. 'What have we got, Ma'am?' he yelled, doing his best to be heard above the helicopter's rotor blades.

Phillips pointed to the van bogged in the mud, locked in the spotlights from overhead. 'Anderson's holed up inside with two potential victims, one of which is a police officer,' she shouted back.

'Is the suspect armed?'

'We think so. We know he has a knife, but as to what else, we have no idea.'

'In that case, we should set up a sniper team,' said Matthews.

Phillips agreed.

Matthews moved to brief his men, who immediately jumped into action.

Phillips returned her gaze to the van. 'What are you planning, Anderson?' she muttered.

It started to rain, a few drops at first, and then the heavens unleashed a torrent of water. Up ahead, the back door of the van opened without warning, and Lachlan Sims appeared. He was being held from behind by Anderson, a huge combat knife locked against his throat. Anderson nudged Sims carefully out into the mud, then slowly moved out after him, his head and torso in almost perfect alignment with his hostage's.

Matthews's snipers were in position, but because Anderson was so close to Sims, there was no clear shot.

Clever bastard, thought Phillips.

Sims limped heavily, very unsteady on his feet. Anderson appeared to be in no rush, holding Sims from behind as he moved in unison, edging sideways and staying out of the snipers' sights. As they reached the side of the van, Anderson began to step backwards, clutching Sims closer still.

Something flashed into Phillips's mind about the Dennehy murders. Rushing back to the car, she jumped in the passenger seat and closed the door to block out the noise, then grabbed the radio. 'X-Ray Eleven, this is Mike Charlie One. What can you see beyond the van? From where we are, it looks like the brow of a hill. What's behind that hill?'

'*This is X-Ray Eleven. It looks like a drainage ditch of some kind. But if that's his escape route, he'll struggle to get through it. The water level appears very high.*'

Phillips recalled Entwistle's briefing on Dennehy earlier that evening: at the time of her arrest, Dennehy had been nicknamed the Peterborough Ditch Murderer – because she dumped the bodies of her first two victims in drainage ditches outside the Cambridgeshire city. 'X-Ray Eleven. How far away is the ditch from the suspect's position, now?'

'*About forty feet.*'

Phillips leapt from the car and shouted to Jones and Bovalino, 'There's a drainage ditch on the other side of that hill. He's gonna kill Sims and throw him in it, like Dennehy.' Without waiting, she raced to Matthews's position. 'Can you get a shot?'

'No, Ma'am. He's tucked in right behind the hostage. If we shoot, we could kill them both.'

As Jones and Bovalino appeared at her side, Phillips turned back to face Sims and Anderson, still moving slowly backwards through the mud. She was certain that as soon as Anderson crested that hill, Sims was as good as dead. She also knew that if they went in after him, mob-handed, Anderson wouldn't hesitate to slit Sims's throat before they could reach him. In that moment, she felt completely helpless, bereft of ideas.

'Guv, if TFU can't get a shot, we should go in after him!' Jones shouted in her ear.

'It's too risky. As soon as he feels threatened, he'll kill Sims.'

'So what else can we do?'

Phillips stared at the two men moving backwards through the field, ever closer to the brow of the hill and almost certain death for Sims. Suddenly, she knew exactly what she had to do. She turned to Jones and Bovalino. 'It's *me* he's been playing games with. *My* attention he seems to crave. I'm going in.'

'No way!' Jones protested. 'Not again, Guv.'

'We can't let you do that, boss,' added Bovalino.

'We don't have a choice. Every murder so far has been an exact copy of the historical crime. This time he's copying Joanna Dennehy. She stabbed her victims and threw them in a ditch. That's exactly what he's gonna do now. I *have* to go in alone. It's the only way Sims is coming out alive. Plus, one of our own is lying in the back of that van, probably bleeding to death. We can't wait any longer.'

'So how do you plan on stopping him all by yourself?' asked Jones.

'I'll talk him down. Make him see sense.'

Jones continued, 'And what if this has been Anderson's plan all along? To draw you out so he could kill you?'

'I don't believe it is. He's a stickler for detail, and Dennehy never attacked women. Only men. And besides, if he does come after me, at least the TFU have the chance at a clear shot.' She offered a weak smile, but in truth, she was terrified. 'We need to hurry. Get me a stab vest and get rid of that bloody helicopter. I need to be able to talk to him.'

THE FIELD FELL EERILY quiet as the helicopter moved higher into the sky. Search lights from the TFU vehicles had replaced the spotlight from overhead, so the ground remained illuminated.

Having pulled on her wellies from the boot of the car, and with a stab vest secured around her torso, Phillips raised her arms in surrender and stepped off the track and into the mud, moving slowly in the direction of the van.

Up ahead, about twenty yards beyond the stranded vehicle, Anderson stopped and pulled the knife tighter to Sims's throat. 'Stay where you are!' he shouted to Phillips.

Stopping for a second, she kept her hands in the air. 'I just want to talk, Gabriel.'

'You must think I'm bloody stupid or something.'

'I'm unarmed. I just want to talk. Please, Gabriel. No one wants to hurt you.'

'Well then, tell them to put down their weapons.'

'If I tell them to do that, can I come a bit closer?' asked Phillips.

Anderson glanced at the team of men, rifles at the ready, and nodded. 'Ok.'

Keeping her hands in the air, Phillips turned to face the team behind her. 'Everyone, drop your weapons.'

Matthews and his men didn't respond.

'Do it now!' roared Phillips. 'That's an order.'

This time, the team reluctantly complied.

Phillips turned back around and worked her way through the sticky mud until she was within ten feet of Anderson.

'That's close enough!' Anderson shouted.

Phillips stood still.

Sims groaned weakly, and Anderson pulled the blade tighter against his throat. 'One more sound out of you and you're a dead man,' he growled in his ear.

From her position, she could see that Sims was in a lot of pain and still losing blood from a deep gash in his left thigh. His skin appeared ashen in the spotlights, his clothes soaked from the torrential rain. Anderson, on the other hand, looked surreal with his beanie, long hair and facial tattoo, his wide eyes almost black. He was totally unrecognisable from the quiet, unassuming doctor Phillips had met at the Manchester Central Surgery just a few weeks ago.

'Detective Chief Inspector Phillips,' Anderson leered. 'I've been looking forward to this.'

'Do you mind if I put my arms down? They're killing me,' said Phillips.

'No pun intended,' Anderson chuckled to himself.

Phillips ignored him. 'Lachlan needs urgent medical attention, Gabriel.'

'Not where he's going, he doesn't.'

'And where exactly is that?'

Anderson nodded backwards, behind him. 'In the ditch.'

'Why do you want to do that?'

'Because that's how this ends, Jane.'

Phillips paused and stared deep into his wild eyes. 'How *what* ends?'

'*The game*, of course. Which I am winning.'

'Why is winning this game of yours so important to you, Gabriel?'

'Call me Gabe.'

'If that's what you want, Gabe. So, please, tell me why winning is so important to you?'

Anderson's face twisted with rage. 'Because I've been as loser my whole life! Constantly told I'm weak. Not good enough. Pathetic.'

'Who told you that?'

'Him! That bastard!'

'Who, Gabe? Tell me who said those things to you, Gabe.' She deliberately repeated his name in an attempt to build a rapport.

'My father, of course. That vicious, nasty piece of

work. From the moment my mother died, it started. "You're not good enough. You're a useless piece of shit."' Anderson began imitating his father. "'Why did your mother die and *you* get to live? You're a pathetic boy! A total fucking loser!" Well, I showed him, didn't I? He's not laughing now. Mr High-and-Mighty Detective Sergeant Sonny. The man who cared more about total bloody strangers than his own son. Well, at least that's what I thought I was, until he revealed his big secret a few days ago!'

Phillips frowned as the image of Bert's maggot-infested body – dead for at least a month – flashed in her mind's eye. 'What do you mean, his big secret?'

'He finally told me the truth. Finally came clean about why he's despised me for so long.'

'What did he tell you?'

'It turns out that, after crying myself to sleep as a child, night after night, year after year, wondering what I'd done to deserve the beatings, the insults, the mental abuse, I'm not even his fucking son. My saint of a mother wasn't such a saint, after all. She had an affair, and *I* was the result.'

'You said your father told you this a few days ago. Where was that?'

'At home. In bed. Barking his orders, as usual. Telling me what a shit son I am, how I'm never there. That he could die and I wouldn't care.' Anderson pointed at himself. 'I spend most of my life at that house. I have a baby boy I never see because of him.'

'Why, Gabe? Why are you always at Bert's house?'

'Taking care of him, of course. The stubborn old shit got cancer, but refused to get treatment in hospital. Doesn't trust doctors after Mum died in hospital, so I've had to look after him at home, sorting out his bed baths, turning him to avoid bed sores, feeding him, even syphoning off extra morphine from all the different practices I work at to ease his pain. How dare he tell me I don't care? I'm the only fucking reason he's still alive.'

Phillips's eyes narrowed. 'Gabe. Your father's dead.'

Anderson laughed nervously. 'Why would you say that?'

'I'm telling you, Gabe. He's dead.'

'You're lying.'

'I'm not, I promise you.'

Anderson scoffed. 'What? So he died in the last few hours, did he? *How convenient.*'

'No, he didn't. In fact, our forensic team believe he died over a month ago.'

Anderson's lip began to tremble as he pulled the knife back against Sims's throat. 'You're lying!'

Phillips raised her palms in surrender. 'You don't need to do that.'

'You're lying, deliberately trying to fuck with my head.'

Phillips's mind flashed to the images on her phone of Bert's ravaged dead body. If she showed him them, would they cut through his delusion, or would they just worsen the situation, make him even more volatile? She decided it was worth the risk.

'I can prove I'm not lying, Gabe. I can prove that your father's dead. If you'll let me.'

Anderson's eyes darted between Phillips and the rest of the officers, who remained in position a hundred yards back on the track.

'My phone is in the right pocket of my coat. I'm going to pull it out,' she said calmly.

Anderson pulled the knife even farther back against Sims's throat. 'It's a trick. You've got a weapon in there!'

Phillips remained stoic. 'It's not a trick, Gabe. I'm right-handed, so I'm going to use the fingers on my left hand and pull it out slowly from my right pocket. That way, there'll be no sudden movements, I promise.'

Anderson paused, then eventually nodded. 'Slowly. But anything funny, I'll cut Sims from ear to ear.'

Phillips reached across her torso with her left hand and slowly pulled out the phone from the opposite pocket. 'See. I meant what I said, Gabe—' She held it lightly in her fingers. '—no funny business. I just want to show you some pictures of your father.'

Anderson nodded again.

Phillips carefully moved the phone to her right hand, keyed in the password, and opened up the photos she'd taken of Bert's body just a few hours ago. She turned the screen so Anderson could see it. 'We believe that this is the body of Bert Anderson, discovered by me and my team at his home this afternoon. Just after you fled.'

Anderson blinked furiously as his mouth fell open. Once again, he tightened his grip on the knife against Sims's neck, but his hostage remained silent, his breathing laboured.

'They're fake! I just spoke to him today.'

'No you didn't, Gabe. Look at the picture again. Look at the bed, the TV, the chest of drawers, the unopened packets of cigarettes. That's your dad's room in the basement of his house, and that's your dad's body attached to the IVs and oxygen that *you* set up. Look at his wedding ring. If it's faked, then where's the living, breathing Bert who normally occupies that bed?'

'You've kidnapped him!'

'No we haven't, Gabe. This isn't Hollywood. We're the Greater Manchester Police. We don't kidnap people.'

Anderson stared at her in silence.

'I need you to listen to me *very* carefully. You're not well. Gabe. Our experts think you may have had a breakdown, which means you're suffering from delusions. Your mind has been playing tricks on you. All those abusive conversations with your dad in the last month, filled with hate and ridicule, they weren't real. *None of it was real.*'

Anderson seemed to wince in pain as the words landed.

'Trust me, Gabe. For the sake of your son Noah, and how he'll think of his dad when he's all grown up, you really need to try and understand what I'm telling you.'

A flicker of recognition passed across Anderson's face at the mention of his son's name.

Phillips spotted it; the chink in the armour she needed.

'This persona you've been living the last few weeks – the Copycat Killer – that's *not* Noah's dad. And neither is the little boy who suffered all that abuse dished out by Bert. Noah's dad is *Dr Gabriel Anderson*. A man who saved lives, not took them.'

Anderson's grip on the knife began to soften.

Phillips pressed on. 'It's time to stop the killing, Gabe. For Noah's sake. Put the knife down and let Lachlan go so we can save his life, and the life of Officer Hastings, lying bleeding in your van.'

Anderson shook his head. He took a step back and released his grip on Sims, who dropped to his knees, then fell sideways into the wet mud.

Phillips raised her right hand in clenched fist, signalling to the TFU to hold their positions. 'It's finished, Gabe. Nobody else needs to die.'

Anderson moved his gaze to Phillips. His eyes appeared totally different now, and his face was suddenly soft and full of remorse. Staring down at the knife in his hand, he began to weep. 'Oh my God. What have I done?' He dropped to his knees next to Sims.

In that instant, Phillips rushed towards Anderson and grabbed the knife. He didn't flinch. Instead, he sobbed like a child, the rain soaking his heaving body. Even the sounds of the TFU team rushing towards him made no difference. He remained on his knees, eyes closed as he wept and moaned.

A moment later, he was secured in cuffs by the TFU, pulled to his feet and frog-marched back towards the awaiting patrol cars.

Phillips grabbed her radio. 'We have two men in urgent need of medical assistance.' She took a knee next to Sims and felt for his pulse.

Jones and Bovalino appeared a split second later.

'I think Sims is in shock. We need to get him to a hospital,' she said. 'Bov, check the back of the van for Officer Hastings.'

As Bovalino moved quickly through the mud to the vehicle, Jones dropped to his haunches and removed his coat before placing it over Sims in an effort to keep him warm. 'Jesus, Guv. How the hell did you get Anderson to give himself up?'

Phillips locked eyes with Jones through her rain-soaked glasses. 'I just appealed to the man, Jonesy, instead of trying to fight the monster. None of us are born evil. Sadly, that's just one of the unwelcome gifts of a fucked-up life.'

59

THURSDAY, MARCH 18TH

Carter placed the drinks on the table and dropped into the booth opposite Phillips. It was their second after-work drink at the Metropolitan Pub in as many weeks.

Phillips smiled as she took a sip of her Pinot Grigio. 'You need to be careful, sir, meeting strange women in pubs. People will talk.'

Carter chortled. 'Just one strange woman, Jane, and I think it's time you called me Harry away from the team.'

The wine was already beginning to relax Phillips, a feeling that had deserted her in the last five weeks as they pursued Anderson, the so-called Copycat Killer. She felt good as she set her glass down on the table between them. 'So, how's things with Mrs Carter?'

He took a swig from his pint of lager. 'Softening.'

'How so?'

'Well, she's getting fed up of being at her mum's. As much as they adore each other, looking after the twins under the watchful eye of a "mother who knows best" is starting to grate on Fran. The falling-outs are happening on a daily basis now. So, I'm pretty sure she'll be coming back in the next week or two. Then it's down to me to try and be at home a bit more.'

Phillips nodded. 'Which is all very well and good until someone like Anderson comes along and bodies start turning up left, right and centre.'

'True,' said Carter. 'And on the subject of Anderson, how's the psych evaluation going?'

'Too early to say. It's only been a couple of days, but, based on Harris's view of him, my guess is he'll plead temporary insanity brought on by the trauma of his father's death.'

'Which, according to Chakrabortty, *he* actually caused by pumping him full of morphine!' Carter added.

'It does certainly look that way, but proving it is another matter. Anderson's the only one who knows what really happened to his father, and mentally, he's completely shut down. Even though his fingerprints are all over his wife's throat, he refuses to believe he killed her, or that she's actually dead.'

'Could just be a convenient excuse?'

'Yeah, maybe, but whatever happens, he's never going to be allowed to walk free. If he is deemed fit to stand trial, we've enough evidence to bury him. If not, then he'll end up in Broadmoor for the rest of his days.'

Carter took another mouthful of lager. 'Your preliminary report mentioned Anderson was linked to the second victim, before they met in the pub, through his son. How so?'

'Yeah. Entwistle was working through the family's history when he spotted Noah had been admitted to the children's ward at Wythenshawe Hospital with jaundice, not long after he was born. Turns out one of the nurses who cared for him was Gillian Galloway.'

Carter shook his head. 'Why kill someone who looked after your own baby?'

'Who knows what was going on in his mind, but it does at least explain why Galloway didn't do a runner when Anderson turned up at the pub for their Tinder date – as opposed to Conrad, the beach bum.'

'Speaking of his family, what will happen to his son?'

'Social Services say Jodie's sister has flown in from Australia. She's applying for official custody as we speak. He can grow up in a normal family, far away from Manchester and the crimes of his father.'

'Sounds like the best place for him.' Carter's glass was now empty. 'Top up?' he asked, stepping out from the booth.

'No. I'm good with this for now, thanks, but I could murder some crisps.'

'What flavour?'

'Surprise me,' said Phillips with a grin.

Carter returned a few minutes later with a fresh pint and a couple of packets of crisps. 'Hardly the greatest selection, so I've got ready salted or cheese and onion.'

Phillips expertly opened both bags so they lay flat on the table. 'Let's share,' she said, popping a couple in her mouth.

Just then, her phone beeped. She checked it and smiled.

'Everything ok?'

'Yeah it is, actually. I've set up a Facebook group for my old school friends. It's a fundraiser to organise a memorial bench for Mr Yates. He always loved Chorlton Water Park. Used to spend hours and hours fishing there. So we're going to see if we can get the council to let us put in a bench for him, down near the water.'

'Sounds lovely. And if anyone can get the council on board, it's the well-respected DCI Phillips of the Major Crimes Unit, right?'

Phillips smiled as she picked up a couple of finger-fulls of crisps. 'Something like that.'

Silence descended for a moment, until Phillips broke it. 'And how is Mein Fuhrer? Cheered up, yet?'

Carter giggled. 'Fox?'

Phillips nodded as she chewed.

'She's cockahoop, actually.'

'Well, that's a first.'

'Rumour has it she's up for the Queen's Medal in the New Year's Honours list for her part in the investigation.'

Phillips closed her eyes and shook her head. 'What the fuck for? She didn't do anything. Well, apart from dish out bollockings, that is.'

'You know Fox,' said Carter. 'No one steals the credit quite like she does.'

'That medal should be going to the two officers that stopped Anderson when he had Sims in his van. If it wasn't for them, we'd have been looking at six murders. PC Hastings is lying in intensive care because of Anderson. He's lucky to be alive. So is Sims, for that matter. As it is, it looks like he'll walk with a limp for the rest of his life.'

Carter raised his hands in defence. 'Hey. Don't shoot the messenger. But don't worry, I've already put both officers forward for gallantry medals. Along with *you*.'

Phillips recoiled. 'Me? What did I do?'

'Er, let me think. You identified the killer, who he would copycat next, *and* his next victim. Not to mention putting your own life at risk to save Sims and Hastings. Need I go on?'

Phillips blushed, and drained her glass in an attempt to hide her smile on her face.

'I do have some bad news though, Jane,' said Carter in a sombre voice, as he stared at his pint glass on the table.

'Oh God. Am I gonna need another drink?'

Carter's eyes locked on Phillips's. 'Possibly. You see, thanks to your efforts, Fox now thinks the sun shines out of my arse. So, I'm afraid it looks like you're gonna be stuck with me for a wee bit longer.'

Phillips put her hand to her chest and let out a huge sigh of relief. 'Jesus, you had me going there for a minute, Harry.'

Carter chuckled. 'Sorry. Couldn't resist.'

Phillips laughed too. 'Well, I'll drink to that,' she said, raising her empty glass in a mock toast. 'Mine's a large one!'

ACKNOWLEDGMENTS

I recently saw a post on a Facebook group page, asking if anyone bothers to read the acknowledgements, and if readers really care about them. Well, if you've got this far, then I think it's fair to say, you probably do. I do too, because publishing a novel is incredibly challenging and takes an enormous number of people to get it ready for expectant readers.

Living your life with gratitude is guaranteed to make you feel happy, plus I was raised to always say thank you, and I'm not about to stop now. So here goes.

As ever, my wife Kim is my rock, my best friend and my soul mate who never falters in her support of me living my dream as a full-time writer.

My gorgeous boy Vaughan. I wake up laughing and go to bed smiling because of you.

Carole Lawford, ex-CPS Prosecutor; once again your guidance on British Law was invaluable in navigating this complex story.

Jo Robertson, the person I trust to read my manuscripts before anyone else.

My coaches, Donna Elliot and Cheryl Lee, from 'Now Is Your Time' and Fabio at 'Fabio Mazzieri Coaching'. Your guidance, support and direction are revolutionising the way I live and work. And a special note of thanks to Dr Erin Fall Haskell, for helping me realise the true power and value of storytelling.

My publishing team of Brian, Jan, Garret and Claire, and my editor, Laurel. Thank you for your inspiration, belief, and incredible attention to detail.

And a special thank you to all the front-line workers who have battled on during the Covid-19 pandemic to keep our world turning and as safe as possible over the last twelve months. You're all superheroes in my eyes.

And finally, thank you to my readers for reading *Deadly Obsession*. If you could spend a moment to write an honest review on Amazon, no matter how short, I would be extremely grateful. They really do help readers discover my books.

Best wishes,

Owen

www.omjryan.com

ALSO BY OMJ RYAN

The DCI Jane Phillips Crime Thriller Series

(Books listed in order)

DEADLY SECRETS (a series prequel)

DEADLY SILENCE

DEADLY WATERS

DEADLY VENGEANCE

DEADLY BETRAYAL

DEADLY OBSESSION

DEADLY CALLER

DEADLY NIGHT

DEADLY CRAVING

DEADLY JUSTICE

DEADLY VEIL

DEADLY INFERNO

DCI JANE PHILLIPS BOX SET

(Books 1-4 in the series)

Published by Inkubator Books
www.inkubatorbooks.com

Copyright © 2021 by OMJ Ryan

OMJ Ryan has asserted his right to be identified as the author of this work.

DEADLY OBSESSION is a work of fiction. People, places, events, and situations are the product of the author's imagination. Any resemblance to actual persons, living or dead is entirely coincidental.

No part of this book may be reproduced, stored in any retrieval system, or transmitted by any means without the prior written permission of the publisher.

Printed in Great Britain
by Amazon